THE ESFAH SAGAS:
EYE OF THE STORM

BY
CHRISTOPHER D. SCHMITZ
AND
SHERIF GUIRGUIS

A DRAGON DICE NOVEL

PUBLISHED BY TREESHAKER BOOKS

THE ESFAH SAGAS

Rise and Fall of the Obsidian Grotto
Cast of Fate
Army of the Dead

The Relic Quests
Ashes of Ailushurai
Rise of the Champions
Drakuwar (coming 2022)

The Cyrean Songs
Chill Wind
Eye of the Storm
Secrets of the Shadowlands (coming 2022)

STAY UP TO DATE ON THE WORLD OF ESFAH!

Get a free copy of book 1 in the Esfah Sagas by visiting:

www.subscribepage.com/getfreedragondicenovels

Subscribers who sign up for this no-spam email list will get free books, exclusive content, and more! You'll get *Rise & Fall of the Obsidian Grotto* immediately… if you would like more details or want to follow the author, you can find his details at the end of this book.

Background

Dragon Dice™ was originally created by Lester Smith and produced by TSR in 1995.It is an Origins Award winning strategy game where players create mythical armies using dice to represent each troop and is one of several collectible dice games that emerged in the 1990s. The game combines strategy and skill as well as a little luck.

After several years, TSR, now owned by Wizards of the Coast, had put Dragon Dice™ on hold to work on other projects. In October of 2000, SFR Inc. purchased the rights to Dragon Dice™.

Most of the races and monsters in original TSR Dragon Dice were created by Lester Smith and include some creatures unique to a fantasy setting and others that are familiar to the Dungeons & Dragons role-playing game. While the world of Esfah, where Dragon Dice™ takes place, has many similarities to that of Dungeons & Dragons, it is distinctly different in many respects. In some ways, there are greater unknowns and its history is both newer and older all at once.

Around the end of 1995 I was a teenager and avid board gamer who had a burger slinging job (which gave me a disposable income) and a car (that took most of my disposable income.) In addition to many other games I played as part of a regular quartet of gamers, Dragon Dice™ was one that we all enjoyed.

I fondly remember how the four of us would cut out of elective classes, study halls, and independent learning periods to meet up for gaming sessions. Dragon Dice™ came in a pocketable carrying bag which made it perfect for that.

We also had a mutual acquaintance. An older gentleman in town owned a new and used bookstore that also carried a limited supply of gaming products. Though he did not stock Dragon Dice™, he had a copy of *Cast of Fate*, the first Dragon Dice™ novel which included a special promo die; I snapped it up right away as the most avid reader of the foursome (which lent itself to me become the dedicated DM for our role-playing game sessions and solidified my path as a story-teller.) The included promotional die was our bright and shiny object for months.

Cast of Fate by Allen Varney was not the only book set in the world of Esfah, though it remains one of the few. As I write and publish more and more fiction (both Fantasy and Science Fiction,) I tend to write the stories that I've always wanted to... and I've always wanted to have a voice in a shared universe. Creating a story within the Dragon Dice™ universe is something I've always wanted to do, so I give a special thanks to SFR, a company composed of true and like-minded fans who have kept alive a product that was one of the gems of the 1990s.

—Christopher Schmitz

FOREWORD

In eons past, when time was young and creation malleable, the four powers of Nature -- earth, air, fire, and water -- the children of Nature, gods in their own rights, brought forth two races of beings to care for their fledgling world, created by the all-father, Tarvanehl. One race, the selumari or coral elves, was created to husband the fluid forces of air and water. The other race, the vagha, a dwarvish race, embodied the stability of earth and the tempering power of fire. Together, these two peoples worked to nurture their infant world into something glorious and beautiful.

But Nature had a nemesis in Death, the spirit of entropy. In imitation of Nature, Death brought into being its own races: the morehl, or lava elves, who worshiped fire and destruction, and the trogs, a race of goblins, who sprang from earth and corruption. From the moment of their creation, the morehl and trogs sowed conflict, defiling the very world that gave them life and corrupting the other races who tended it. War sparked over land and possessions. Soon, hordes of dispossessed selumari, vagha, morehl, and trogs swept back and forth across the lands of Esfah, locked in endless battle.

In their struggles for supremacy over the fledgling world, the First Races pressed other magical beings into their service. The morehl were the first to do so, bringing up fire-breathing hellhounds and web-casting driders from the deepest caverns below Esfah. The trogs followed suit, leading trolls, harpies, and other monsters into battle. In response, the selumari called forth coral giants from the ocean and swarms of sprites from the skies. The vagha enlisted gargoyles, androsphinxes, and other creatures of the crags.

Conflict raged across the face of Esfah, and Death delighted in the carnage.

Back and forth across the world, darkness battle against light. Each side pushed harder yet for victory and the battles grew ever savage and desperate. New races arose, each pressed into the fray of the bloody struggle that seemed to have no end in sight.

Saddened by the bloodshed, Nature, the goddess-mother Ghaeial, dealt death to preserve life. Death, the bastard child Malgrimm – son of Ghaeial and

Selurehl, the god known as Void – reveled in the chaos, terror, and pain that war brought.

A time of champions arose to safeguard the realm. Wars continued and an entire age passed. Pockets of tenuous peace grew from apathy – a new trick engineered by Death to soften the resolve of Nature's troops, almost seeming to abandon his playground for the comforts of the Abyss – but his attention never truly waned.

Esfah has never known true peace. It is not in the planet's makeup: this is where the children of gods war on their behalf. Both old and new races struggle ever onward – creatures inspired to greater ends, forever in search of either an end to the bloodshed, or carnage renewed, as each is bent towards his or her own ends.

Esfah cannot know peace. Malgrimm, the god known as Death, will not allow it. Only a few know his true name – and to speak it aloud is to court Death himself.

For a short video overview of Esfah's origins, visit

https://youtu.be/JhF8RPFkF9I

For up to date information on the world of Esfah, and all things related to the Dragon Dice universe, including products and specials, check out:

http://www.sfr-inc.com

Acknowledgements
And
Dedication

Joe Joiner, the author of Chill Wind, passed away in 2014. Nearly a decade after Joe released the original version of that story, the literary world of Esfah finally comes into its own and I would like to dedicate this version of its sequel, Eye of the Storm to Joe, his legacy, and to the Joiner family.

Joe left behind notes and some story scraps that were compiled, revised, and added to, posthumously helping create a Chill Wind prequel titled Thunderfist & the Dragon. He also left behind a few details in the final notes of Chill Wind: that he ahd hope to write a series following the children of Geril and Thrag. We learned of a very young Ra'al who stayed behind in Icehome via the story and his notes revealed Geril's future child who was to be named Coryn.

Aside from the title and those two names, this was all we had to go on, and so we hope we did a service to Joe and all the other denizens of Cyrea.

—Christopher D. Schmitz

The Shadowlands
The Shadowlands
Gyrea
The Shining Sea
Maris Sea
The Eeylands
Faeleise
Maris Coast
Lemeliandor
Tarvenish Ocean
The Birthlands
Dereb'Liandor
Tarvenish Ocean
Doban
Telvat Sea
Charnock
Far Seas
Gnome Home
Sontarra
Meridie Sea
Hiriath
Scattered Isles
The Broken Crown
Lost Diadem Isles
Leagues

Prologue

Year 1020, Second Age

Four dwarves followed a fifth out of the vaghan city of Balgavarr Reaches. The small coterie moved with a speed that did not readily come to mind with dwarves.

They stopped when the gates of the city could no longer be seen.

"All right, tell us why you pulled us from our beds, Dragonsbane?" The oldest of the four vagha stared at the young vagha who led them out of the city. "This is not about the peoples' insistence that the council make you King, is it? Some on the council would find such a late night meeting suspicious, given the circumstances."

"I needed to share something with you. And we had to be well away from the ears of the council." Dragonsbane looked past the other vagha and into the distance, where the city rested for the night.

"This is rather odd… quite alarming." Another vagha eyed Dragonsbane suspiciously. This was a matter for the council, and Dragonsbane had ties to the ruling body of Balgavarr—that he did not pursue action through the proper channels unnerved the others.

"The matter at hand is too risky and dangerous to discuss with the council," Dragonsbane answered. "Especially given the trouble I've had of late with Elder Lahmyn, whom I do not trust. It concerns the hidden cache under the temple of Ailuril in Tulgesh. The council has a one-sided approach…They would force my hand if they knew I could access it, especially Lahmyn and house Kiyh…"

The four other vagha all looked at the younger one with wide eyes.

"How do you know of the weapons?" the eldest demanded.

"Is the location no longer secret?" the second eldest asked.

"Did you cross the maze?" the fourth asked. "How did you pass the riddle?"

The younger vagha signaled for quiet with both hands. "I did, but it doesn't matter how I did it." He exhaled a hot breath. "The morehl know it is there, and I think, soon, the Death god will know also… If he does not already."

The dwarves huddled closer together and looked expectantly at their youngest member.

"We have discussed this in the past." The eldest looked at his colleagues. "Could Lord Death extract the secret from the minds of the dead builders or not? We think not, otherwise, he would have opened the cache long ago."

"Something has changed," Dragonsbane insisted. "They were searching for it—the morehl of my past, but you know the tale." He turned his head from side to side and then disclosed, "One of the agents of Death died inside the maze, right where the cache was."

The entire group fell silent. They had not considered that the Death god could interrogate one of his own worshipers who had slipped beyond life while inside the dungeon.

"This could change everything," the eldest vagha hissed. "Now Death has a presence *inside* the maze. Did you remove the body from the labyrinth?"

Dragonsbane shook his head. "No, I could not. The earth melted, sucking in all the cache and the body of the Death worshiper. She remains there, beyond my reach."

"Then the cache is in grave danger," the fourth vagha said. "If Lord Death resurrects his agent, she could remain inside the maze, where the cache is, and tell its secrets."

The second vagha put his hand to his mouth. "We are doomed," he groaned. "We don't stand a chance if Lord Death can get his hands on the cache."

"That is why we must move it," Dragonsbane said. "Well, not exactly. Moving it will not be possible, but stone-magic is in our blood. And I have chosen you to help me accomplish the same end."

The other vagha all stared at their fifth member.

He flashed a crooked smile. "I have a plan for how to keep Death from gaining this treasure."

Lightning shone brightly in the sky for just a moment, casting shadows over the face of Esfah as torrents of rain poured down.

The darkness was almost complete, with clouds that completely covered the stars. It lent a certain tone of loneliness to the night. The rain muffled most sounds, and the squelch of slouching feet in the muddy ground went unheard. A roar of thunder rolled across the world in a shroud of magnificent booms, ensuring the footsteps could not be detected The thunder sounded like Ailuril, the goddess of air, playing enormous drums and calling the world of Esfah—or the worlds beyond—to heed her.

Five vagha pushed forward through the mud, riding upon dragonkin mounts. The vagha worshipped Firiel and Eldurim, not Ailuril, but they could not ignore her warnings. Nevertheless, they proceeded with caution.

They each rode the proud drakufreet until they reached their destination. Each kept two bundles tied tightly to their mount, and each pulled behind a cart covered with tough leather hides.

The procession seemed surreal; such magnificent beasts pulling plain carts was something the locals never dreamed of seeing. They usually passed through tiny villages, many leagues in the south.

Tonight was no ordinary night; this night, the five Vagha planned to cheat Death. They would conquer the lord of the unseen and steal from his grasp the thing he coveted most in the Cyrean region.

Four magicians, maybe the last of their generation, and an honored war hero stole through the night, unbeknown even to their kin and loved ones. The mission was so secret that each decided to erase it from their minds after its completion.

This journey might be the first of its kind. And in some ways, it could be last –at least, that is what they hoped for. The group marched until they reached the ruins of the ruler's Palace of the city of Tulgesh, then the procession slowed, and finally stopped.

Dwarves were not uncommon in the ruined selumari city. Many Balgavarrians were present here, and in the far north, after they had sent builders to repair war damage from the lava elves.

Nervous sounds occasionally came from the beasts who sensed the trepidation of their riders. All five dismounted and gathered in front of a large slab of mostly erect marble. Dragonsbane approached the stone and said, "This is our cover."

"What do you wish for us to do with this stone?" the oldest vagha asked him.

"I want you to shape in the likeness of my late friend, the areosan king, Thrag." Dragonsbane caressed the stone. It was a dwarven monument, commemorating the fallen heroes that had fought in the Tulgesh war and saved many selumari.

"Why him?" The second vagha asked.

"What better way to hide the entrance than under the feet of such a great protector. He is the most revered hero of the battle of Balgavarr Reaches." Dragonsbane smiled at the group and walked a bit away from the stone slab.

The eldest dwarf smiled and rubbed his hands together. He pulled a gem-like sightstone from his pocket and squeezed it, waving his free hand at the stone slab.

At first, the slab screeched and shuddered, but then pieces chipped and fell out of it. It stiffened and lengthened; almost seeming to wobble and melt. The shaping went fast from there on.

Within a single hour stood a new grand statue, four times the height of its inspiration.

"I don't remember that Thrag had such long claws or huge fangs," Dragonsbane commented on the finished work.

"Call it artistic interpretation." The vaghan mage shrugged. "This is how I remember him, anyway."

While the single magician worked the statue, Dragonsbane worked with the others to summon their connection to Eldurim, the earth god. They melted the inside of the nearby tomb like wax, melting and remolding the passages so that the old labyrinth, and even the original entrance to it, were barred by solid stone. They could not change the cache's ultimate destination, but a corps of powerful casters could rebuild the dungeon leading to it—and this time, agents of the Dark One would not know the way in, or how to pass its dangers.

"I guess it is our turn to make the new maze." The three other vagha started to feel the ground between the old dungeon and the new statue until they found a favorable spot.

The three mages knit their wills together and began to shape the earth.

A long tunnel burrowed under them, branching and widening at key points, creating an elaborate set of rooms like the labyrinth Dragonsbane crossed before first finding the cache.

It took hours, with the mages drawing only on the powers of Eldurim, but finally, they finished. The three casters dropped to the ground, barely able to keep their eyes open.

"The structure is done." One of the three tired mages announced as the sun began to rise.

"Then it is my turn." The eldest handed a torch to Dragonsbane. "Follow me."

The elder magician created stairs leading downwards, and then outfitted the tunnel leading to the first room with the first puzzle, with two corridors branching out from within. The prize had to remain well protected.

As the mage worked out the details, Dragonsbane followed with the torch. Far after the dawn went through its birth and matured into a full day, they worked.

Finally, the mage stopped and handed parchment covered in verses to Dragonsbane.

"It is done, Dragonsbane," he said. "This will be the key to the first chamber. You will have to add the rest to match the maze's route."

"You should make a map for it," the mage said as he led Dragonsbane back to the surface. "It will be quite difficult to penetrate once we've removed our own memories via the incantation.

Dragonsbane gazed on the parchment for several moments before pocketing it.

"I will make four maps, each detailing how to pass one of the four puzzles." Dragonsbane said, holding tight to the frail hand of the mage as they wound their way back up

After they arrived back on the surface, the other three mages held a single, pearly stone between them.

The fourth spell caster approached them and placed a shaky hand on the stone. "Dragonsbane, this artifact will wipe our memories of the events covering these last few days." He flashed a thin smile to the younger dwarf. "You must take it and destroy it. A good axe should do the trick." The elder dwarf winked.

Dragonsbane watched as the mages chanted together. The stone shone brighter than the day's sun for a single moment, before growing cloudy and gray.

The four mages fell backward immediately, deep in a dreamless sleep.

Dragonsbane sent a fast prayer to Eldurim and began dragging the sleeping bodies back towards the dragonkin mounts.

Within half an hour, he was back on the road, heading towards Balgavarr.

It made the perfect cover. One hundred vagha already worked at forming Tulgesh's walls. Soon, they would work on a new development: evolving the northern city of Icehome into a fortress for the frostwings.

These four mages would only remember that they had helped craft the statue near the center of Tulgesh—a condition of the vagha's service to the selumari leader, Matrek, the most renown coral elf leader to emerge from the war. Nobody would ever know that they'd helped bury the most dangerous artifacts left upon the continent of Cyrea, after the Magestorm Wars.

Today, he buried a burden. Tomorrow, he would rebuild entire cities.

Geril Dragonsbane laughed; his life was nothing like he had expected it to be.

Chapter 1

Year 1140, of the Second Age

The wind sang a forlorn song through the corridors of Castle Ice. It told eerie tales of long-traveled journeys, having passing through lands no living creature would dare to touch.

But the castle didn't care for the song of the wind, not like those who walked its corridors. The castle merely endured them. It was built high on the mountain around the original cave city that had been carved by its areosan original builders.

Even though the wind claimed reign over all its long, winding corridors, the frostwings owned the castle.

Icehome's inhabitants, and the original cave's builders, were almost exclusively frostwings. It was common for them to seek the will of the wind and the air goddess's never-ending song. That song ran in their blood, or so they said.

The areosan race, the frostwings, stood tall and proud, covered in thick hide and fur of grays, whites, and blues to help them blend in with their frigid surroundings in their native north. They harnessed the power of the wind with their powerful, bat-like wings.

Prince Ra'al walked slowly through one of those wind-haunted corridors. With each step he took, the song increased in pitch.

He didn't know if the wind was furious at him, or if it urged him forward; he never claimed to understand the song. Ra'al was as areosan as they came, but he never felt as if the wind sang in his blood or that his blood had been touched by its frosty fingers.

Most of his people claimed affinity with elements of the air: some attunement to the goddess Ailuril. Some of his kin even claimed they could read news of the past or foretell possible futures in the gusts' shrill, cold notes.

Mainly, though, it gave the areosa their innate ability to control climate, and create ice out of the air when necessary. Most of the walls of the castle were formed from, and decorated with, ice.

It was a formidable weapon in battle, one that frostwing warriors often employed. Who needed to carry projectile weapons when one could create spears of ice and hurl them at their enemies from extreme heights?

Ra'al was not one of those lucky warriors. He had no such affinity. Even though his father was known to have been finely attuned to the wind, he had never found its song. He could not hear it He'd never been able to perform the smallest mystical task and he could not summon the famed areosan icicle javelins that his people used in battle.

He shifted the leather thong that crossed his shoulder. A long, leather quiver held a cluster of shortened javelins made of wood and steel – the weapons he used in place of ice. None ever looked at it or spoke of it, for the prince's sake.

Regardless, Ra'al smiled through his felinoid muzzle. He still liked the tunes it played through the corridors, but he'd never yet tried to put any meaning to them, though he was told that this song was part of his blood, his legacy, just as it had been his father's.

Heavy tapestries fought for wall space with the wind. He'd passed these tapestries thousands of times over the years, never really giving them much thought.

Not today, though. Today, Ra'al stopped and stared at the intricate, woven scenes of battle, *these warriors clearly heard the song of the wind.* They depicted tales of the glorious victories his people earned over their main enemy, Malgrimm, the one God whose name promised to bring the grave to your doorstep and should never be spoken of again. He was simply called *Death.*

This much he knew: his people were touched by Death, but not the same touch endured by all the species of Esfah. Their ties with Death were far more intimate. He was a patron god responsible for forming their race, just as the other gods had crafted Esfah's other races.

As it happened, Death thought to enthrall creation and failed; the first generation of frostwings resisted his dread call. Ever since, they had fought against him and his festering influence on Esfah.

Ra'al whistled softly as he walked under the shadow of the tapestries. Centuries of heroes and embroidered warriors seemed to look down at him in anger, disappointment, and shame.

More likely, the images on the tapestries were just images. But he did feel a mild sense of disappointment, all the same. His mother kept hammering him day in and day out to make a name for himself, much as his ancestors had before him.

He wanted to please her. He really did, but it annoyed him to feel so much pressure on his shoulders. Ra'al continued walking the corridor to attend a meeting with his tutor later in the day. But he didn't want to train for battle on an empty stomach.

Ra'al stopped. During one of the last five training sessions, his tutor managed to make him spill his breakfast on the training ground; maybe he was better off skipping breakfast. The only other frostwing who grated his nerves as much as his mother had to be that instructor.

Being a prince was nothing like in the tales or songs he'd heard. Ra'al contemplated that for some minutes, then concluded that bards, as a lot, were a bunch of liars. None of them had ever been a prince or had even lived in close quarters to one, hence their misconceptions.

Instead of breakfast, he headed to the upper ice gardens of the castle. This was the place he most liked in all of Icehome. Sometimes he sat and composed songs, his interpretations of life as a frostwing. Ra'al was an introspective sort.

Occasionally he even composed songs about Icehome. But he never shared them with anyone.

This was his calling, he knew it, even if his mother didn't condone it. Ra'al loved to compose songs. Ironic as it was, his songs were not for frostwing ears. The frostwings were more than content to listen to the only song that mattered to them, the song of the wind.

Sometimes he entertained the idea that he would become the first bard who was a prince. Maybe he could clarify all those errors regarding the lives of princes and princesses.

Pleased with his idea, Ra'al picked up his pace and headed towards the garden. As he tried to cross through the main hall, however, someone called for him.

He turned to see Coryn running to catch him.

Coryn was a vagha, a dwarf; she was his closest friend…but also the source of much grief. Coryn sa'Geril was an emissary from Balgavarr Reaches, Icehome's southerly ally.

Despite this, he and Coryn had practically grown up together and were taught much of the same things. Ra'al appreciated that she even had an amazing singing voice.

He was pleased to see her. Now, he could take her to the garden where he hoped she would sing his latest piece. Though he composed, Ra'al knew his singing voice was painful, even to his own ears. He sounded sometimes like a wounded lion and others like a strangled man.

"What are you doing here?" Coryn panted.

"What do you mean, what am I doing? I live here." Ra'al gave her a lopsided grin.

Coryn nudged him in the stomach, and Ra'al lost all thought of breakfast.

"I know snow-head, I meant why are you not out and about?" Coryn was about to give him another nudge, but he jumped back. "I've been up for hours."

"You have a very strong jab for a lady." Ra'al looked seriously to Coryn. "Anyway, what is there to do?"

"*Everything.*" Coryn spread her arms and shouted to the whole world; a few sparrows nesting in the upper rafters of the grand hall took flight. "We can go on an adventure, or maybe visit other places, or we could just meet new people in the square. They say adventure is good for inspiration, and who knows, you might find a new song in that."

Ra'al narrowed his eyes, guessing that his mother had put her up to speaking with him. "Adventures are overrated, and new people are often thieves, cutthroats, and liars. You would end with less inspiration than you started with." Ra'al looked critically at his friend. "Close your mouth Coryn, the sparrows sometimes empty their guts mid-air around here. Gods know, your diet is already unhealthy with that spicy stuff you use, and that would make it even worse."

"Seriously, Ra'al, I want to travel. I am bored of this place. I want to visit all of Esfah if I could... and it's called *fire sauce*, and it's a delicacy." Coryn matched Ra'al's pace, almost running to keep up with the large frostwing; her gait proved the difference between their lengths of stride.

"I just want to stay here. I don't think traveling would make any change in my life. Most probably, it could only change for the worse." Ra'al said and pressed his lips tight.

"That's just because you only know this place. If you go out to the world, your perspective might change," Coryn spoke in her natural, loud voice. Ra'al thought she assumed everybody around her was deaf. He also knew she got that trait from her father, whose booming voice could easily fill a room.

"Did you not hear the news?" Coryn chirped.

"Not that I care, but what news?" Ra'al was keen to know the local gossip, and Coryn was always happy to supply it.

"Some traders came from the east. They told amazing stories of horrible events and great courage." Coryn's voice rose to a crescendo by the last of her words. "Tales of magic mazes and courage in the face of undead hordes. Apparently the dead came back to life in northern Charnock."

"So... the usual?" Ra'al scoffed.

"What do you mean 'the usual?' I am telling you, they told of vagha bands and selumari facing great odds in the south—past the Birthlands, even. They said they fought with Death himself."

Coryn flipped her hair and huffed, livid at Ra'al's attitude. "They say the Gods' own have returned: champions chosen by the gods to defend the age."

"And you believed that? I mean, these are obviously tall tales," Ra'al said, oblivious.

"There are adventurers out there, and they are making a change for good in Esfah! They are the new heroes for our age. One day, *I* will be one." Coryn looked to the ceiling as if posing like a hero from the many paintings around Castle Ice.

Ra'al barked a laugh, , skipping away from Coryn to avoid her inevitable jabs.

He stopped and asked, "What exactly do you think you will gain through an adventure like that?"

Like Prince Ra'al, Coryn came from a ruling family. Her father was a kind of king, but was appointed by the people of Balgavarr. As such, she had lacked nothing in her life. Daughters of kings did not live lives of discomfort.

Coryn was silent for a moment before answering, "Knowledge of the unknown."

"This is too grand, and ultimately vague. It doesn't convince me." Ra'al started to walk again, yet slower. He did enjoy his discussions with Coryn, and he wanted them to last longer. Plus, he knew she wouldn't be able to keep up with his long strides.

"Alright, you want something more defined." Coryn nodded thoughtfully. "So here is a very specific reason: experience through action, not just reliving tales through literature."

"Still vague." Ra'al jumped two steps to the side as Coryn tried to punch him. "Besides, what is wrong with books and sitting in a quiet corner, reading tales of epic adventure?"

"Hah," Coryn barked. "As if you would read anything other than poetry."

Coryn started to run after him, intent on striking him with a balled fist. Ra'al, who despite his claims of loving a calm life, had the strength and dexterity necessary to keep the dwarf always within reach, yet never able to touch him.

Their potentially violent dance caught the eye of some courtesans and within moments, a crowd gathered to cheer on the combatants. Frostwings always liked a good fight.

Eventually, Ra'al, raised a hand of peace to Coryn and remembered his earlier hunger. He stated, "I am ready for breakfast, and quite prepared to skip morning training, shall we?"

She licked her lips and nodded. Both strutted out of the main hall to the disappointment of the gathered audience.

"I don't think that anything we wish actually matters," Coryn said as they walked towards the dining hall.

"It should, but I know what you mean by that." Ra'al took a deep breath in. "Our parents are sure to send us abroad on some mission, and soon. We are adults, after all, and that carries a certain duty. Kits half my age have endured outpost deployments and your coming of age was very recent." He was older than her by a decade, but their cultures had vastly different ways of reckoning age and maturity.

Coryn shrugged knowingly. She'd only recently aged past her first half century. While the areosa had recognized Ra'al as an adult for many years now, Coryn was a dwarven adolescent, though certainly ready to be an adult. Balgavarr would likely call upon the daughter of Dragonsbane—the descendent of Thunderfist—for an adventure like this one.

"Well, it might not be as bad as you think." Coryn gave a short laugh, wondering what heroic name they might come to call her. "You might even meet your equal on your travels, oh mighty Ra'al."

"Very funny," he scowled.

"Well, you have to try seeing the bright side of things, even if circumstances take you away from home and friends." It was Coryn's turn to sigh.

"Do you know something that I don't?" Ra'al stopped and faced Coryn.

Before she could answer, a frostwing wearing a court sash came hurtling towards them,

"Prince Ra'al," he panted. "Your mother and beloved queen, Rashingot, requests your presence." He panted some more and added, *"Immediately."*

Ra'al smiled at the interruption, accidentally baring his teeth; Ra'al's fangs shined through his smile with unintended malice. The feral messenger squeaked and jumped two paces back.

The prince excused himself from Coryn and headed for the throne room.

In less than ten minutes, Ra'al stood before his mother. He hoped that this wouldn't prove to be another one of her daily lectures. He had a hard enough time meeting frostwing standards without her help.

"My beloved son, approach me, please." The queen signaled him closer with her jeweled hand.

"Your majesty." Ra'al obeyed court protocol. But he dragged his feet as he approached the areosan throne.

The queen pointed to the chair next to her throne and insisted, "Sit."

Ra'al sat beside her, trying to hide his discomfort.

"You know, Ra'al, this is a difficult time." Ra'al sighed. He'd heard these words a hundred times before. "Peace makes ruling a challenge. When all the eyes of your subjects fall on you, you have to prove yourself worthy of your seat, over and over and over."

"But your subjects are not the only people who will scrutinize you. The frostwing elders must also be appeased; they will have to accept you as their king if you are to ever ascend," Queen Rashingot insisted. "It is their faith in their leader that keeps challengers to the throne at bay. If they suspect a challenger more fit to rule, they would allow a rival's demands for a rite of combat."

Ra'al rolled his eyes. He had little ambition to take the throne in the first place, and so that made her lecture moot.

"And you know that the elders would accept much other than a hero as king. With this enduring peace your father helped earn, even the smallest conquest or display of courage would be considered." Rashingot continued as Ra'al breathed slowly. He hoped that it might end soon so that he could get to the garden and read some poetry afterward.

The queen finally finished, smiled, and looked expectantly to Ra'al.

Ra'al had been here before. He knew that was his cue, so he said, "Of course Mother, as long as my service would not take me away from the kingdom, I am willing to do my best."

This was his regular answer, and it usually pushed the queen into the second half of her speech. Then, Ra'al would spark up the same debate he and his mother frequently had, and as a consequence, the queen would become upset and send him away.

Once or twice a week he endured this, but he'd gotten better at his part in the act. After wasting an hour in the royal hall, he would have at least three days to do as he pleased.

But something felt different this time. The queen's smile widened, and Ra'al could see a familiar gleam in her eyes. She reserved that glare for political opponents whenever she knew she'd secured a surprising victory.

"Perfect, my beloved. I found for you a task most needed for the good of our kingdom, and it is practically at our doorstep."

Ra'al's panic showed apparent in a quick flutter of his wings.

"What is it, mother?" Ra'al gulped. The prince was neither lazy nor a coward, but he fashioned himself a poet, and poets didn't usually perform feats of daring. One was bound to break an arm or a hand doing that. How could they commit letters to paper in such a state?

"Icehome needs an emissary to speak on behalf of the kingdom, someone who can guide important trade and territory negotiations." Queen Rashingot radiated warmth. "Since you are one of the most studied areosa in all Castle Ice, and know all the treaties along with your ballads, you are perfectly suited to this. And, since you dislike traveling far beyond the borders of our kingdom, you should have little issue with this mission."

"But I will have to leave the kingdom?" Ra'al swallowed at the hard lump forming in his throat.

"Well, not exactly. The vagha have been our allies since your father, Thrag, formed our alliance." The queen smiled so broadly that Ra'al wondered if it might have stuck on her face.

"But that alliance was before my time," Ra'al complained, and as he tried to steer the discussion back to the usual debate, his mother laughed.

"This is exactly why I want *you* to negotiate: to extend our diplomatic reach within new lands. This would make you a hero just as your late father was. He fought with magic and sword, and you will fight with paper and tongue."

"So this is because I can't use magic?" Ra'al looked straight and hard at his mother.

"Ra'al, any disability you have is all in your mind. I have never counted it as a hindrance. Perhaps it is an effect from some latent talent which will bloom when needed." The queen smiled gently at her son.

Ra'al was trapped, and he knew that there was no talking his mother out of sending him on the mission. But he risked one last trial. "Okay, but I get to choose who accompanies me. I want Coryn to come along." He was certain that his mother would refuse. If his role was supposed to be a royal matter, only frostwings should be trusted—even if Geril Dragonsbane and his line were more like family than allied political leaders.

"Why, of course." The queen's wings vibrated in excitement. "And you are not just limited to the vagha...Take anybody you want! Your task is to negotiate with our most formidable neighbor, the morehl. Even now, they are suing for peace with their neighbors south of the Sareen River."

"Thurisa and Tulgesh?"

She nodded. "You will first make contact with the selumari in Tulgesh to establish the nature of their business; I assume they are growing desperate to open their economy to the outside. Internal trade has languished for them over these last many decades."

Ra'al held in a moan. His fate was decided, then; he would have to travel for many tendays to fulfill his mission—it would take four of them at least by the time he returned to Castle Ice. He felt doomed.

"But…" he stammered.

"Call your friend if you wish, or I will call her. It would be better that way, actually. I will send a messenger to fetch her within the hour. I also wish to send a letter to her father. Geril Dragonsbane will know to expect you both when you pass through," Rashingot said.

"So, I guess I had better get prepared for the journey. Maybe I will return in one piece," Ra'al said, trying unsuccessfully not to mope.

"I am glad that you started seeing things my way, beloved son." Rashingot reached and patted his head, completely ignoring the sarcasm of his final comment.

Ra'al turned to leave, mumbling under his breath.

"Wait, there is a bit of crucial information you must heed." She reached out to stop him.

"What information?" he asked cautiously. Everything his mother said or did had layers of nuance—she'd developed keenly honed political skills after Thrag fell defending Balgavarr. Those skills helped her retain the throne all these years. Sometimes, she even set traps and tests for her own kin in order to teach them lessons—though Ra'al thought them more exercises in maliciousness.

She kept her voice low and for his ears alone. "I am sure it is nothing, likely far-fetched rumors, but traders recently brought news of unrest from among the undead in the far south…" she trailed off thoughtfully before adding, "My own sources have confirmed an increase in their number in the northern wastes of the Shadowlands." Stray skeletons and half-frozen corpses were sometimes spotted wandering through lonely passes in the northern reaches, but the mindless, shambling agents of Death were seldom of any real concern, and they typically disappeared on their own, likely falling into the Heimdarl Crag, or wandering into the frozen sea.

"Coryn mentioned the undead earlier, but I assume these are merely tall tales." Ra'al said.

Rashingot set her jaw. "I am afraid there might be some merit to them. I hear reports from my trusted scouts that sightings of larger numbers of undead roam in the depths of the Shadowlands."

Ra'al knew that 'scouts' meant her personal spies. She kept an intricate network of information traders that ran deeper than he could imagine.

"Should I be worried?" Ra'al hoped she would consider letting him stay home because of the danger.

"Not yet…" she trailed off, confessing something in a tone that made even his areosan blood run cold. "But a day may come when you will need many friends and the strength of allies to win the day. Take advantage of this journey. . Perhaps it will help you find your strength and finally learn to be a true frostwing. The dead have wandered in the north for millennia. While it is unlikely they are anything more than a nuisance, that may not be the case when I am gone and you must rule."

Ra'al silently gazed at his mother, and then nodded. He stated sincerely, "Alright, mother. I hope that this time I will make you proud."

"I know you will. Go with the blessings of Ailuril. Prepare well for your journey." She squeezed his hands and then watched him depart.

Chapter 2

Ra'al paced in his chambers, bothered by a sinking feeling in his gut. His travel trunk lay half-filled near his wardrobe.

He felt like he'd missed something he needed for the journey. It bothered him that he couldn't locate whatever it was and nagged in the back of his mind.

Consumed by his thoughts, Ra'al growled; his mother proved again that she was the sneakiest frostwing ever born to Esfah. His efforts were no match for her scheming wit.

Pacing some more, he felt that prolonging the packing was like dragging out the last few hours before an execution. He puffed some air out, stopped pacing, and started jamming cloth, books, and the smaller items into his travel trunk. If he had to go to his death, at least he would do it fashionably.

The prince clutched his quiver and glanced at the javelins splayed on his bed. He momentarily thought of abandoning it. The bandolier was a constant reminder that he could not hear the wind... not like other areosa. He sighed and grudgingly strapped it in place on his body before further packing.

At the moment when he couldn't stuff anything more into the trunk, the door to his chambers flew open. Coryn almost jumped with every step. "We are going on an adventure, you and me." She squeaked, excitedly grinning. "I couldn't believe my ears when the messenger came from the queen, may the gods bless her heart."

Ra'al murmured under his breath about the backstabbing of sly mothers. Because of Queen Rashingot's relationship with Coryn's father, she'd always treated the dwarf like family... only more like a doting aunt than the harsh mother Ra'al knew her as. She'd given Coryn exactly what she'd wanted, meanwhile, Ra'al had to endure his least favorite pastime: traveling.

"I see that you are already packed." She clapped with a grin. "We are off to unknown lands, facing untold dangers. We will have nothing but our wits and the strength of our arms." Then she struck a pose with one hand on her hip and the other clubbing the air.

"Where in festration do you come up with all this excitement?" He looked at her with wide eyes. "You know what, I don't care, not anymore. You are just as bad as my mother, sometimes," he seethed.

"Come on, Ra'al. This is your chance to leave your mark on history." She jumped from one foot to the other, her energy testing Ra'al's patience.

"Coryn, I would much prefer to leave my mark upon my bed." He slumped and fell onto the stuffed mattress. "I would rather be a peaceful prince, the prince who never left home, or better, the prince who lived to be old!"

"Pfft. You're exaggerating *everything*, as usual." She waved her hand in dismissal. "You will live to be ancient, and you will leave a mark as a great hero—greater even than King Thrag. I know it in my bones."

"I suspect that whatever is in *your* bones has to do with the cold weather in the castle." He smiled mischievously. "Maybe if you rub hot oil on them, you'd stop jumping and squeaking all over the place."

She punched his shoulder, although a lot gentler than her usual. "Come on, stand, and face the winds that bring us to the shores of exotic and forbidden lands."

"We are going to Balgavarr, and then the south-east border. It is well mapped, you know." He stood and brushed his wings off.

Coryn stopped jumping around for a second, laughing. "I know that, of course. It still doesn't make it any less adventurous."

Ra'al mumbled under his breath about the cruelty of life, the three goddesses of Fate, and chirpy, optimistic friends.

"Besides, we will take several guards with us," she said in a lower voice.

"A whole company?" Ra'al said hopefully.

"No, I don't think it will be more than a few personal guards at best." Coryn shook her head. "It is not *that dangerous,* after all."

"At least we will die with people from home there to witness it." Ra'al pulled the trunk with one hand and hefted it above his shoulder.

"That's the spirit." Coryn jumped around him like a happy sparrow. Ra'al hated sparrows. The way Coryn dumped her optimism on him only reminded him of the way sparrows released their bowels on his head. "They will sing about our deeds for ages to come," she continued, jumping as she punched the air and kicked at it for effect.

"And so, it begins, the journey of one prince forced to face the dangers of the world because of his mother, and the crazy friend who followed him to his death." Ra'al left the chamber and Coryn trailed after him, laughing to tears.

Ra'al and Coryn stood before Queen Rashingot, dressed and prepared for the voyage south. A corps of escorts stood behind the two emissaries. Mostly frostwings, they included a few dwarven traders, two ghwereste, and a motley collection of other free folk. The caravan tightened straps and made final preparations while Ra'al and Coryn said their goodbyes.

Much of the convoy included wagons filled with raw supplies and other goods meant for the markets or forges of Balgavarr Reaches and its outlying towns.

Behind the queen, a number of the areosan elders stood warily. They looked over the prince, who'd shown little interest in flying through King Thrag's wind wake until now. A few wore approving looks, if only to curry favor with the queen.

"I will do my best to make you proud, mother," Ra'al said with a bow.

"I am certain you will." Rashingot turned aside to Coryn. She slipped a sealed canister to the dwarf. "See that your father gets this when the convoy passes through Balgavarr."

Coryn turned it over in her hands. The gilded tube was of dwarven design and had a rotating set of dials keyed to an unknown cypher, which would unseal it. It was one of the more secure ways of sending messages, and she immediately knew it held some great secret. "I'll see it done." She slipped the message tube into her traveling robes.

The queen turned back to her son. "And see that these traders make it safely to the mountains."

Ra'al nodded reluctantly. The trip would have taken only a fraction of the time by wing, but Rashingot took the areosans' responsibility to protect their dwarven allies very seriously.

He turned and headed towards the caravan, the travelers climbing onto their mounts. Ra'al looked down at his friend. He said nothing, not wanting to bring down her elated mood. She walked with a light step, practically hopping with excitement for this yet-unknown adventure.

Ra'al tried not to resent her for her sentiments.

Many days passed uneventfully before the blues and whites of the Shadowlands' topography broke away before the grays, browns, and deep green of conifers and Ironwoods. The mountains loomed in the distance, breaking through the haze of low-lying vapors beyond the wilds.

The caravan came to a stop at one of the smaller villages near the lower half of the winding Kafnysan road that coiled through the mountain range, ascending to the peaks. Balgavarr Reaches laid further up the mountain. Their march had taken two tendays, and Ra'al had slept under the stars for the longest consecutive period in his life. But at least the journey had remained largely uneventful.

Coryn jumped ahead. "I have to see my father. Don't you dare leave without me." She looked sternly to Ra'al as she rummaged through her pack for the secured message given to her by Queen Rashingot.

"I wouldn't dream of it," Ra'al chuffed. He thought Coryn completely delusional; the feisty vagha might have finally snapped. He had no desire to take this trip in the first place, and the fact that his best friend was his co-adventurer was the only thing that made it bearable. There was no chance he'd leave without her. "I'll see that our companions each get to their destinations safely."

He turned to see if he was needed at all, but his fellow frostwing travelers were already directing traffic, making sure metals and materials meant for the local forges were on the correct forks in the road. A ghwereste—a member of the animal hybrid feral folk—and a human headed for a local tavern. The vaghan travelers seemed to know their way from here, as this was their homeland. By the time Ra'al turned back to Coryn, she was a considerable way down the road, already climbing the mountain.

Ra'al's mouth turned to a grimace. He felt slightly unneeded, but he'd have to wait for her to return from Balgavarr. The prince growled slightly and then made for the tavern to book a room. The journey to Tulgesh would go quicker from here, without the convoy to slow them down, but Ra'al had no intention of roughing it another night.

The morehl, red-skinned lava elves, entered the boundaries of the city in the waning period between dusk and nightfall, keeping to themselves as much as possible. In little time, they were the talk of the town, at least on the lower-end where they'd entered the gate. Citizens stared at the travelers with glistening eyes mounted upon blue-skinned faces. No red-skinned enemies had dared enter the city of Tulgesh since sacking it more than a generation prior.

Tulgesh's tower shaded over the poorer parts of town, chilling it slightly more than the normal heat of the rest of the city. Any lava elf daring to travel this deeply into coral elf territory had either a lack of sense or an overabundant confidence.

They did not go to the castle. They made no proclamations. Instead, they booked rooms adjacent to a local tavern, as if Tulgesh was any free city in any other part of Esfah, where the races lived in mixed company. They acted undisturbed by the bitter hatred of the folk around them. That further inflamed the rumors about the red elves; their indifference caught the local selumari off-guard.

Even the innkeeper who served them watched them suspiciously, despite being paid handsomely for the food and drink. Still, his posture remained tense, as if he was ready to turn on them in an instant.

Racial memories didn't easily die, and for a long period, the morehl were considered the nemesis of *everybody* on Cyrea. Even the goblins and pockets of reptilian sarslayan had broken with them. The suspicions of the local townsfolk were not unfounded.

The group of lava elf travelers sat around a table in the furthest corner of the inn, almost shrouded by the shadows. A tall, tin cup of ale had been poured and left in front of them; none touched the dwarven drink, which had likely been poured as a private insult.

"I am not sure coming here was wise," an elder morehl spoke softly. "I don't know what the purpose of this visit could be. You can see that we are not welcome here." He directed his words towards a young morehl sitting at the corner of the table. The young lava elf had his head bent and didn't react to the words of his older companion.

"We need allies. It is the primary objective for our mission," the younger said. "And after what we found in the forest…what we acquired in secret? Those allies must be the kind of folk even a powerful sage would not run from—remember, it was our kind that burned their ancient home in Yentosh."

The elder crooked his jaw and nodded slowly.

"That we have not been sent to offer peace to the king, disagrees with the wisdom of the emperor. Emperor Saugor, ruler in Mount Uruzak, is the wisest morehl on Esfah." A morehl sitting beside the young one at the corner whispered in heavy tones. His red skin almost darkened to the color of wine as he spoke.

"Keep your temper in check, Yarichek." The older morehl said. "The part of this plan that worries me has nothing to do with the wisdom of the king." He looked at the young morehl by the corner. "It has to do with his son."

"You can address me directly, Marnash. Honorifics could be deadly in a hostile tavern." The young morehl beside Yarichek leaned forward to face the older elf. "I agree with your advice not to directly address the king, but our agreements end there. What can be done, will be done." The young morehl fell back into silence.

"But Prin…" Marnash stopped midway in saying what he wanted to say. "I mean, Garesch, we are in enemy territory. We must advance with caution."

"The war is over Marnash, it was over before I was even born." Garesch looked hard at Marnash. "We already have a peace treaty with our neighbors, and this is not a hostile land—at least, it should not be."

"Didn't you see how the town's people looked at us?" Marnash still whispered, but there was a tone of urgency in his voice. "Or how the innkeeper acts around us? Gods know we paid him double what he deserved for his filthy rooms."

"You were the one who advised approaching influential merchants as mere emissaries, not as guests under the crown's mercy." Garesch stared at Marnash in challenge. "Or did you change your mind? Would you rather sleep on the soft beds in the castle?"

"You think King Matrek doesn't know that we are here? You think that he is not calculating our moves and plotting how to counter them?" Marnash barely held back from waving his arms in the air. Garesch could see the strain in the older morehl's eyes.

"He signed the peace treaties decades ago, giving us more land than we deserve, even though we lost that war," Garesch hissed, bending his head, "a war that claimed so many of his countrymen."

He continued, "And what did we do with this land? Nothing, it lays as waste, and as a point of weakness at our backs. This is the main reason we are here."

"It was part of her long and cunning plan…that frostwing queen," Marnash practically choked on his words. "She supported our retaining it; she knew that we were stretched too thin and we couldn't care for those lands—and that the trogs would eventually crawl out from Big Wet and infest them. She *knew* she would claim them back with her vagha allies. She gave nothing, and that she will get back. She has manipulated this whole situation."

"Are you to tell me that the dwarves, the frostwings, *and* the selumari are never to be trusted?" Garesch intoned softly. "That trying to broker an alliance with them against a far greater force is foolhardy, and a complete catastrophe?"

"None of them are to be trusted, and an alliance with them would never hold true." Marnash held the edge of the table with both hands, squeezing hard on the wood. "They will break their oaths as soon as we turn our back to them."

"That is the exact same reaction that rules the people of this town *when they see us*." Garesch still had his head bent as he talked. "To them, we are the enemy: a nation of thieves and murderers. We are everything they hate." He raised his head with a completely rigid face. "This has to change, and we are here to achieve that."

"Garesch, I don't think this is the opinion of your father, the emperor." Marnash ignored the looks of alarm on the faces of his companions, yet he blinked three times in a row, which none of the other morehl glimpsed but Garesch, who blinked in return. "He would not be pleased to hear of your thoughts."

"He will grow to accept them." Garesch reached for his ale and drank it in one gulp. Even if dwarven drinks tended to disagree with lava elf taste buds, he vowed to never show weakness before those troops under him. It was the morehl way.

The travelers stiffened and went silent as the barkeep approached them. He wore a blank face to disguise his indifference. "A letter," he said blandly, and waved it back and forth to determine which lava elf was their leader.

Finally, he dropped it on the closest elf and left.

The red-skinned traveler handed it to Marnash.

"Thank you, Werdth," Marnash said, quickly scanning it. When all prying eyes had left him, he slipped it to Garesch.

The prince read it in his lap. His eyebrows rose. "An invitation."

Coryn arrived at the main gate of Balgavarr Reaches and nodded to the sentries posted outside. She did not know their names, but their faces were familiar, and they let her hurry pass without any hesitation.

The dwarf ran through the Great Hall and up several flights of steps, turning aside and into the winding corridors that led to her father's home. She burst through the door to a surprised looking Geril sa'Ghuren.

"Oh, Coryn," he said. "I was expecting you sometime today…but not quite yet.." Geril turned, snatched a bound bundle, and handed it to her. "I bought you something I knew you'd like, a present for the road. You'll need some new boots to be a proper traveler."

She smiled, always happy for new foot-gear. Coryn had hoped to surprise him, but Queen Rashingot had obviously sent word ahead of the caravan. The two dwarves embraced briefly, and then Coryn produced the message tube. "A message from Castle Ice," she said.

Geril eyed it curiously and then accepted it. He keyed in the combination and then opened the tube to remove a number of parchments. He scanned them quickly and then nodded. "Rashingot has sent you on a mission with Ra'al?"

Coryn nodded enthusiastically. She knew he would have to grant permission since she was, technically, on assignment in the north.

Geril continued before she could chime in. "It's good for him to get out and experience the rest of what Cyrea has to offer." He drummed his fingers on his lips for a moment. "I don't think we *need* a vaghan emissary stationed in Icehome full time, do you?"

Coryn cocked her head. "You're asking if we need an official spokesperson in the court of our closest ally?"

"Well, do we? What did you normally do all day?"

She shrugged. "Tried not to die of boredom. It was dreadfully slow there. I wouldn't wish it on my worst enemy."

Geril grinned. "That's what I thought. You should accompany Ra'al —you were never much for sitting still, anyway, and Castle Ice will always be there when your mission is accomplished."

"You won't be overstressed knowing I'm in potential danger?" Coryn fussed over her father with a grin. He was as close to royalty as the mountain had ever produced. "Your apartment looks like you've not entertained in *ages*. We could always lay over here for a couple days and – "

"Dear Coryn, I am strong as an ox and far more stubborn. You have nothing to worry about," her father guffawed. He'd showed no signs of moving on to another woman after Coryn's mother had passed two decades ago, though his quarters might have been improved if he had shown any interest in another mate.

"Who cooks for you? Who mends your tools? Who will listen to your stories of valor and bravery?" Coryn asked, a sudden maternal instinct coming over her. "I am thrilled to take part in this mission, but fear leaving you here and thinking you might worry over *me."*

He cocked his head, knowing she was overreacting. Geril was still in his prime and many folk, especially the eligible ladies of Balgavarr, looked down on his reluctance to move past the death of Coryn's mother. "Elder Lordan keeps me in line, as he has done all your life." Her father winked at her. "Besides, I have the entire city of Balgavarr to care for me. As for the tools, I can always swipe some from the dying council elders after their funerals." He laughed. She punched his shoulder with a loud smack.

"And do they listen to your stories of valor and bravery? *Ha.* When have they?" she growled.

"They tolerate them. Truly listening is *your* duty, daughter." Her father nursed his bruised shoulder. "But, stories pale in comparison to the real thing." He puffed his chest and placed his hands on his hips. "You will make me proud. I have no doubt."

"So, you are *not* worried about me going to see the morehl?" Coryn asked.

"I can't deny that I have my doubts. They are a dishonest species; it is in their death-borne nature. But they haven't come knocking at Balgavarr's doors yet." He looked seriously into her eyes. "You know that my hackles rise whenever I'm around the morehl—they murdered your grandfather in cold blood... and Ra'al's father, too."

Geril looked softly to the stony walls around them. "I have tried to honor Thrag's memory as much as possible, but Ra'al is now an adult—he's been one for some time now. He will muster the strength to rule if he truly wants to; and if he can't, then perhaps the throne should fall to another... It is the areosan way."

Coryn listened with half an ear and looked over the papers upon Geril's desk. Writs, stamps, and writing tools were strewn across it, joined by the new papers Rashingot sent.

"Do you still think the lava elves will one day come for your maps?" Coryn tried to pull her father from his dour reverie. A tightly bound map stood unassuming and vertical at the edge of his desk, contained in an unassuming scroll case made of lavender leather. She knew that the case had three mates he had placed in secret places around Balgavarr.

"I don't know, but I will have to change their hiding place again soon. Maybe in earnest." His smile faded. "Someday, you or your descendants might use them—or at least pass them off to the Champions of the Gods, should this age ever produce them." His eyes worriedly flitted to the letters written by Rashingot in off-kilter letters. Coryn caught only the phrase *bloodless are gathering in growing numbers*, before his elbow covered the report. "The cache must remain buried until a hero who is worthy comes along. They should stay secret—and even I was no hero."

She kissed her father's forehead, and said, "I think you're wrong and are perfectly worthy. I will be back soon. The Reaches are on the route back from where our mission takes us. We must swing through Tulgesh first. Certainly, Ra'al and I will stop for a visit."

Geril smiled at his daughter. "I'd like that very much, but Tulgesh more than doubles the distance of your visit." He bobbed his head east. "The lava elves' border is that way, and it is not far."

Coryn grinned. "I know. I think Rashingot is trying to make a point to her son. But first consulting the selumari has its wisdom. We can negotiate the strongest position if we know we are all unified."

Geril nodded and then bid his daughter farewell. As soon as she had departed, he turned his attention back to Rashingot's letters.

Ra'al spotted Coryn duck into the tavern. The frostwing quickly polished off whatever it was the bartender had given him; he hadn't paid attention, but he had largely indiscriminate taste buds when it came to brews. The drink did nothing to improve his mood.

He stood and made for the door when Coryn spotted him. Once on his feet, the areosan towered over the other patrons who were mostly dwarves.

"Why is your axe wearing a dress?" Ra'al looked suspiciously at the weapon hanging over Coryn's back, hiding a sour mood with humor. They departed together.

"It is not a dress." Coryn tried to punch him, but he jumped away from her. "It is a cloth to cover the blade; it protects my axe from the elements and keeps the edge as keen as the day it was forged."

"Not a dress then. Got it." Ra'al still looked at the axe. "Even though it has frills and sleeves." He jumped away from Coryn, laughing. "Still, *not* a dress."

Coryn gave him a sharp look. Then, she went on and on about the next leg of their trip as if nothing had happened. It certainly shut him up.

Their short walk through the village felt long to Ra'al, mainly because Coryn wouldn't quit chirping about the horrors they might face on the way. He marveled at her eagerness to meet the myriad terrors, however unlikely any real encounter might be.

Ra'al, on the other hand, hoped to avoid both known and unknown dangers. He heard either was bad for his health. He kept his silence as Coryn continued to prattle. Ra'al ignored her, humming to block her out of his mind.

When they'd walked a circuit and neared the entrance to the inn, where the frostwing had secured them lodging, Coryn yanked him out of his introspection. She repeated, "I said, what do you think about *that?*"

"About what?" He tried to move, but Coryn knew the soft spots of his wing and pressed firmly. "Ow, ow, stop it Coryn!"

"Where were you?" She moved her free hand in the air animatedly. "Probably doing your mind hum thing to avoid paying attention, right?"

"I *did* pay attention," he complained. "Up till your description of a behemoth and how it can tear a person limb from limb without shedding a drop of sweat."

"That was several minutes ago." She released his wing and waved both her arms in the air. "Next, I told you about the ghwereste and their amazing fighting skills, *then* I talked about the morehl emissaries who we will undoubtedly meet with for negotiations on behalf of Icehome… *that's* something you ought to know more about."

Ra'al snorted a hot breath. He had little desire to parley with a race that he'd been taught was dangerous all his life. "Hah, peace and morehl should not be included in the same sentence." He bent to Coryn's level and said, "They are directly bonded to Death. They will always do his bidding." He straightened. "Besides, they are a bunch of backstabbers and liars to start with. I don't know how much we can really expect of them."

"Agreed." Coryn bobbed her head. But the irony was not lost on her; the frostwings had also been bonded to the Death god at their creation, according to the histories.

They ducked into the inn and smelled the earthy odors that were colored of clay, soot, and fresh hewn wood. A few diners lingered in the lobby, and the prince's areosan companions from Castle Ice gave him a subtle salute. One approached and directed them to their rooms. "We leave at first light," he said.

"It'll be good to spend a night in a bed before the next leg of the trip," Ra'al said.

The soldier grimaced. "It'll be a shorter leg, at least," he said. "Much like these dwarven beds. It may prove a cramped night, Prince Ra'al."

Ra'al scowled. He should have expected nothing less.

Coryn slapped her friend on the back, as far up as she could reach. "Come on, Ra'al. Beds are for sissies." She began walking towards her room.

Ra'al hung his head and followed.

Chapter 3

The air rushed past Coryn's face and bit her cheeks as she clung to Ra'al's back. For the first time in her life, she envied the beards of the male vagha. At least they didn't suffer wind-burned faces.

She shifted uncomfortably in the belted harness areosan artisans had made for her to ride upon her friend's shoulders. As strong as Ra'al's arms were, he could not hold her forever, and carrying the extra load tired him. Neither could she hold on for hours on end while they traveled through the skies.

Coryn had heard the tales from before her birth, stories of how Thrag carried her father north so soon after receiving an injury from the lava elves. What made the tale so legendary was the areosan king's stamina and her father's stubborn endurance. Combined, it allowed them to reach the safety of old Icehome and gather reinforcements before Uruzak's forces came in range to assault the Reaches.

A direct route to Tulgesh through the air would dramatically cut down the travel time. While the trip would take them a few days, it would take as much as a tenday for their luggage and supplies to arrive in the selumari city, and that was only because of "the luge": a kind of utility slide that dwarven artisans had built to connect Balgavarr with the base of the Kafnysan Mountains. The ferry station at its base would deliver their goods across the Sareen and to Tulgesh as soon as possible, but only because of a shortcut the vagha had cut through the Aldens, the persistent woods south of the mountain range.

Coryn could tell by the way Ra'al sweated through his fur that he was losing steam. They would have to land soon and rest, as they'd done regularly for the last several days. From her bird's-eye view, she'd seen the expansive Plains of Seshara like she'd never imagined. Far beyond them, like a gray mist where sky met land, the Uruzak Mountains spoiled the eastern horizon.

"We must rest," said a weary Ra'al.

She could barely hear him over the whistle of the air past her ears. Before them, the clouds broke while Ra'al and his four escorts glided to a lower elevation.

"There!" squealed Coryn. She pointed ahead at the shimmering coast and the city perched upon the bay. "There's Tulgesh."

She sucked in a breath through her teeth. She'd visited many years ago with her father, but had never seen it like this. The walls and structures closest to the water appeared to be sculpted from living coral and towers of glistening white rose, while cerulean stretched high from their bases where they surrounded the royal castle. In the distance and at an equal elevation, tiny figures could be seen flitting around the city's perimeter in lazy arcs. Coryn knew they must have been eagle riders. Beyond them, a coral airship hung in the sky with its dirigible bladder inflated, so it could easily hover. They were a rare sight, and she'd never spotted one, even from a distance. Her father had told her about riding one many decades ago, when Tulgesh was still in ruins from the lava elf invasion.

Ra'al gulped a lungful of frigid, thin air and redoubled his efforts. They'd glide the rest of the way and arrive at the elven city without stopping to rest.

Soon, an eagle picked up sight of them and came closer. Coryn produced a flag in each fist, one for Icehome and one for Balgavarr, so the rider could identify them as friendly. He saluted and buzzed past them at a safe distance.

Ra'al shuddered momentarily, and Coryn thought her friend might drop for a moment. "You got this buddy, you're doing great."

"Easy for you… I'm doing all the work," he growled back. "As soon as we reach the city, we're finding the nearest inn so I can sleep for twelve hours."

The frostwings landed a short time later at the furthest edges of Tulgesh. Ra'al's wings practically gave out ten cubits above the ground and both rolled to a graceless crash landing.

His shortened javelins spilled out from the quiver and scattered across the ground. He scrambled after them to hide his embarrassment.

Coryn nearly tumbled out of her harness. She hurried to help him retrieve them and said nothing, as if they didn't exist at all.

The other five frostwings alighted nimbly behind them as the dwarf unstrapped herself, stretched, and stood to her feet.

Blank stares met the newcomers as the mostly blue-skinned faces watched the areosan visitors and their dwarf companion. Frostwings were a rare sight below the Kafnysan Mountain range.

Ra'al did his best to catch his breath. The group began heading into the town, and those citizens who stopped to stare resumed their daily lives as if nothing remarkable had happened.

"There," the areosan prince insisted. "That's the first inn. Let's go."

"That dump?" Coryn sounded surprised. Cedar shingles in need of patching boasted more than a little dry rot, and its foundation crumbled in one corner. "Surely we can find better…"

"A hot meal and a nap," Ra'al said. "It's all I really want. You just rode on my back for three days. You can give me this, at least."

Coryn shrugged and then followed Ra'al inside. It was only a little past lunchtime, and the smells of a warm hearth overpowered the odor of decayed, creaky floorboards.

An aged human male quickly dished up a plateful for each and remarked about his rare guests' appetites. Ra'al declined to say much, simply taking the room key and warning Coryn, "Do not wake me for at least three hours."

"Yeah, yeah. You're tired. I hear you."

Ra'al caught the mischievous glint in her eye. "I mean it, not even if my bed catches fire. We've got a few days before our luggage arrives and we can explore the city before announcing ourselves at Matrek's court. We will need his council regarding trade and boundaries for the morehl."

"Fine," she shrugged, thinking those details sounded incredibly boring.

He closed the door, and she heard the sound of him collapsing onto an undersized mattress. Moments later, he snored loud enough to rattle the door planks.

Coryn turned to her companions and realized she barely knew them. She could only recall one of their names. Before the awkwardness could overwhelm her, a selumari entered the inn. His body language felt wrong for a place of such low means, and he almost cringed at the sight within. Judging by his fine clothes, she guessed he was from a wealthy house.

The coral elf's eyes lit when he spotted Coryn and the frostwings lounging in the lobby. "Oh good! I found you."

Coryn raised a brow. Before she could ask any questions, the coral elf thrust a scroll into her hand. "My lady wishes me deliver this to you." With a bow, he turned and left.

"Curious," the adventurous vagha mumbled before unrolling the parchment.

"Wake up, Ra'al! Get up—something has happened," Coryn squealed, jumping about like a playful wolf cub.

He squeezed his eyes tighter for one final moment, certain that it couldn't have been more than two hours since he'd collapsed into bed. His eyes fluttered open and, through the window, he spotted Soll still high in the sky. It bathed the city in mid-afternoon light. He noticed the ratty accommodations and sighed, mumbling, "How far have I fallen..."

"Come on, Ra'al," Coryn insisted.

He glowered at his friend. Ra'al knew her well enough to recognize that the tone of her voice did not indicate danger. "What is it?" he groused.

"I've met someone..."

"And I'm sure you'll be very happy together."

"No, you stupid snow-head. I met a queen, and she has agreed to sponsor our stay in Tulgesh." Coryn clutched the scroll she'd sent earlier. "I just got back from meeting her, and she's lovely. I think you'll…"

"Matrek is king in Tulgesh," Ra'al interrupted, putting his hands on his hips. "And he has never married."

"Yeah," Coryn spat. "I didn't say she was *the selumari queen*… although she *is* a coral elf… and I think she's some kind of royalty, too. But I know she does not rule Tulgesh."

Ra'al cocked his head.

"She's offering us a place to stay, and the rooms are far nicer than this dump," Coryn continued. "And she wants to meet you and talk with us both. She is something of a world traveler but has never been to the Shadowlands."

A moment of silence passed between them as Ra'al thought it over. Coryn sweetened the pot by saying, "She's having a feast prepared for this evening."

No sooner did she say "feast," that Ra'al's stomach growled in a twisting knot. All the recent physical labor that sapped his stamina had kicked his metabolism into overdrive.

"Fine. Alright," he said, gathering his few belongings from the bedside and following her towards the lobby. He looked for his other companions. "Where are the others, already feasting in the halls of your *queen?*"

Coryn gave him a thin-lipped smile. "Gone."

"What do you mean 'gone'?"

Coryn didn't answer.

"Coryn…What do you mean?"

"I sent them back to Icehome. We shouldn't need an escort if we're under the queen's care."

Ra'al rocked a step back with surprise. "We don't even know this person."

"I do. Well, I know *of* her," Coryn said, and sat up straighter. "She visited Balgavarr Reaches in her youth, before she became a world-traveling queen. Besides, she might have even more influence than Matrek. Cyrea is small compared to the rest of Esfah. Queen Naemyar is originally from Tulgesh, but she is the queen of Niamarlee in Eastern Charnock… and she is the heir and owner of Riechus Aqualines."

"The shipping company?"

Coryn nodded. "Our entire mission concerns trade negotiations. What a better way to further your mother's goals than to arrive at the meeting table with the backing of one of the biggest trade moguls in all Esfah? It's better than a handful of soldiers, if you ask me, and less likely to spur conflict."

Ra'al stroked his chin, pondering her logic. Her support might make King Matrek's offers obsolete. Ra'al nodded. "Well, this feast had better be amazing."

The duo caught a rickshaw and crossed town. They entered a more affluent part of the city; buildings grew more opulent as they drew nearer the water. Finally, they passed the gates of an elegant, private estate.

A doorman saw them in and escorted them inside the house where the queen's selumari majordomo took over. "I am Lotep. Queen Naemyar's head of staff. I offer her apologies," Lotep said, "but Queen Naemyar had urgent business to attend to. The feast is still prepared, and she wishes for you to eat without her. I will see you to your rooms afterwards and a tailor will meet you in your quarters to fit you for tonight's gala."

Coryn's eyes lit up. "A gala?"

Lotep nodded, even as Ra'al's face fell. The coral elf servant flashed the duo a suspicious look, seeming to measure them up with his eyes.

"It will occur this evening," Lotep assured her. "The queen hosts them often. They are a vital part of connecting with her network. Naemyar believes that, as it is in statecraft, relationship building is the key everything."

Ra'al looked ready to complain on principle…But that was before the food arrived.

Ra'al wore only part of what the tailor laid out for him: a regal, silk tunic. The lightweight fabric felt smooth against his fur and it breathed well. He entered the castle's ballroom, which danced with the lights of a thousand candles. The light came from the great chandelier hanging from the ceiling, where a glimmering hue cascaded into the room's center in beautiful prisms.

Dignitaries and courtesans fluffed around in all colors of silk and velvet, their Prismatic accents sparking around them with opulent effect.

Two very long tables stood at either end of the room, filled to the rim with all kinds of local and international delicacies meant to appease an estimated two hundred guests.

Ra'al walked slowly around the hall, trying to avoid all of them. Several stopped him for idle chat; though it was immediately clear that few had ever spoken with a frostwing. The north was inhospitable, and comfort seekers did not fare well there. The irony was not lost on Ra'al.

Queen Naemyar sat upon a throne-like chair and presided over the gala. It was made from carved black wood, which made her look regal and inviting.

He paused before the patroness and gave a short bow. A few onlookers recognized the lack of a deep, formal bow and sucked air through their teeth, understanding Ra'al's movements subtly indicated his royal position. "Greetings, Queen Naemyar," he stated. "I am Ra'al, of Icehome, at your service."

"Pleased to meet you," she said with a smile. "You and I must find a time to chat later. I do hope you find Tulgesh to your liking."

Ra'al nodded formally, accepting her eventual invitation, and then he moved along, searching for his diminutive friend.

Coryn was here somewhere, he felt certain. She was likely the first one in the room. Ra'al would have bet that the vagha was already dancing with someone.

He pitied her poor dance companions. Not only was Coryn a graceless dancer, but she wore her steel battle boots everywhere, likely even to this ball. Many shins would be bruised before the end of the night.

Still, spending time around Coryn seemed like the perfect shield from the curious folk trying to engage him in small talk, and so he searched for her in earnest.

The search did not go well. At most, Coryn's height was barely chest level of the average guest. The crowd was made up of dignitaries including selumari, a cluster of blue-skinned empyreans who looked like bodyguards for other important folk, and a few odd humans here and there. A few gray-skinned elves, frehlasuhl, faded into the background to perform scullion work. They were masters of remaining unseen.

A flash of red skin caught Ra'al's eye. A group of morehl sat huddled together near a corner of the room. Their skin shone deeper in the candle light and made them appear more sinister. Typical of lava elves, they wore the darkest of black attire and remained aloof as wallflowers.

Just as Ra'al finally pulled his eyes away from them, something sharp and heavy crushed his left foot, followed by a cheerful, "Hello."

He winced. "Hello Coryn. I see that you are wearing your boots to the gala, as I'd expected." He hobbled to the nearest table and leaned on it to rest his bruised paw.

"Battle boots fit any occasion, and they are perfect for dancing." She smiled. "You should have heard my accompaniment to the royal band's music."

"So, you were that occasional, off-tempo boom in the background?" Ra'al jumped a cubit to the left as Coryn tried to step twice on his feet.

"Not so funny." Coryn grabbed his wing and pressed.

Before Ra'al could retaliate, an older looking vagha approached and extended his hand. The vagha wore the attire of a foreign dignitary, which told Ra'al of his station and pedigree. "Ki'Harol sa'Lahmyn, at your service."

The dwarf waited for a moment until Ra'al, nudged by Coryn, took his hand.

"Pleased to meet you esteemed Harol sa'Lahmyn." Ra'al gave him a measured smile.

"Coryn told me that you are both to undertake an adventure," Harol said matter-of-factly, causing Ra'al to internally groan.

"A trip to the eastern side of Cyrea, not an adventure." Ra'al looked fiercely to Coryn.

"I know. Still, you have to take every precaution to come back fast and safe." This was a dwarf after his own heart: no talk about how exciting the trip would be. "Many dangers on that side of the continent," Harol continued, looking away.

Ra'al matched his stare and locked eyes on the morehl guests, who looked even more unhappy to be at this party than he.

"Master Harol is an emissary from Balgavarr to Tulgesh," Coryn piped up. "He and I met at the start of the gala."

"And how is Tulgesh, Master sa'Lahmyn?" Ra'al asked casually.

"Just Harol, Please. Tulgesh is on a razor's edge, as should all of Esfah," Harol said. "At least those of us who are in the know. The rest of the huddled masses are ignorant of the dangers that intensify across Cyrea." He turned his head from side to side slowly, as if checking to see if someone might be eavesdropping. "There have been sightings of the risen dead all over the continent…especially the north. I'm sure you also get reports from your father's command?" he asked Coryn. "Something evil stirs in the frozen wastes."

Something the emissary had said struck a nerve.

"I've heard other rumors. I am starting to think that this is a global phenomenon occurring all over Esfah." Ra'al said, a shiver running down his spine.

"Add to that how alienated the nations are, and it conjures a bleak image." Harol looked right and left, as if he feared being heard. Harol glanced to the side and captured Coryn's gaze. "Don't be fooled by elven hospitality, girl, at least not from any but Naemyar. The selumari still blame Geril Dragonsbane for losing the treasure from the Magestorm Wars, although few even know what it is, let alone how he lost it."

. "But surely, if Death stirs his acolytes again in Cyrea and the call arises, a new generation of heroes would rise to stand against him?" Coryn stressed. "Surely help shall be given from the gods when it is most needed."

"The legend of the Chosen, the Gods' own Champions?" Harol tapped his plump lip with a forefinger. "I've heard stories from across the globe of this so-called group. He trailed off momentarily. "Perhaps we can only hope that these legends are true." Harol gave Coryn a searching look.

The younger vagha turned her head away. Something in Harol's wild eyes unnerved her.

Ra'al noticed her expression and interjected, "Till dark days come, we have this gala, the music, and the dance." Something screamed at him not to do it, probably the notion of a broken toe, but he reached for Coryn's hand and said, "Would the lady Coryn grace me with this dance?"

Coryn was more than grateful to get away from the deeply scrying eyes of Harol.

Soon, the mismatched pair melted between the throngs of dancers. Coryn stomped with all the grace of a young umberhulk.

Ra'al was tall enough to look over the crowd and keep tabs on Harol. The dwarf followed them with his eyes for some moments before Lotep, Naemyar's servant, arrived and had a brief conversation with the dwarf. After that, Harol turned and left.

Lotep found Ra'al in the crowd and met his eyes briefly. The elf bowed cordially and then followed suit.

Ra'al decided after the fourth time Coryn stomped on his foot that it was time for him to retire, too. He didn't stop to address the morehl when they passed, and he tried not to think about what they might be up to, or why they were here.

He would have his fill of morehl soon enough, when he and Coryn traveled to meet the lava elf ambassadors north east of Thurisa, where the Plains of Seshara met the vagha's borders of Uruzak and the Sareen River.

Ra'al shot one last look back at Coryn and thought, *and now, we've got to meet the lava elves without our protective detail.*

Ra'al woke up the next morning with strange pains and aches. Then, he remembered: he'd gone dancing with Coryn last night.

He groaned as he moved from bed to dressing room. He pulled the silken robes over his body that he'd worn last evening.

He rummaged through his belt pouches and retrieved a small bladder of ointment – one that was given to him by his old weapon-master. It was meant to ease the pain from new calluses that sometimes grew from intense practice or from hand bruises earned with clumsy grips. He rubbed the salve upon his feet.

The ointment was magical, but according to the consistent, throbbing ache in his feet, it didn't seem to be working. Maybe it didn't work against dwarf-induced dance moves.

The first time he danced with Coryn was many years ago. He told her mid-way through their second dance that she should quit weapons' training and concentrate on dancing.

Coryn had blushed and asked if that was a compliment to her weapon skills, or an insult to her dancing. Ra'al answered that it was a petition on behalf of future enemies who might encounter her wickedly designed metal footgear.

He laughed to himself as he walked out of the room, remembering the beating Coryn had given him after the celebrations were done.

As he walked through the opulent corridor, Ra'al decided that the ointment was indeed working; now, he only hurt every other step. Or maybe it was just that Coryn favored her left foot during their dancing session.

Ra'al decided that if he actually claimed his father's throne, he would pass a law banning all female vagha from dancing. After a few more steps, Ra'al figured it might be best to simply prohibit dancing in steel boots.

He was so lost in these thoughts that he nearly crashed into the selumari butler.

"Forgive me, Prince Ra'al," the coral elf squeaked and bowed.

"Sorry, I didn't see you." Ra'al smiled widely, a move that showed off his well-cared-for canines.

The butler gulped at the sight of the fangs. Primal instincts ran strong in most folk. Trying to regain his composure, the butler said, "I was sent to tell you that Queen Naemyar requests your presence."

"Understood." Ra'al bobbed his head and followed the messenger towards Naemyar's chamber. The door opened to show that Coryn already stood in front of their hostess. Though Coryn's optimistic face appeared gloomier than normal.

Ra'al watched as Naemyar approached. She wore a more serious expression than she'd worn last night.

"I fear there is not much opportunity for small talk or formalities. We have a pressing matter to discuss." She led them both to a small meeting room at the back of her chamber.

Ra'al's heart beat faster as their benefactor clutched a sightstone inset with a sapphire gem. She mumbled some words beneath her breath and cast a simple spell to create an orb of silence. "It is quiet secure," she promised. "We will not be spied upon."

The chamber reminded Ra'al of his mother's war room at Castle Ice. From there, Icehome and Balgavarr had engineered a victory over Uruzak and the volcanic mountains' allies. Rashingot rarely used it since, and the last time he remembered her there, Ra'al was still a kit. He and Coryn had once sneaked into that very room when they were adolescents, and the look on the face of his mother had been terrible.

Ra'al shook his head to clear it.

Naemyar invited both him and Coryn to sit.

"I have met with some morehl visitors. You may have seen them last night," Naemyar said. "They came to me because of my seat on Tulgesh's Trade Council. They thought my family ties and connection to the shipping and trade industry might help sway public opinion in your favor."

Ra'al nodded, finally making the connection.

She continued, "The lava elves are seeking an alliance. Something that should be great news for all Cyrea."

"But it isn't?" Ra'al expressed worriedly.

"It might have rendered your upcoming visit to the border needless," she said. "Yes, I know much of your mission, even before Coryn told me of it. King Matrek is aware of it, too, and he and I have an *understanding* when it comes to sharing information."

Coryn put it together first. "Uruzak is offering common guard on the disputed land," she said in a rush. "They'll be pitching the same idea to all the major kingdoms of Cyrea. Much like our free cities, they are hoping for a kind of free territory."

Naemyar nodded. "I told them it required time to formulate the terms of such an alliance, and they simply left." The displaced queen rubbed her hands together, her brow furrowed.

"Something happened to ruin these plans?" Ra'al guessed as he looked from Naemyar to Coryn, who shook her head.

"Not exactly," Naemyar said. "I placed servants all around the palace."

Ra'al pressed his lips thin. This selumari had much in common with his mother.

"Well, one of those ears heard something disturbing." The queen continued rubbing her hands and it set Ra'al's nerves on edge. He waited for her to continue.

Coryn blurted out, "First, their leader might be the imperial prince. Second, he is up to something dangerous."

"Good to know." Ra'al shrugged. "But how does that impact *my* mission?"

"Coryn isn't exactly correct," Naemyar said.

"Of course, she's not," Ra'al chuffed.

"Any delegation is only as strong as its leader. This delegation is headed by the lava elf next in line to ascend the throne." Naemyar inhaled a long, slow breath. "Short of them escorting Emperor Saugor, no delegation should be as strongly supported.

"If he is indeed the prince, his traveling delegation is important for two reasons. The first is that he travels soon to Frostshoal, an area so long disputed, it gained its own autonomy through national conflict avoidance."

Ra'al's ears perked up. Frostshoal was a place any poet would dream to visit. Many great stories started in Frostshoal and it was famous for entertaining bards of high repute. His heart remained in Icehome, but he was invested in this new detail.

"The second reason is the object of the prince's quest. At the very least, there is some dishonesty in him—his diplomatic travels mask something he wishes to keep secret." The queen sighed. "My ears pick up many secrets and the morehl indicated that Frostshoal, 'has something to do with the Magestorm Wars.' And *that* is the core of all of my fears."

"Why?" Ra'al looked from Naemyar to Coryn, who looked especially crestfallen.

"Scraps of legend mention a huge weapon cache, created during the Magestorm Wars and hidden after it was won. It's practically a myth; only wizards and their disciples know much of it," Coryn said and clenched her fists. "It's a well-guarded secret."

The queen raised her head high, looking haughty. She nodded to acknowledge Coryn's information. "This is true; my father was something of an expert on that era, and I still remember much of what he told me. Not that we have time to talk about old legends…

"If they seek this cache, we should suspect them of preparing for an all-out *war.,*" Coryn said and struck the table.

Ra'al's mind sped up. He did not want to play with the notion of re-igniting the Cyrean War. More than anything, he just wanted his life to pass idyllically – as boring and comfortable as could be.

War, he decided, had to be prevented *whatever the cost.*

"Alright, Naemyar, what should we do to stop this morehl prince?" Ra'al said, stretching his wings to their full seven-cubit span for emphasis.

"I think you should join the prince and his group on their trip to Frostshoal." The queen looked him over, impressed at the areosa and his muscular physique.

"And what should we say to convince him to take us along?" Coryn asked, turning from Ra'al to the queen.

"You can join as co-travelers. Say that you wish to reconnect with the descendants of the heroes of Balgavarr," the queen said excitedly. "Your father was one, Ra'al. So was Coryn's father. Everybody knows that."

Coryn caught onto the queen's excitement. "I know a couple of descendants who live in Frostshoal; it would make a perfect excuse!"

"Who lives there?" Ra'al pulled back his wings and sat with a thud upon the heavy wooden chair. "And please, no long-winded stories about the war."

Coryn flushed with embarrassment. "Never mind then, I don't need to know the descendants. What was the second thing?"

"Perhaps Prince Ra'al tires of old stories." The queen smiled, her eyes twinkling with amusement. Perhaps she was a fellow fan of historical battles. "But I think the data is relevant to what I am asking of you. So, Coryn dear, tell us more."

Coryn sat upright and prattled enthusiastically. "We know that the beast folk contributed to the war, specifically in Balgavarr. They eventually retreated from the public eye. Many now live among the humans in the Plains of Seshara and in the Wilds of Dur'Sona."

"Yeah, yeah, bla bla bla, and they are also in Frostshoal," Ra'al mumbled, "I know what you're getting at."

"But I didn't get to the interesting parts," Coryn said in a choked voice.

Queen Naemyar raised an eyebrow. "For someone rumored to loathe conflict, you should really work on your bedside manners." She flashed a smile at Ra'al.

He bobbed his head with a polite grimace.

"While with the lava elves, you must thwart whatever the prince is up to," the queen said on a long breath. "Once you know what he's planned, alert me, and I will send the forces necessary to take them into custody, should a diplomatic solution prove impossible. I have already secured King Matrek's aid..."

"Finally, some action!" Coryn barked.

"And risk igniting war with Uruzak?" Ra'al raised his eyebrows. "Is King Matrek usually so reckless? Why would he let two foreigners disrupt the peace he's worked for decades to bring to Tulgesh?"

Naemyar's face remained neutral. "Matrek is also on the Trade Council. He is aware of the risks and has weighed the dangers carefully. Any soldiers we send are not likely to be coral elves...Unless the conditions demand it."

Coryn hung onto every word, but Ra'al saw the truth of it straight away. His mother's training taught him to see the truth hidden in history's "facts". If something went wrong, Tulgesh would escape the worst of Uruzak's wrath because Matrek had not been directly involved. Any disastrous outcomes would be the fault of the vagha, areosa, and whatever private mercenaries they hired.

The frostwing mulled the plan over. Much of it overlapped the mission his mother gave him. If they had to kidnap a lava elf prince by the end, a hostage negotiation could have the same end result as a diplomatic solution, albeit more tense. And if the morehl were planning some major war effort for the mythic weapons, then his diplomatic mission would be moot, anyway.

"So what should we do now?" Coryn asked eagerly. Ra'al ignored her, assuming it would never come to a full-fledged battle. As layered in subterfuge as the plan appeared, only a worst-case scenario would put them in any *real* danger.

"Now, you must wait. I shall call on the red-elf prince." Queen Naemyar stood. "The vessel they have booked passage belongs to Riechus Aqualines." With a broad smile, she mumbled an incantation and put away her stone to release the spell of silence before dismissing them.

Prince Garesch stood in front of the queen with his colleagues. They'd been pulled from their beds by a very insistent coral elf messenger. The blue-skinned courier felt obviously uncomfortable in the lava elves' presence.

He didn't mind her calling on them, but Garesch was intrigued to know what had been so important for Queen Naemyar to summon them on the day they intended to sail away from the selumari city.

The fact that she called at all was strange. They had concluded their formalities the night of the gala, and she had agreed to contact him directly, and at a later date, to address any land-stewardship arrangements. Garesch couldn't fathom a single reason for this audience, and he was anxious to hear what she had in mind.

But first, she inspected Prince Garesch and his companions. "You intend to circle the continent until you reach Frostshoal?" she asked.

"This is the plan, yes. A trip meant for alliance welding," Garesch said, showing enough deference to keep her talking.

"That is a noble endeavor," Naemyar said and gave the prince a genuine smile.

"We aim to gather as many allies as possible, Your Majesty." Garesch was raised in court, too, but he couldn't understand what the queen was asking of him.

Naemyar's smile widened. "I understand your ship was supposed to leave soon. Unfortunately, it has been delayed for maintenance repairs. No more than a day, at most."

Garesch arched a black eyebrow upon his otherwise smooth, crimson skin. "Is it your intent to inconvenience a corps of royal ambassadors from Uruzak?" He kept his voice as even keeled as possible.

"Quite the contrary," Naemyar insisted. "That is why I have summoned you, to explain firsthand and smooth over any misconceptions of ill-intent. However, I hoped it might make time for a visiting prince to accompany you aboard the same vessel. I'm sure you understand. I could not refuse the request of a royal passenger and must show preference to royalty above a company of ambassadors."

She held his gaze as she spoke, and the lava elf already knew she suspected his true lineage. Garesch had not told her he was a prince, and she squinted as she scrutinized him. It was only the tiniest flexing of an eye, but in that moment, he understood that she knew. *Damn, she's good*, he thought. *Better than most morehl, and we have the natural aptitude for it.*

Regardless, she kept up the pretensions. "I'm certain you won't mind, and perhaps you already met Prince Ra'al at the gala. He is on a mission of similar purposes."

"Similar purposes?" Garesch remained neutral, but he was pleased that the game had progressed, even if he felt his identity had quickly become the worst kept secret in Tulgesh.

"Yes, Prince Ra'al and his companion are searching for the heroes of Balgavarr's heirs." Naemyar kept a placid posture, playing the same game as the young prince.

"This is a noble endeavor, Your Majesty," Garesch said. "One befitting the future King, of course.

"Your mission, and his, represents more of what we need in these troubling days," she said.

"We would be honored to have the son of Thrag and his company aboard our ship. I shall inform my company of the delay."

Naemyar gave him a stiff bow. "I appreciate your understanding. The additional guests will be provisioned as soon as possible. I will send word to the harbor and seek word from the captain. He will give you a more accurate idea of the revised departure time."

Garesch nodded, returned her bow, and then departed. He was well aware of the smirk upon Naemyar's face when his back was turned.

Coryn and Ra'al made a mad dash through town. They aimed to replace the supplies still in transit via Balgavarr's couriers. They made quick purchases of clothing and sundries, as well as backup weaponry and two new travel trunks.

Once they arrived at the port, they greeted the captain of the *Coral Skip*. The ship was not the biggest vessel, nor was it a shabby one. It would prove serviceable enough for their needs.

Ra'al followed his friend up the gangplank. He stood at the rails and looked back as Tulgesh grew further away by the minute. Soon, it lay far behind the vast wall of water, leaving Ra'al only his wits and his chirpy little friend to stand against the company of devious morehl and whatever nefarious plans they had laid.

64

his wits and his chirpy little friend to stand against the company of devious morehl and whatever nefarious plans they had laid.

Chapter 4

After a few hours at sea, Ra'al smiled smugly. He felt
pleasantly surprised not to have suffered any sickness from the
constant rocking of the ship gliding across the waves. He mused
that his familiarity with flight and its shifting air currents might
have prepared him with a kind of airborne "sea legs."

Coryn, on the other hand, had emptied her stomach twice
and had never felt so miserable. To Ra'al, she smiled through her
pain – still refusing to admit that adventures could contain such
deep misery.

Ra'al gazed into the waters of the sea. Deep blue
surrounded the ship in every direction and he relished its beauty. A
poem filled him like the thousands of other poets before him, and
he yearned to write it down before he lost it.

A silver-backed fish flipped and shined in the morning sun
like a shooting star. It dipped back into the sea where, moments
later, a seagull swooped and picked the silver-back up with its
beak. Before the bird could pull away from the surface, the toothy
maw of a large sea creature with red eyes snatched it and pulled it
under.

"It wasn't a very poetic scene, anyway," Ra'al muttered.
He decided that he'd had enough sightseeing for the day. He
stepped gingerly away from the rails, seeking company from the
seasick Coryn instead. Ra'al and Coryn had kept their distance
from both the other passengers and the crew ever since the ship
had set sail. The sailors were a crude lot of mixed selumari and
humans.

Garesch and his group followed in similar fashion.
Although the morehl huddled together and whispered amongst
themselves, the crew had been indifferent to them. Dregs and
roughnecks seemed less disturbed by old racial grudges.

Ra'al did his best to avoid looking suspicious to the red-
skinned enemies. He didn't want to tip them off that they were

being spied upon, but he kept an eye on them as closely as possible.

Coryn struggled to stand by his side, her constant sickness causing her to sway and swoon. They tried to watch the lava elves from across the deck.

"So, did you catch any of what they were saying?" Coryn belched and turned yellowish-green for a few seconds.

Ra'al waited for her color to almost return to normal before he answered, "We are standing, or wobbling in your case, more than twenty cubits from them." He reached quickly to grab Coryn before she fell onto the deck. "How do you think I can hear them?"

"Well, you have enormous ears, even for a frostwing." She clutched on his arm for dear life. Her words slurred, "Plus, you have this thing with the wind and its songs or whatever."

"I might be a frostwing, but the wind doesn't sing to me." Ra'al looked down at Coryn, who plucked at the hairs of his arm. "And I certainly can't hear anything clearly more than ten cubits away, especially if it is a whisper."

Coryn looked up to him with misery in her eyes.

"Don't give me that look," Ra'al said, and looked back at her like she was his little sister.

"I know for a fact that every single frostwing can hear the song of the wind." Coryn threw her arms in the air, twisted her entire body like a professional contortionist, and landed on the deck.

Ra'al stole a look at the morehl to be certain that they were not laughing at her predicament, then reached down and pulled her up.

"So, Ra'al, prince of the frostwings, why do you lie to me?" Coryn held onto Ra'al with both arms, as if she were drunk.

"Did you take something for the nausea?" Ra'al leaned closer to look in her eyes. "This can't be just seasickness."

"A sailor gave me a special concoction to fix my seasickness." She belched loudly. "It works. I don't even feel my stomach anymore."

"I think you should go lay down, Coryn." Ra'al started to drag the vagha towards her hammock in the passengers' quarters.

"No, not yet." She swayed and careened toward his body, fixing him with a serious gaze. "Why do you lie about the wind, Ra'al?"

"Coryn." He pulled her nearer and bent down to whisper, "I have never heard the song of the wind. Maybe I am different, or maybe I am cursed." The weight of the leather quiver at his back weighed heavily upon his shoulder sling.

"Cursed. I knew it," Coryn said and fell again onto her back.

Ra'al groaned, grabbed the vagha by the waist, and picked her up. He carried her like a bundle under one arm as he headed for their cabins under the deck.

After four days of impromptu puke-fests, Coryn finally managed to earn her sea legs. Ra'al applauded that she barely lost any food now, which was good, because every time she did, fish swarmed around the ship to eat whatever she offered.

Though some sailors would say her sea legs were not such good luck, as her constant chum plumes had often provided them with endless supply of easy catches on the line and lure.

As Ra'al and Coryn sat for breakfast, the captain of the *Coral Skip* came to their cabin.

Captain Harna bowed. "Good day, my lady, good day Your Highness."

"Good day, captain," Coryn said, and popped a large piece of bread and buttered dry cheese in her mouth.

"I hope you enjoy your breakfast," the captain said.

"Immensely." Coryn dipped a large morsel of bread into the infamous Fire Sauce from her homeland. She made certain it was soaked from all sides before pushing it into her mouth. In their mad panic to re-provision at Naemyar's expense, she'd spotted a dwarven vendor selling it in Tulgesh near a vaghan supply store.

"I wanted to inform you that we will soon pass near the plaguelands of southwestern Cyrea. There, we might expect scalder attacks." Harna bowed deeply. "The faeli often attack ships. They've managed to repel all invaders to land as they expand their hold on Cyrea...even the morehl fear the twisted creatures. I encourage you to go nowhere above deck unarmed until we are sure to be clear of the threat." He nodded with an assuring bob of his head. "Do enjoy your breakfast." Then, he left.

"Did I hear some irony in his voice?" Ra'al cracked opened his seventh egg and slurped it down. "How am I to enjoy my breakfast now?"

"Maybe he never saw a vagha eat before. Fire Sauce is not for anyone." Coryn pulled the vinegar-like, spicy condiment to her mouth and drained the small bowl.

"Well, I guess breakfast is over." Ra'al stood, and as he'd done for the last four days, hit his head on the ceiling of the low-roofed cabin. He winced. "I think we should prepare for battle, just in case of an attack." He looked at Coryn with eyes that seemed to accuse her for getting them into this mess. "This is how I go... killed by faeli and sunk off the coast of the Shining Sea," he sighed.

"I got enough Fire Sauce inside me to scorch any foolish scalder who thinks of approaching this ship." Coryn jumped excitedly, completely ignoring his expression. "Plus, I'm wearing these new battle boots my father gave me and I am *dying* to try them."

Ra'al winced as he recalled her regular battle boots. Somebody was in for a world of pain. He just hoped it wasn't him.

Anyone aboard the ship and not working riggings or rudders was divided into one of two groups. Most faeli had wings, so an attack could come from any angle. One half stood at the ready on the starboard, and the other on the port side. The most capable sailors trimmed the sails, so as to quickly and efficiently speed beyond the danger zone.

Ra'al stood next to Garesch with Coryn, two other morehl, and a mixed retinue of selumari and human watchers on the port side.

"I think you should smile more often," Garesch said to the prince, his eyes looking intently at the sea.

"Well, thank you, I think I would." Ra'al smiled widely at Garesch.

"Seriously, it terrifies most folk; I think the scalders might just turn around once they see those teeth." Garesch continued watching a spot a hundred cubits away.

"You must be joking," Coryn, who stood only chest high to Garesch, said. "Ra'al has the finest pair of frostwing fangs I ever saw."

"My point exactly." Garesch winked at her with a slight smile.

"Yeah, people mistake our teeth for a tool of war." Ra'al pointed to his three inch fangs. "But, in fact, we frostwings use them to sing back to the wind…Unless we really have to bite someone."

"You don't say." Garesch smiled wider.

"In a fight, our wings and hands are more important." He brandished his retractable claws, where they gleamed in the morning sun, clutched upon his weapon. "The fangs are more for decoration." Ra'al turned to Garesch and guffawed, noticing how Garesch eyed him curiously.

"As I said, Ra'al is one of the finest frostwings I ever saw." Coryn said and twisted her boots, scraping the wood of the ship beneath the balls of her feet.

Garesch shook his head with lips pulled thin. "I guess I would rather stand next to you in battle than against you, Prince Ra'al." His voice took on a diplomatic air.

"I can say the same." Ra'al nodded.

After the first hour, the demeanor among the ship's crew lightened. It would take another four or five days to sail around the full length of the plaguelands, but attacks, when they came against any ship, typically came within the first half-day of crossing their boundary.

After the ship passed the most dangerous waters, weapons were sheathed. The passengers at the rails returned to sightseeing.

"See those bubbles over there," Garesch said, and pointed into the water... "Something that breathes air must make them."

"Not fish, then." Coryn peered curiously.

"No. Usually sailors avoid spots with bubbles." Garesch looked back at the crew who worked their posts. "They will never cast their nets on bubbles. Who knows what they might dredge up?"

"So, not whales, I presume." Ra'al squinted to see what might lie beneath the waves. "I think whales would be an ordeal for a ship this size."

"Most whaler ships are about this size, but they are better equipped." Garesch pointed to the harpoon at the bow. "For instance, that harpoon doesn't have the force to pierce a whale's heart, but it could possibly deter a leviathan, which doesn't have the blubber to guard its vitals."

"There are leviathans in these waters?" Coryn asked excitedly. Leviathans were rare, oceanic monsters.

Garesch shrugged. "Not that I know of." "I suspect it's in case we encounter creatures that faeli pirates might press into service."

"You are very well versed with sea life. I mean for a morehl," Ra'al said to Garesch.

"I dreamed of being a sailor at a younger age." Garesch suddenly stopped what he was about to say, and the pause made Coryn and Ra'al stare at him. Then he continued, "But I had other duties that made that dream impossible. Besides," he laughed.

"Lava elves are not well suited to the sea. And I eventually got my share of sailor tales to last any living morehl a lifetime."

"I also wished for something else as my destiny, but alas, not everything we wish for can be achieved." Ra'al said.

"Something as wild as being a morehl sailor?" Garesch chuckled.

"Far wilder actually," Ra'al said. "I wished to be a poet, and a bard who sang tribute to the great heroes of the past."

"And here you are, creating your own story, one that will be a tribute one day." Garesch smiled. "Not so different after all."

"Yeah, yeah." Ra'al looked far into the horizon and remembered their cover story. "The heirs to those champions who fought against your kind all deserve whatever recognition they can get."

"Your pursuit fascinates me." Garesch let the diplomatic faux pas slide and half-turned to face Ra'al. "I wish you could indulge me in the details of the whole endeavor."

"Well, the person at the heart of this whole project is Coryn," Ra'al said and shrugged. "I am only here for my handsome looks."

"I can't believe that." Garesch looked hard to Ra'al. "You are the prince, you are the leader of this expedition, and lady Coryn is just one of your aides and companions."

Ra'al could see the lava elf was onto them, and he decided to reveal his suspicions. A lifetime spent frustrated with his mother's cloak and dagger methods made him prefer a more direct approach. He asked, "Where are you and company actually heading, and why?"

The lava elf stiffened. "It is none of your business. And I resent your spying on us in the first place," Garesch snarled.

"We don't have to spy on you, Prince Garesch; we know you have ill intentions." Ra'al's wings spread open to their full span

Coryn groaned, and muttered, "You weren't supposed to tell him that…"

Garesch whirled and faced Ra'al with two daggers drawn. "I guess talk is for weaklings, after all, Prince Ra'al." Garesch licked the edge of one dagger. "Let's see if those claws of yours live up to your father's statue."

As Ra'al growled, Coryn stepped between them.

"What in the name of the gods are you two doing?" she shouted sharply.

"Nothing to bother you, Coryn, just some playful sparring," Ra'al hissed.

"I don't think this is the time to fight, Ra'al. We are all stuck together on this ship, after all," Coryn pressed, still between the two combatants.

"We are *not* spying," she shouted at Garesch. "But we *were* told that you plan to steal something and should be wary of you." She only had to fudge the truth a *little*. "It might have had something to do with my father's…"

"I don't even know who your father is," Garesch snapped back. "Why should I steal anything from him? You accuse me only because I am a morehl?"

"No, but how can we trust you, if you come in denial of your real title?" Coryn argued.

Ra'al beat the air with his wings once, forcing both Coryn and Garesch to grab the rails as the sudden gust pushed them.

"Ra'al, stop this right now," Coryn shouted as she stiffened, knowing exactly how ironic it was that she'd slipped into diplomacy when Ra'al had opted for violence.

"Well, I was only reacting to his *majesty,*" Ra'al snarled. "I will stop when he stops."

"Alright, let's talk, then." Garesch sheathed his daggers.

"I think that would be a far better course of action." Coryn whipped imaginary dust off her clothes. "We are bound to the ship, and we are deep at sea. This fight could not have ended well." She looked around the deck and spotted amused faces from the crew. They'd had no intention of stepping in to stop any fight; it would have proved the most entertainment they'd seen in days.

"I will start by saying that I hid my identity with good purpose. Beyond Uruzak, Cyrea is openly hostile to morehl." Garesch straightened his clothes "And I would make an easy target as the son of Saugor. Now, I have a right to know why you forced *your* way into my journey after I had fairly chartered this vessel."

"We really *are* seeking the sons of heroes." Coryn momentarily looked at the scuffs her boots had left on the deck. "We can prove our claim."

"Then do so," Garesch dared her.

Ra'al looked from Coryn to Garesch and then relaxed his wings.

"I can tell you in detail who we are searching for, as long as you tell us your own story," Coryn bartered. She lowered her head, which made her look even shorter.

"I will be more than happy to tell you; although; I don't really think you will believe it." Garesch sighed. "Just know that I really do travel beyond Uruzak to make allies."

Ra'al's stomach grumbled. "To our cabin, then. Let us find something to eat as we discuss our corporate, hidden agendas."

Siting in the morehl prince's private quarters, Ra'al was keenly aware of the sentries posted outside the door. He found the food mostly enticing, even the lava elf fare. It included unique dishes such as fried silk-eel, blood meal, and of course, spores and lichen from a variety of toxic fungi that only morehl and frehlasuhl could safely eat. Ra'al picked off the mushrooms.

Coryn produced a jar of her favorite Fire Sauce and placed it on the table as a sort of peace offering.

One of Garesch's men, a red-skinned bladesman named Werdth, delivered a tray of fish, accompanied by large loaves of warm bread and jugs of ale.

"You go ahead." Coryn took a small piece of bread and a half a fish. She picked at them lightly. "I am not that hungry."

"I am not that fond of fish, but that sweet sauce has a soft spot in my heart," Garesch said as he pulled the fire sauce beside him and dabbed some onto his fungus and a cross section of eel.

Ra'al was crunching the second fish when Coryn tapped her hand on the table.

"Alright, Prince Garesch," she announced, "Like you, we are also seeking alliances." She took a tiny bite from her bread, which made Ra'al choke on his fish with surprise; he realized why she wasn't scarfing down her food. *Was Coryn doing "the proper lady thing?"*

"So, you also know that the undead are rising and that the entire continent is in danger?" Garesch drained the Fire sauce into his mouth and followed it with a large piece of bread.

Ra'al blinked twice, imagining an overdose of capsaicin from the magma peppers the stuff was made of. The dwarves grew them on the west side of the Kafnysans and he'd heard of hungry trogs gorging themselves on them and dying from the internal burns.

"We have heard rumors," Coryn said. "We are seeking heroes to lead the fight, if it comes to that, and we think that the heirs of the last generation's greatest warriors could be the people who can rally our countrymen for such a mission. People follow heroes." Coryn wiped her mouth and hands as she removed the bones from her small fish piece. *She is definitely doing "the Lady thing," * Ra'al thought.

"Yes. There is one in particular that we seek," Ra'al spoke between mouthfuls, reinforcing the half-truth he and Coryn had spoken of earlier. The undead problem was a side issue, and not a task officially given to them—their real mission was a morehl one. "He is beastfolk. One of the feral ghwereste."

"I have heard of the prowess of feral folk." Garesch sat back with a content look on his face. "Yet, I don't recall any heroes mentioned in our songs of the Balgavarr War, though from our perspective, they were made out to be villains. But I can see past Uruzak's point of view."

"There is one whose name is widely known, although the songs don't specifically name him as ghwereste." Coryn settled back in her chair as she folded her arms in her lap and looked serenely at Garesch. She was taking this "lady thing," too far. Ra'al shook his head, trying to keep from grinning.

"And that would be?" Garesch looked at Ra'al's expression, seeming confused by it, and then turned back to Coryn with a smile.

"Eihwaz." Coryn exhaled what felt like a held breath, as if she'd searched her memory for a name and only just remembered it.

"I know that name, he was legendary." Garesch widened his eyes. "I didn't know that Eihwaz was one of the feral."

"He was." Ra'al reached for his fifth fish as Coryn made a clicking sound in the back of her throat. He ignored her and starting munching on his fish. "I am certain that your kind, who lost the war, are not in full possession of all the lore. At the very least, parts were left out. A remnant of survivors from the genocide at Seshara took refuge amongst the frostwings of Icehome. Their children and grandchildren came to the aid of Geril sa'Ghuren and Thrag in their hour of need—partly to aide friends and partly to take revenge on the morehl for the injustices which began in Seshara."

Garesch tilted his head as if he'd just learned an interesting fact. He said softly, "That would certainly explain my difficulty in securing any peace talks with the ghwereste."

Ra'al interjected again, "Eihwaz's grandson is rumored to be a local hero, much as his grandfather was." Coryn flashed Ra'al a look of warning and took a deep breath. He was mostly firing from the hip just to see how she would spin them. She was glad to have learned enough lore and statecraft from her father and her tutors to concoct something believable. "Eihwaz is crucial to our quest."

"I see." Garesch waved his hand as if to point at something unseen. "But don't you think that the whole mission seems rushed? Is it not strange that you decided to join me at this very time?"

"Unsettling reports arrived on the day of Queen Naemyar's gala, Prince Garesch." Coryn smiled as serenely as possible. "The plan was discussed over the weeks prior to your arrival, but the sudden urgency of the news rushed our decisions. The timing is coincidental, but still pressing."

"More plausible." Garesch pointed his index finger and waved it at Coryn. "But this leaves an important question." He paused for effect. "How did you know that I am a prince?"

"I heard a delegate at the gala speaking of your likeness." Coryn chewed on her lip, and Ra'al gulped at the brazen lie. "Your identity made no difference, though. Ra'al and I had to catch the next available boat to Frostshoal, regardless of its passengers."

Ra'al suppressed a laugh; Coryn was good. She was almost as good a liar as his mother, which is who he expected she learned this skill set from. He remembered his mother concocting similar tales for situations in Castle Ice.

The lava elf hesitated. "Alright, I will accept this for now." Garesch narrowed his eyes slightly. "Even though I find certain details implausible."

"As long as we are in partial accord, we should all be able to get along." Coryn extended her hand to Garesch, who shook it.

Then, he extended his hand to Ra'al, who shook in kind.

"So, no fight to the death, then?" Ra'al smiled widely at Coryn and Garesch.

Chapter 5

Two more days passed uneventfully for Captain Harna's passengers. There was little required of them, and little intrigue other than playing stones and trying to unravel the subterfuge of the morehl mission. Such an idyllic trip might have been Ra'al's dream. He lay on the starboard deck like a sun-dried fish, trying to spy new stars above him in the evening sky. He inhaled a breath of the fresh, salty air to clear his head.

The horizon was awash with the glittering jewels. He waxed poetic as the heavens spread over a deep blue velvet tapestry. Staring into the sky, Ra'al felt the pressure of his ancestors weigh upon him, much like he did whenever he passed the tapestries in Castle Ice's windy corridor.

He would not call the feeling *homesick*, yet something made him search the stars for answers to questions he could not voice.

Ra'al felt that the heavens owed him some explanation. *Why couldn't he hear the song of the wind? Aside from his recent snafu, why was he normally a reluctant warrior, even though he was more than capable? Why did his mother urge him to draw blood from foes he never met? And why was Coryn rhythmically tapping her metal boots on the deck beside his head?*

He angled his head towards her. "You know, you are ruining a perfectly good evening."

She ignored him, but furrowed her brow. Coryn kept tapping her new boots.

Ra'al groaned as the rapping vibrated inside his skull. There was no escaping a lady in a bad mood, especially if she was a dwarf.

He jumped to stand beside her. His frame towered over the anxious vagha. "What is wrong?" he asked in a gentle voice.

"Something…I don't know. I can't place it. I have a strange feeling that I something is out of place." She kept thumping her foot and Ra'al started to feel like his heart beats misaligned; they pulsed instead to the rhythm of her pounding the deck.

"Take a breath and think slowly." Ra'al knew Coryn well. They were almost siblings. That they came from different parents, races, and cultures was beside the point. "Now, what is it?"

He suspected that Coryn's mind had jumped ahead of her brain, projecting fears and failures into her subconscious just to spite her; Ra'al was also familiar with the sensation. He guessed that if she slowed her mind, her brain might catch up; such had been with his past experiences.

Late the night before, they had spoken again with Garesch. Something that he'd said might have upset Coryn.

He hadn't felt bothered, but her mind worked differently than his. "Is it something to do with what the prince told us last night?" He probed, though breathed softly so as not to upset her further.

She exhaled sharply. "Maybe, but I am not sure."

Ra'al patted her shoulder with an assuring smile and gave her time to mull over her thoughts. He turned to gaze at the horizon.

It had turned inky black, and for the moment, felt much too silent.

Ra'al searched the vastness of the sea surrounding them and whistled with wonder. If this was not proof of the power of Tarvanehl, the god who shaped Esfah, then nothing would suffice.

The immense expanse of water boggled the frostwing's mind. But the dark waters didn't impart the ethereal homesickness like the heavens did. Instead, it made him feel whole, calm, and less lonely.

Coryn kept tapping, but it didn't bother him anymore. Ra'al smiled as he remembered some of the teachings of his earliest mentor: *a silent warrior may hold an eruption below his skin, and none would be the wiser*. He'd never thought himself such a person.

"I know what is bothering me," Coryn suddenly said.

He turned to ask her more, but before he could ask the first question, a cry went up from the lookout in the crow's nest. A warning bell clanged.

"We are under attack! All men to the deck."

Ra'al ran to the source of the call, rounding the bow and halting as a score of scalders climbed over the ship's rails from the port side. They were twisted, misshapen elves with corded muscles, overgrown noses, stunted wings, and protruding jaws, as if caricatures of Esfah's denizens.

Another group flew over the ship, shooting fiery arrows at the deck. Half of the deckhands faced the invading faeli, as the other half worked to quench the fire before it could spread from blazing quarrel to deck board or sail. The defenders attacked with raised blades, trying to kill or repel the invaders.

The frostwing prince took to the air and gained greater elevation. He reached into his quiver and rained down a number of shortened spears upon the flying scalders, scattering them and taking some out of the battle. Some of the injured fliers fell to the ship, wounded by Ra'al's steel and wooden quills, and faced combat on deck.

Coryn grabbed her war hammer and rushed to the fight with a wild cry. After scattering the airborne threat, Ra'al landed and unsheathed his claws. He hadn't strapped on a weapon before heading to the deck for his evening stargazing, besides his quiver, which he rarely removed.

Ahead of Ra'al, four scalders brandished wicked-looking clubs, while behind him, the *Coral Skip's* crew shouted and screamed.

Coryn shifted the mallet between her hands. She smashed knees and chests of the enemy with loud crunching sounds.

Ra'al pushed his way towards the nearest scalder and slashed its chest with one hand, then the next, taking a cut on his forearm in the process. He advanced and hooked another faeli with a wing, forcing the enemy to the ground. The prince dispatched him and then kicked another, sending him reeling.

The scalder stood and licked its face, juggling a short sword between his grip and snarling a challenge.

Ra'al knew that scalders were not known for skilled tactics, but this one obviously stalled for time. He turned and spotted two more scalders creeping his way. Ra'al unfurled his wings and leaped.

He rose twenty feet above the deck, where he spotted the scalders' rafts off the port side. Ra'al counted seven of them, each brimming with growling warriors waiting for their chance to assault the ship—the faeli's wings were too small to carry off plunder should the vessel sink in the chaos. They could barely fly if loaded with much more than their bodyweight.

Ra'al shouted, "Rafts at the port, seven of them!" Then cut down two scalders. He stabbed a third with a blade taken from a dead raider. As the scalder collapsed, Ra'al leapt and landed at the *Coral Skip's* rail.

He spotted Coryn, who screamed with rage as she charged into a scalder. Her mallet made a loud crunching sound as it connected with the surprised faeli's skull.

She didn't hesitate before running to the next enemy and planting her boot on its face. She pummeled his face with a nasty squelch.

Coryn, panting, looked at Ra'al and gave him thumbs up.

Ra'al shook his head slowly. *Those enemies don't stand a chance.*

He turned back to the rafts and smiled widely at the sight of more scalders clustered near the grappling line that tethered them. Before Ra'al could jump to the skiff, Garesch and three of his men charged ahead of him. They looped the flats of their blades across the rope and rode it like a zip line.

Scalders reeled in surprise, not expecting such brazen counter moves.

The morehl fought with incredible precision. But Garesch moved even faster than most lava elves. Like a machine, he systematically slaughtered the pirates. Every step Garesch took was accompanied by sprays of faeli blood that splashed across deck boards and the frothing waves.

Ra'al jumped to the next nearest raft. The force of impact rocked the craft and dropped three of the ten scalders aboard it. He flapped his wings to regain his balance; his enemies did the same.

Ra'al sucked in a deep breath and steeled himself against his enemies. His mother had never let him be a pampered prince, even if he had earnestly desired it; Rashingot refused to allow such a fate for the son of Thrag. Ra'al was areosan, and as a frostwing, he'd been trained in the arts of war since he was a kit standing barely a cubit tall.

Scalders and frostwings had much bad blood between them, dating back a thousand years when the faeli first appeared. Bloody history rarely died without reconciliation, and Ra'al twirled both his reclaimed swords and roared at the advancing enemies, ready to extract his pound of flesh.

Two scalders nearest him stopped in shock and the rest of their kin bumped into them.

Ra'al advanced.

The startled scalders didn't get the chance to defend themselves before Ra'al's blades decapitated them both in a scissor swipe. He blocked the swords of the next wave, but one of them managed to plunge a fiery bolt through his right wing, leaving a bloody hole in its center.

Ra'al roared in pain and turned to impale the assaulting scalder on the hook of the same injured wing. He slashed another with his swords.

Other scalders joined the fray. One of them leapt ahead and tried to cut Ra'al's head off. The fiend caught him off guard, and Ra'al's eyes widened with the panicked realization that he could not escape. Time seemed to slow as the assassin brought his sword down.

The killing stroke did not connect. The faeli fell backward, instead, knocking three more of its kind to the deck. A dagger protruded from the assassin's heart.

Garesch waved at him from the next raft over and flashed him a wink.

Ra'al bled from cuts on the arms, torso, and wing, but only four invaders remained aboard the craft.

He returned his attention to the nearest two enemies and almost slipped upon raft's blood-soaked boards. Ra'al barely caught his balance as the scalders mobbed him. He struggled to block and parry. Halfway through, he heard the Coryn's cries for aid.

At least six scalders lay dead at Coryn's feet. Members of the *Coral Skip's* crew were separated from her by a crowd of enemies, and one of the faeli fired shot after shot from his crossbow, keeping them from helping her.

Ra'al unfurled his wings and tried to take to the air. Pain wracked his body, forcing him to pull his injured wing back.

A morehl jumped to Ra'al's side and pushed back his enemies.

Ra'al growled through the pain and gathered his strength for a final push. He turned to face Coryn, worried more about his friend's life than the enemies closest to him. Ra'al couldn't spot her. He only noticed Garesch, clambering back up the tether rope. The morehl dropped back aboard the vessel and drew his curved sword.

The frostwing roared through the pain and surged into the sky, gaining elevation. Ra'al spotted Coryn's body splayed across the floor. He howled and dropped down upon the advancing horde.

Hot, red anger fueled his sword hand and plunged into the fray, cutting the first scalder almost in half before severing the arm of another at the shoulder. He advanced towards the morehl, let go of the pain in his wing, and hacked at the faeli as if they were only cordwood.

Within seconds, he had mowed the group down. Frothing with battle fervor, he turned and searched for any surviving scalders, but found none. The remaining rafts had disengaged and headed back towards the darkness of the sea.

Ra'al felt dizzy as he looked down. Nasty cuts had opened and bled red rivulets through the deep blue of his hide. He nearly collapsed, but the crew nearest his side kept him on his feet. Others cut free the grappling hooks from the tether lines and released the derelict crafts.

As soon as Ra'al could string two steps together, he went to Coryn's side.

"Hey Coryn, I would sure like to hear some of that tapping right about now." He leaned close to her face to listen for an answer.

Coryn weakly punched him in the chest, which made him wince. "I don't do tapping, snow-head."

"So, are you ready for some more scalders, then?" He smiled at Coryn as she pulled herself up to sit.

"Sure, grab me some mead and let me loose on the next batch." Coryn grinned groggily.

Garesch knelt beside them. "Are you both alright?"

Ra'al winced as he faced the morehl prince. "I don't see a scratch on *you.*"

"I am fast, even for a morehl." Garesch gave him the same wink as before.

"Thank you, Prince Garesch." Coryn looked in Garesch's direction. "If you didn't come when you did, I guess you would be giving me to the sea right about now."

"It was my duty, lady Coryn." Garesch knelt and kissed Coryn's hand. Both Ra'al's bushy eyebrows climbed high on his forehead.

Coryn nudged Ra'al out of his stupor.

"Indeed, thank you for saving my life, too." Ra'al bowed as low as he could.

Coryn furrowed her brows at Ra'al and then flashed a radiant smile at Garesch.

"As I said, it was my duty." Garesch bowed back to Ra'al. "We agreed some days ago to be in cahoots. I would not let the southern wretches kill my partners." Uruzak still harbored a grudge against the invaders who stole land from them when the faeli migrated to Cyrea…And then broke repeated vows of service in exchange for it.

"Still, you faced great danger jumping in the midst of those raiders to save me. This was beyond the simple code of duty." Coryn held tenuously onto Ra'al's arm and tried to bow. "Thank you again."

"Don't mention it." Garesch stood. "You have both sustained injuries that will continue to fester if left to their own." He whistled to one of his men. A lava elf knelt by an injured member of Garesch's troops and mended a cut in the morehl's torso. It leaked steam and blood that ran almost black against the elf's crimson skin.

The medic raised his head and looked to Garesch expectantly. Injured crewmates sat in a line against the railing, awaiting medical attention.

"Marnash, when you've finished with the serious injuries, please have a look at the prince and the lady," Garesch said. The elf medic nodded and then returned to his work.

Garesch bowed to Ra'al and Coryn and walked away.

After he disappeared from the port side completely, Coryn pulled Ra'al's massive head closer. "Now, *that's* a hell of a warrior." She sucked in a breath as she struggled to remain seated. "If we were really collecting heroes for a cause, he would make a fine addition to the quest."

"Agreed. The morehl is a killing machine." Ra'al winced. Coryn slid back in her position and grazed one of his dozen arm cuts. He wondered if she'd taken a hit to her head, or simply forgot that locating heroes was only a cover story.

Coryn laughed. "You didn't do bad yourself. You took on an entire scalder squad on that raft."

"*Huh,*" Ra'al grunted. "Well, you were amazing. I didn't even need to help you much! Figured I'd get a kick or two with those steel boots of yours if I tried." She tried to lift her feet and then recoiled. "I… I think my legs are broken."

As the two friends laughed and bragged on each other, the morehl healer stepped closer.

"If the prince would allow me, I would like to care for her ladyship first." The lava elf bowed, and then knelt beside Coryn.

Ra'al moved to give the morehl space to work his magic. He knew of magic and how it worked, even if the frostwing struggled to harness it—luckily lava elves shared overlapping magic elements with both the vagha and the areosa. Without an elemental connection, a healer's magic would have never worked. At least, not without something stronger, like the help of magic items found in the Magestorm cache Coryn's father had famously lost.

The lava elf held a small nine-sided stone in one hand and touched Coryn's forehead with the other.

Ra'al could hear the bones of Coryn's legs grinding. They grated like two pieces of wet sandstone rubbing together as they mended. Ra'al hadn't even known that Coryn's legs were broken.

Coryn had kept her resolve until now. She gnashed her teeth and growled a repressed moan. Finally, a sigh rumbled from her chest. The dwarf's eyes rolled back, and she snored in deep slumber.

Ra'al looked up as the morehl turned to him.

He bowed deeply. "Can I take a look at your wounds, Your Highness?"

"Yeah, yeah, do your magic, friend," Ra'al said and waved his hand in a flourish.

The morehl looked him over once, and then put the stone he clutched into his pocket and pulled out a different one. It was black as coal and seemed to absorb light. He clutched it in his left hand.

"This magic is different," he murmured. "The element we share is not an element of Esfah. It is Death magic, but it will heal you all the same... Though with a price."

"A price?"

The lava elf looked down the deck, where the others arranged the four limp humans who had fallen against the faeli incursion. Two crewmates laid a fifth in the line. They shook their heads. "He'll be gone in a moment."

In shuddering, ragged gasps, the human sailor's chest heaved and convulsed.

The morehl medic leaned down and whispered something into his ear while drawing a broken circle on the victim's chest. With a startled gasp, the sailor arched his back, and then fell limp.

Returning, the medic placed his hands on Ra'al and drew a complete circle.

"What did you say to him?" Ra'al asked.

The lava elf frowned. "Better you not know." Marnash frowned and warned, "There will be pain." A moment later, agony wracked Ra'al's body, and he stiffened as if struck by lightning. Once the pain reached an unbearable point, it suddenly quit.

Across the deck, the sailor gasped his last and his chest fell still.

Ra'al panted like a dog on a hot summer day as his cuts knitted shut. Most of the pain came from a tear in his wing; it felt as if someone had pulled upon the strings of his soul and used them to stitch the edges of the wound together. *Black magic never produces a pleasant sensation,* he thought as he fell back against the deck rail, dizzy and exhausted. The morehl bowed before moving onto the next person.

Ra'al tried to push away the stupor. When he finally managed to sit unaided, Coryn's eyes fluttered open, too.

She hummed something. He crawled closer to her head and leaned cautiously down.

"Did you say something, Coryn?" Ra'al whispered to his prone friend.

"Yes," she panted. "The king."

"What about the king?" Ra'al flinched away from the flailing hand of Coryn.

"Before the attack, I said something was bothering me. I realized what it was… something Garesch told us about his quest the other night." She reached out and took a hold of Ra'al's arm. "He never mentioned his father, King Saugor. Not even once."

"And this means?"

"It means he is acting on his own, without sanction from Uruzak," Coryn whispered.

"I still don't understand. How did you reach this conclusion?" Ra'al asked.

"Would you mention our quest *without* talking about how much the queen, your mother, insisted you take the lead? You'd talk about her, play on her authority as a point of your credibility." She sighed as she pulled harder on Ra'al's arm and moved into a sitting posture. "It makes your mission legitimate."

"Alright, I get your point." Ra'al helped her stand. He crawled to his feet as well.

"We have a rogue prince as our ally." Coryn smiled viciously. "Knowing that will make it easier to do the job. And if *he is* up to no good, that might salvage our diplomatic mission…" she trailed off. Both had silently agreed that Rashingot's original mission had to take a back seat to whatever intrigue they'd been pulled into.

Ra'al glanced down at her and she repeated their secret duty. "Discourage the morehl's mission." But Ra'al didn't hear any conviction in her voice. *With the undead gathering in the Shadowland wastes, maybe a rogue morehl was exactly the sort of ally Icehome and Balgavarr needed…provided he wasn't trying to kill them all to curry favor with his father.*

Chapter 6

"Land ahoy!" yelled a sailor hanging from the mainmast.

Ra'al, Coryn, and Garesch left their cabins and went to the deck to see the port of Frostshoal, looming larger on the horizon as they approached.

The frostwing counted more than forty different ships docked at the distant piers. A barque style vessel like theirs was the nearest, with bright blue sails and a newly polished body. Next to it huddled three brigs painted in brilliant colors. *They must have been the pride of the owner's fleet,* Ra'al thought. All the ships on this side of the city were in good condition, though he knew smaller ports dotted the shores on either side of the city, where the disreputable and overtly cavalier merchants went.

More ships came into focus. No less than fifteen smaller clippers unloaded their contents at the same time. The large bales they unloaded were likely tobacco, the regional commodity with the highest customs. Frostshoal was a "Free Port," meaning that customs were lax and were often managed by bribes. Shipping those kinds of items through Frostshoal reduced shipping tolls by circumventing the worst of regional taxes.

The colored sails on the ships made the port a colorful one. For Ra'al, it felt like he'd entered the spring festival back home, only it was ten times bigger.

After docking, Ra'al followed Garesch, who weaved with his men ahead of them on the pier. The morehl and his group closed on another group of lava elves from a ship that had docked further ahead on the wharf.

Ra'al approached the newcomers to listen to what they discussed with Garesch.

"You better tell your mates to hang onto their purses," the morehl said to Garesch and laughed. "Seems to be a new gang of wallet pinchers roaming the town, and as you know, what is taken by Frostshoal is lost to Frostshoal."

"So, the old enforcers are gone from the scene then?" Garesch asked the sailor.

"No, they are there, but they've closed their eyes to the whole operation." The sailor shrugged. "Better bribes from the thieving types, I guess."

Garesch thanked him and turned to Ra'al and Coryn. "I think hanging your wallet from your belt is ill advised." He pointed to Coryn's wallet.

"It is a matter of vaghan pride to show off a full wallet." Coryn frowned at Garesch.

"Suit yourself then." Garesch shrugged and left Ra'al and Coryn before rejoining his group.

They tried to follow after Garesch, but he was soon lost among the myriad crowds that milled about the town.

Everything seemed strange and exotic, even for the homesick and crowd-shy Ra'al. Vendors on small carts crammed around the exit of the port streets that led to the town. Each one offered wares they never imagined. From food carts that made their stomachs growl, eyes glitter, or water, there was a display of every possible palate from Esfah. If a visitor liked animal meat, they could find the flesh of every creature permissible to hunt, plus an equal amount to dubious, strange, and illegal animals. Several vendors flaunted meals claimed to be cooked from those forbidden meats.

One even claimed to have cuts of dragon meat. Ra'al wrinkled his nose at the rancid fillets and seriously doubted the vendor's authenticity.

From jewels and cloth, pottery plates made so thin, Coryn could see her hand through them, and strange musical instruments that Ra'al yearned to try, and the town thrived on trade. And there was much to go around.

As they left the port and entered into the town proper, they saw bigger shops, sometimes the size of mansions, that specialized in craft and art from every nation in the land. A sign on one of those shops claimed to have selumari wrought weapons, vaghan armor, and morehl flintlocks.

Coryn and Ra'al stopped in front of that structure, trying to understand how such a place could have all those items in its hold. Coryn noticed an advertisement on one of the shop's windows, declaring that their items were favored by the fearsome ghwereste of Seshara.

"Wasn't Eihwaz a tigerfolk?" Ra'al turned to Coryn.

"Yes." She confirmed and pursed her lips as she read the claim on the shop's front.

"Do you think we should actually find Eihwaz's grandson, at least to convince Garesch that we really are searching for those heirs to the champions of Balgavarr?" Ra'al asked Coryn.

"It was not a totally fake claim." Coryn smiled at the look of confusion on Ra'al's face. "In our conversations while you were sleeping, Queen Naemyar implied we should find the new Champions, if possible. They might prove crucial to our fight against the undead."

Ra'al raised a single brow.

"Well, maybe if you weren't always sleeping, you'd have a bigger picture of the state of Cyrea, snow-head. She seemed far more worried about an eventual undead uprising in our private conversation."

Ra'al frowned. "So, the undead rumors are true, then?"

"Yes. She thinks it's worse than the other members of the Trade Council think… or, I guess, my father and your mother." Coryn pushed air through her mouth slowly. "Only Naemyar seems to be taking steps to prepare, but she's keeping them quiet. I don't think she wants to lose credibility and look like the child who cried drake."

The frostwing bobbed his head, understanding his friend had intended to follow through with the search before they ever left Tulgesh, and it was for more than just maintaining their cover. "That changes everything about our mission." Ra'al clenched his fists. "Do you have any idea how much time we have to get back home?"

"First of all, it changes nothing." Coryn shook her head. "Second, why are you asking about going back home?"

"We need to be there to defend our people, that's why." Ra'al threw his arms in the air. "We should get back as soon as possible if there is a threat—and if not, then we must return to our diplomat."

Coryn tapped her boots. "Don't you understand that altering our mission is the one thing that can turn a sure chance of defeat to a hope of winning the war?"

"No, I don't understand how it would do that. We are following morehl around a foreign city." Ra'al threw his arms in the air again. "How could that help us win a war?"

"Sometimes I wonder if you were dropped as a child." Coryn kicked Ra'al in his leg. "We are collecting heroes to face the coming tide; if we can do that, we can shift the odds of surviving such a war to our favor."

"So, we get a couple of extra people to fight with us. How is that going to break the enemy hordes?" Ra'al rubbed his knee as he gave Coryn a mean look.

"We don't want simple people…We want *heroes*." Coryn blew a trapped breath out to show her exasperation and re-explained it to Ra'al. "People follow heroes. They take an example from their deeds, and this is what will give us a chance to win the war."

Ra'al stood silently for some moments. "Okay, but we both know that being the son of somebody doesn't make anybody a hero."

"That's why we search among those heirs to the champions, *at least one must be a hero*." Coryn smiled and thumped Ra'al's bruised leg lightly. "Or else we'll have to make our own. You could even be one."

Ra'al couldn't help himself when he started to laugh uncontrollably. "I am *not* hero material. I was *forced* to leave home. I didn't go willingly, remember? And that's when our primary mission was just *talking*."

"I do." Coryn patted his arm. "I also remember how you dealt with those faeli pirates. *That* was heroic."

"Huh," Ra'al snorted. "I was just trying to stay alive and push the threat away from my friends; that doesn't make me a hero."

"Maybe not, but it is a start." Coryn jerked her head from side to side. "Heroes are not the larger-than-life figures you hear about in the songs. They are everyday folk who decided to stand up for their loved ones, once, twice, and as many times as it took to push harm away from those they loved."

Ra'al coughed to hide his shock at the depth of her words.

Coryn pulled his hand. "Now, come on, we have to find a tigerfolk." She dragged Ra'al through shop after shop, trying to gather information on the hangouts of any tigerfolk around town.

Eventually, they found a side market known around parts of Frostshoal as one favored by tigerfolk who sold hunting spoils.

The market was placed in a narrow, long, and winding alley. Several, very low-end sellers had wares spread on blankets or battered tarps. Windows opened into the buildings on both sides of the alley. They were the only way to deal with many of the shopkeepers or make any kind of transaction. The duo made a few inquiries.

Eihwaz was a name recognized by most shop owners, almost as a kind of patron saint. However, most of them remained evasive to the whereabouts of any descendants.

One peddler advised the pair, "You should not ask questions about Bastawr. You might make trouble for those of us who don't pay the peacekeepers' bribes." They assumed Bastawr was a descendant of Eihwaz. They'd pieced together information that he occasionally supplied a few of the poorest vendors with free carcasses from his kills in the wild, but that he was also considered a volatile figure by those close with whatever passed for law enforcement in Frostshoal.

The shopkeeper refused to elaborate beyond a name, to the frustration of Coryn, who insisted on knowing more. The vendor eventually shut her window, severing their conversation.

"Well, at least now we know that his name is Bastawr." Ra'al munched on a sandwich he'd purchased from a kiosk nearby.

"Yeah, but our search hasn't progressed one scratch from there." Coryn blew through pursed lips. "How can we find the one we seek if we don't have any idea of his whereabouts? Is he in Frostshoal, or is he in the wilds?"

"I don't know." Ra'al took another bite of the sandwich as he took in the surrounding scenery. "But things usually find a way to resolve themselves. This always worked for me."

"That's because you were always a prince, things always *had* to work for you." Coryn scoffed. "And that was because regular people made them work."

Before Coryn could say more, a whisper interrupted them, "Pssst, you two, come over here."

In a nook between two buildings, a stranger stood in the shadows and beckoned for them.

Before the pair could make a decision, another stranger approached. Both wore ratty cloaks of nondescript cloth and would have barely stuck out in any crowd had they not signaled them. "So, you are searching for Bastawr." The stranger made a strange clicking sound. "Unsavory sorts might take an interest in you for that, you know. Ghwereste aren't typically glory seekers."

"No, we didn't." Ra'al smiled a full-fanged smile. "Are you of the unsavory sort then, friend?"

"Oh no, no, no, I am just a helpful citizen of Frostshoal in search of a good trade." The two strangers started to laugh.

"And what do you trade, then?" Coryn eased her axe from her shoulder strap and swiftly fit it tightly in her grip.

"No need for weapons here, they won't do much for you." The stranger who still stood shrouded in shadows snickered. "We trade in information…If you are interested."

"We are interested." Ra'al cracked his knuckles. "If you have something worthwhile, we will pay."

"No, friend." The stranger made the same clicking noise again. "You must pay first, then you get your information."

"I don't like this arrangement." Coryn shifted the axe from one hand to the next. "I think we are good without it, thank you."

"It is a shame," the stranger said. "But we doubted you could pay, anyway."

Coryn felt a sickening feeling in the pit of her gut. She reached to her hanging wallet and touched nothing. She bent over and frantically searched the ground as both strangers laughed hysterically.

"Ra'al, we've been robbed." She pulled the axe into a fighting stance and moved in the direction of the strangers.

"So long, now-poor vagha." The stranger and his comrade scaled the building to their right with lightning speed. In seconds, they were at the top, and then they were gone from view.

Coryn shouted and ran after them. She started to climb a stack of crates and pallets to reach the rooftop, but at a far slower pace.

Ra'al tried to unfurl his wings, but they got caught in the narrow space and wouldn't open.

He ran to the end of the alley as he shouted at the crowd. "Where is an enforcer? We will pay. We were robbed in that alley."

Folks looked in his direction for a second, then ignored him.

Leaving the narrow market, Ra'al could finally use his wings. He unfurled them and flapped into the sky. Three beats later, he was at the level of the roof and he set down at the edge of the alley. Ra'al ran in the direction of the building where the thieves ascended.

Ra'al was fleet-footed for a frostwing and he sped past one building after building and soon caught up to Coryn. She was bent double, trying to catch her breath.

"Where did they go?" Ra'al demanded.

"I don't know," she panted. "I lost them by the fourth building, they jumped off to a side street, I think."

"Okay, point the way." Ra'al picked up Coryn under one arm and started to run.

"Hey!" she shouted at him. "You could have asked first."

"No time." Ra'al tried to save his breath as he jumped from building to the next.

"Here," Coryn shouted. "They jumped off here!"

Ra'al splayed his wings mid-run and leapt from the building, Coryn screaming.

He landed nimbly and released Coryn. Ra'al looked left and right.

Nothing, the thieves left no sign of their passing.

He started to breathe slower and grimaced. "They are gone."

"Even if we caught up to them, I think they would have escaped." Coryn arranged herself as she stood beside Ra'al. "They were beastfolk, and I think we could never catch up to them, not on unfamiliar turf."

Ra'al stood silent as he looked around him in the street. It was a residential lane, and no windows were open to ask where the thieves could have gone.

He exhaled a long breath. Defeat set in and he hoped that Coryn left some of her money back in their quarters. Otherwise, this trip would end very soon. Ra'al was about to ask Coryn about their funds when they heard the sounds of a scuffle.

Both of them broke into a mad run, hoping they might find the thieves.

As they cleared the street, they watched as a tigerfolk with a long pole made short work of the thieves; there were four, not two, as they had assumed. They must have had accomplishes.

The tigerfolk incapacitated the lot with swift strokes of his staff. He then knelt and retrieved Coryn's fat wallet and walked slowly to the stunned pair.

"I think this belongs to you." He handed the wallet to Ra'al. "I heard your call, but you flew away so quickly. I had to follow from the ground level." He bowed to Coryn as she let out a squeal of surprise. "I found these guys running and laughing, and I knew that they must have had something to do with your robbery."

"I don't know how to thank you," Ra'al said to the tigerfolk. "You saved our quest, enforcer. My eternal gratitude is not enough. My name is Ra'al, and this is Coryn."

"And I am Bastawr." The tigerfolk bowed to them. "Pleased to meet both of you."

Ra'al started to laugh, then Coryn followed.

"I fear I don't understand the reason for your laughter." Bastawr stared between the two in confusion.

Ra'al finally managed to stop laughing. "Apologies, but the truth is, we were looking for *you* when those thieves stole Coryn's purse."

Coryn grinned. "If we hadn't been robbed in the first place, we might have never met you."

"This is Esfah; the goddess Mitta ensures nothing is coincidence." Bastawr smiled widely and referenced the middle fate goddess. "And I am pleased to have met you, but why were you searching for me?"

"That's a rather long story." Ra'al looked at the food vendors in the distance. "Maybe we can talk somewhere private, and with food."

Bastawr pointed to the north. "We have one of the best international cuisines in all of Esfah. It is perhaps a ten-minute walk."

"Then let's head there." Ra'al already felt the need to eat after the chase.

"Lead the way, Bastawr," Coryn said and followed.

An hour later, and after demolishing several dishes, the three sat facing each other in the rustic inn and discussed the events of the last many months, including the reports of the undead rising. They did not disclose their orders to spy on and disrupt lava elf activity—nor the orders from Rashingot to parley a treaty.

"I think I have been ignorant of the rising threat." Bastawr took a breath in. "And not just because Frostshoal is relatively insulated from it by the sea. The enforcers in Frostshoal had taken a step back from the greater Shadowlands; more and more, lawlessness rules here and legitimate business is in decline. Only a few people like myself care enough to keep the town's cogs turning."

"I am sure you have lots on your plate." Coryn drank from her pint of ale. "And I know that asking you to join our efforts might be asking too much, but know you are needed."

"I have tried convincing myself to stay in Frostshoal for a while now." Bastawr shook his head. "But things have changed so much in the last few years. And I know that your effort requires many abled people to stand with you."

"The truth is, we are recruiting a collection of heroes, folk of pedigree as well as talent." Ra'al put down his mug. "When the time comes to stand against the dark tide, people need to know that they are following the right champions—the right causes."

Bastawr laughed. "I may not make the grade. I mean, I can lead soldiers, as I was trained in the art of war since my young years; in fact, my grandfather was born in Icehome prior to their alliance with Balgavarr." He shook his head. "But sadly, I am no hero of any kind…certainly not a champion like those Gods'own adventurers from the south that penny bards tell tales of at the pubs."

Coryn cocked her head. She hadn't heard the new stories the ghwereste referenced.

"Coryn has different views about that than I." Ra'al laughed. "You should hang around her more often to understand her logic."

"You already assumed that I would join you?" Bastawr threw his head back and laughed for some moments. "Alright then, let's go and find the heroes who will help save the world. My heart left Frostshoal long ago."

They spent another hour at the inn before heading out.

Instead of returning by the same route they came from, Bastawr suggested following another route. They traversed the town and passed by the long shore. The night had already set in and the sounds of the town changed tone from the constant calls of vendors hawking their wares and the chatter of people trading money to people laughing over loud music and revelry.

Bastawr explained that most of the inns and taverns employed musicians and bards to perform through the night. All a patron needed to do to enjoy the show was order a drink. He explained that the best bards encouraged the patrons to consume drink after drink until their wallets were emptied or they were carried out to the curb for pickpockets to deal with. Frostshoal often employed the best entertainers.

Their ghwereste guide took them nearer to a district with plentiful lodging and a lively night scene. A familiar red-skinned figure caught their eye.

"Isn't that Garesch?" Coryn stopped and pulled Ra'al back. Ra'al halted Bastawr in turn.

They all moved into the shade of a huge wych elm, an exotic tree that was probably brought to the port town as a sapling.

Garesch stood adjacent a human in colorful clothes. He and she were engaged in a heated discussion.

Coryn noted that the morehl prince stood alone with one exception. One of his red-skinned companions stood on the far side of the square, trying to remain aloof. She assumed he was Garesch's bodyguard.

Finally, the lava elf produced a purse and handed it to the lady. She opened it briefly, allowing the spies to glimpse the coin within.

"I don't know who this Garesch is, but that one…" Bastawr pointed at the woman in the colorful clothes. "She is a notorious pirate who goes by the name Ry'Ober."

Ry'Ober produced a distinctly purple-hued container from her jacket and handed it to Garesch. The prince shook hands with Ry'Ober and departed towards one of the nearby inns.

"That package was a map, I am certain of that. I've seen it before—and I would know what it looks like." Coryn clenched her teeth. "The morehl have my father's map, Ra'al."

Chapter 7

Ra'al and Coryn returned to the *Coral Skip* and waited for the morehl prince. They pretended not to suspect the lava elves had lied about their intentions against Balgavarr. Together, they introduced Bastawr to Garesch once he arrived back on the ship, only he returned alone with no bodyguard. Garesch insisted that they take dinner together.

Their meal was peppered with questions from Garesch, who grilled Bastawr about living in Frostshoal and the struggles of living up to the reputation of his war-hero grandfather.

Bastawr answered most of Garesch's questions politely, even the ones that crossed the borders of politeness. Morehl were forward about their curiosities, as a general rule. Eventually, the questions began to feel more like an interrogation than a conversation.

Coryn intervened, announcing she felt very tired and would prefer to retire. Ra'al concurred and Garesch released the company.

Two hours passed since Garesch and Coryn pulled Ra'al and Bastawr into her cabin for an urgent discussion. "He has my father's map," she insisted as she sat down at the edge of the bed. "This is the worst thing you could imagine happening."

"I still don't understand how a map could be worse than the undead." Bastawr leaned by the wall of the cabin, facing Coryn.

"It is the map to untold power, and it should never have been revealed." Coryn breathed slowly, but kept the details vague.

"Coryn's father told her that his map should be given to the champions of the gods, but only when the time came for it to be used," Ra'al explained.

"So, it leads to something of extreme power that could be used if the undead came, right?" Bastawr looked from Coryn to Ra'al, who both bobbed their heads. "Then it should be used now, if the undead are proved to be on the rise."

"It is a trove of items, specifically, but the map users should only be men and women deemed worthy by the gods," Coryn blurted passionately. "And I don't think that Garesch is that worthy champion—none would be if they had to steal to get it." She glowered at the door. "Furthermore, if the lava elves are pursuing the forbidden cache, it means they are likely not pursing the peace they have claimed—it means Cyrea could face war on multiple fronts. If the lava elves have been playing us all along, we'll be fighting undead at the front and have morehl putting daggers in our back."

"What if the *gods* don't choose their champions?" Ra'al asked her. "What if *we* have to choose them?"

"Then there should be signs, and all signs are sent by the gods." Coryn stomped the floor hard. Silence enveloped the room and the three people gathered inside.

"Alright, what should we do about the map?" Bastawr looked from Ra'al to Coryn.

"We steal it back from them," Coryn said in a low voice. "Tonight, just after they go to sleep."

"I can't imagine how Bastawr or I can sneak about Garesch's quarters and steal anything." Ra'al laughed. "Even if Bastawr is the lithest of tigerfolk, I doubt he would make a good thief, unless Garesch and his group are dead, or deaf, whichever is easier to pull off."

Coryn took a deep breath. "I will do it."

"With your steel boots?" Ra'al smiled widely. "You might as well heavily tap dance into Garesch's quarters and all around his bed."

"I have soft leather boots, too." Coryn looked down and fiddled with her fingers. "I got them in Tulgesh before we left."

Ra'al's jaw hung open and Bastawr laughed as she withdrew a set of vagha clothes in pitch black. "What were you planning for in Tulgesh? Secret evening assassinations?"

"I knew that you were a resourceful lady the moment I saw you in that street." Bastawr chuckled. "I bet if you happened upon those thieves before I did, they would have met a far worse fate."

"Alright, but there are guards at his door." Ra'al waved his hands to stop the laughter from Bastawr and Coryn. "How can you pass them?"

"I won't have to." Coryn winked. "You two will lower me from the deck to Garesch's window. I can manage it from there."

"I can already tell this is going be one of those nights," Ra'al snorted and rolled his eyes.

Ra'al held the rope over the railing on the port side of the deck while Bastawr engaged the two sailors at the helm with local nautical horror tales. The areosa's inner bard paid half a mind to the tigerfolk's stories, and he understood why the sailors found them so enthralling.

As the rope swung and jittered behind him, Ra'al tried to adjust its weight so it wouldn't scrape against the rails or the hull of the ship.

He recalled how he came to be in this strange, awkward, and painful situation. Coryn arrived earlier in a dark outfit, black as the heart of the void, and looking completely ridiculous with the axe strapped on her back.

"I understand the full suit of black, I even appreciate the leather boots, but why on Esfah do you have that massive axe bound to your back?" Ra'al shook his head.

"A vagha never goes anywhere without an axe, or some weapon, at least…" Coryn frowned. "I thought you knew that."

"Yes, but why the huge axe? Why not a dagger?" Ra'al smiled a lopsided smile. "I fail to understand your logic."

"Don't be silly. You know I love this axe." Coryn said.

"Of course. How silly of me."

"Come on, grab a rope and help me tie it around my waist…Now dangle me over the rail, we have to finish this fast." Coryn demanded and ignored Ra'al's stifled laughter.

Currently, Ra'al maintained a weird posture to hide the fact that he dangled a rope over the rails with a dwarf grunting and puffing as she opened the window to Garesch's cabin.

Suddenly, the rope went slack. Ra'al peered over the rail, but didn't see Coryn or hear a splash in the sea, so he assumed Coryn managed to sneak to her target.

Some minutes passed as Bastawr raged in laughter after yet another exaggerated story.

Ra'al started to relax. Perhaps Coryn's heist idea was not so bad after all. Coryn would come up the rope soon with the map, and perhaps Bastawr would stop laughing every few seconds? Perhaps Ra'al could get a snack? He'd felt a growing unease in his stomach for some time now.

But the unease worsened fast when he heard shouts. There was a scuffle below.

Ra'al ran the distance from the rails to the entrance of the cabins in three strides and found Bastawr by his side.

The morehl were awake, and they massed on the door to Garesch's cabin.

Ra'al didn't ask permission to see the morehl prince. He bolted through the gathered morehl and busted into the room.

As he entered, he saw Garesch holding Coryn from behind with a dagger pressed against her throat. A purple leather map case lay open and on the bed.

"What in the name of Death are you trying to achieve, frostwing?" Garesch pressed the tip of the dagger harder against Coryn's throat.

"Let her go Garesch, and face me instead," Ra'al growled.

"I caught her rummaging in my trunk. She is a thief." Garesch twisted Coryn's body around to face Ra'al. "Why on Esfah would I let her go?"

"Because if you touch a single hair on her head, I will take you apart limb by limb." Ra'al unsheathed his claws.

"Do not throw out such threats in vain, frostwing. You are outnumbered five to one." One of the morehl behind Ra'al pulled out his sword. All of them stepped into the cabin.

"You know *friend*, you are at a disadvantage here." Bastawr stood by Ra'al's back, facing the other morehl. "If you knew much about close-quarter fighting, you'd see your numbers and weapons are at a disadvantage."

Bastawr roared and slashed the arm of the morehl, forcing him to drop the sword. "We, on the other hand, don't need any weapons aside from our own naturally grown ones." Bastawr bared a savage, fang-filled smile.

"Do that again and I will cut her throat." Garesch snarled.

"Don't do this, Garesch," Ra'al warned.

"You don't get to pass orders. First, my servant Yarichek disappears, and now this." Garesch licked his lips. "What did you do to my servant?"

"We didn't even know he was gone," Ra'al said sincerely, dropping his claws slightly. "And why should we bother with anyone's servant?"

"Admittedly, Your Highness, Yarichek was always your father's man, not yours," One of the morehl behind Ra'al admitted. "For all we know, he could have run back to your father for reasons he's kept to himself."

"That doesn't permit them to enter my cabin! They must pay for this," Garesch shouted at his men.

"Be careful of what you say, Garesch," Ra'al growled. "I am about to lose what patience I have left and you might learn to regret this."

"Everyone, stop it!," Coryn screamed. She rolled her eyes with resignation. "It wasn't even the map."

"Are you certain?" Ra'al asked her in a much calmer tone.

"Yes." Coryn jumped once, bringing the shaft of her axe to crash into Garesch's chin and allowing her to twist free. "I am sorry, Prince Garesch, but I had to make sure." She turned to her friends, "I'm not really certain what it is, but it did not come from my father."

The morehl rushed further in the room with their weapons flashing.

"Stop," Garesch shouted as he rubbed his chin and blinked away the tears. "I don't understand what in the Void is happening here. Explain yourself." He barked at Coryn, who had stepped into the safety of her peers.

"I am sorry. I thought your transaction in the town with Ry'Ober was to purchase my father's map." Coryn took a deep breath in, then continued. "But it was not, and I owe you an apology for my rushed and thoughtless actions." She bowed in front of Garesch. "I am willing to take whatever judgment you should pass for this. Just know that I thought I was doing something noble and of great importance. I came to take back what I thought was stolen from my family."

"What on Esfah are you talking about?" Garesch sheathed his dagger behind the folds of his garments. His face twisted with confusion.

"My father has a map that leads to something precious, but terrible." She swallowed with an audible sound. "It is a family curse, a burden and a secret, and I am sorry for believing that you stole it. A frehlasuhl tried to claim it on behalf of Uruzak in the past."

"What is on that map?" Garesch asked.

"I am sorry, but I have no right to tell you, and no wish. It is intended only for the champions of the gods." Coryn stood, looking him straight in the eye. Then she waved her hand in dismissal. "Let's just leave it at that."

"But what was on the Ry'Ober's map, then?" Ra'al looked to Coryn for an answer.

"I am not really sure." She looked to Garesch in turn.

"Perhaps some tea to calm everyone's nerves." The prince sighed, seeing a chance to dispel the tension. He motioned to his man, who rubbed his wounded hand from Bastawr's attack. "Werdth, bring us hot water."

The servant nodded and went in search of the tea service.

"I knew this was going to be a long night." Ra'al retracted his claws and groaned.

Less than half an hour later, the group of combatants sat around a pot of very dark, spicy tea served with dried fish crackers.

"Let's first clear the issue of your servant, Yarichek." Coryn munched on a dried fish that refused to yield under her teeth for several moments. "We don't know anything about him or his whereabouts."

"I would prefer to believe you." Garesch looked to his group, five of them bowed in acquiescence. "Even my men think he went back to my father…or worse, was a double agent with other orders."

"I hope you don't take offense for asking, but why would he do that? And why do you handle the entire trip in such secrecy?" Bastawr looked to the morehl with a puzzled face. "I mean, he is your father, but you talk about him as if he is a rival."

Garesch smiled. "Let's say that my father and I don't see eye to eye."

"So, this expedition of yours was not sanctioned by him, then." Ra'al winked to Coryn. "My fast-thinking friend assumed that much."

"Not completely, no." Garesch shook his head slowly. "I will be honest with you, and I expect the same of you—and a dose of confidentiality will go far to building trust."

"Agreed. Honesty should clear these waters and help us move forward." Coryn clasped both her hands.

"My father actually opposed my efforts to broker peace with Uruzak and the rest of Cyrea; he called it 'tactless nonsense'." Garesch sighed. "And I think that he might be on the foul side of the coming war."

"You mean that your father could be an agent of Death?" Ra'al raised both eyebrows.

"I am almost certain of it." Garesch looked to the morehl, and one of them held a hand to his chest in a strange sign.

Garesch made the same sign to the morehl and continued, "We all know that he had an alliance with a warlord in the Shadowlands. A very long and unnatural alliance."

Ra'al assumed that this was some sort of code to disclose their secrets. He was not so versed in the customs of the morehl, but this seemed too obvious not to see.

The morehl who nodded to Garesch shook his head. "It is a widespread secret known by most all morehl. His hidden ally is an undead warlord."

"It might be more than mere rumor as Marnash has said." Garesch took a deep breath. "Add this to the fact that my father hates - *loathes* - the other races and considers all of them to be our enemies. He thinks that our race should lord above the order of races and that the others somehow stole our divine rights." Garesch looked down at his hands. "I can't accept his vision for our people. Something screams inside me that all his teachings are wrong."

Silence spread fast, and everybody looked at the floorboards for several moments.

"Although not entirely shocking, this could be the worst news I've heard as of late." Bastawr finally broke the silence. "First, I learn of undead movements all around the mainland, and if that was not alarming enough, I get an intimate declaration that one of the most powerful kings in the continent might be an ally to these forces of darkness? Further, he is a racist with a vendetta against anyone but his own kind? These are dire times."

"I am sad to say, it could be even worse than that." Garesch placed his clasped hands in his lap. "What Coryn saw is one of four parts to one map. Yarichek may have stolen one of the other parts and taken it to my father."

"What were the maps for?" Ra'al asked.

Garesch looked to Marnash, for some moments. The morehl made the same sign to his chest. "We are not entirely sure."

It sounded like he held something back, but the others did not press him on it.

"All we know is that they are keystones to something very powerful and ancient called the *mist stones*." Marnash pursed his lips. "We fear that, if Yarichek reaches the king, these powerful stones would fall in the hands of Cyrea's nemesis. We also believe that such a powerful artifact could change the tide of the coming war…at least, the leader of the undead in the Shadowlands believes it so. I expect my father will trade them to secure an alliance with them, which has gone cold since the Battle for Balgavarr."

"Then he has to be stopped." Bastawr hit the table. "If such power can change the tide of a war everyone knows is coming, then Yarichek has to be tracked, and the map retrieved."

"This might not be the only item of power that is planned for use in the coming war," Ra'al said in a low voice. "There are others."

Coryn stared angrily at him. "Ra'al!"

"Let's be fair, Coryn. We promised complete honesty," Ra'al pleaded with Coryn.

Coryn frowned deeply. "It is not for us to decide. *It is the gods' decision.*"

"I am sorry, lady Coryn, but we need to know what you are both talking about." Marnash looked intently at Coryn.

"It is about Coryn's map, Marnash," Ra'al said firmly. "Her father's map."

"Ra'al! At least give me the right to state what is at stake here." Coryn's voice rose in a crescendo.

"Please do, lady Coryn." Garesch turned in his seat to face her.

Coryn took a deep breath. "The map is not just a map to an item of power. It is for all the items of power that survived the Magestorm Wars in Cyrea," Coryn said, and then paused for a second, turmoil clearly written on her face. "So, you can appreciate the need for secrecy. This knowledge is not something to be trifled with."

Again, silence reigned supreme.

"After the Magestorm Wars ended, there was peace for a brief time in Cyrea. The majority of the magic weapons that the gremmlobahnd had created were gathered into one trove and sealed away for a millennium. My father found a way to access them…that was the spoils at stake in the Balgavarr War. Enough mystic weapons to outfit an army—more, in fact." Coryn prayed her faith in the morehl prince was not unfounded.

After some moments, Garesch said, "You are absolutely right, Coryn." He shook his head. "These weapons should be called upon only if circumstances demand it."

"For now, we must retrieve the maps to the mist stones." Marnash stared hard at Garesch.

"Leave this to me, then," Bastawr said. "The wilderness is familiar to me, and I am an excellent tracker."

"And a fierce warrior, as Coryn and I have witnessed," Ra'al added.

"But what do these mist stones do?" Coryn asked. "And how can they be used?"

"There are few folk we could ask, and time is not on our side." Marnash put his hands back on the table. "They are an arcane creation meant to aid the Sages, but there are none we know how to reach. Lady Naemyar is likely to know. I believe that lady Coryn is acquainted with her? She may have the right means to connect those pieces of the puzzle."

"Indeed, I think you might be right." Coryn nodded. "She is well versed with the history of Esfah; her father wrote several books of history, I am told. If she does not know what these mist stones are, someone in her network will."

"Then we have to seek her out as soon as we can." Ra'al shook his head at the irony. "We have to turn back to Tulgesh."

"You go after Naemyar. I will chase after Yarichek, and we shall meet in Balgavarr." Bastawr flashed Ra'al an equally menacing smile. "I'll retrieve this wayward map, if it can be done."

Chapter 8

Garesch stood adjacent to Ra'al and Coryn on the ship's deck. The sun had not yet come up. "I will join you on their journey to Tulgesh," he informed them. "This mission is vital to the survival of your people, *and* of mine."

Coryn raised a brow. It seemed to her that the dwarves had a more vested interest, or at the very least, their presence would ensure that, if Bastawr failed, these elves had nothing to do with it.

"The elves of Uruzak can never become what they *should be* if we do not help our would-be allies survive the coming storm. And I must not let my father have his way, if he is indeed playing for both sides of the war."

Bastawr told them that he had to retrieve his gear, but he would track down Yarichek, if possible.

"We'll join you in the city," Coryn told him. "We should stock up on rations as well. You can show us where."

Bastawr smiled. "I can show you where, but ghwereste, especially the tigerfolk, rarely need supplies in the wilderness."

Soon, they marched through the markets of the city.

Ra'al was not eager to carry any extra weight, but Coryn was eager to purchase merchandise. The company of the morehl agreed to carry the dried foods and extra provisions at the frostwing's complaint.

As they trekked through different stalls and shops, Garesch stopped by a weapon seller that posted a sign stating they carried enchanted weapons.

When they entered, the proprietor was fast to point out that their large number might scare off other customers, which was odd since it was too early for the sailors sleeping through the alcohol haze of last night to be buying anything off the merchant.

Still, Garesch accepted the merchant's demands and took only Ra'al, Marnash, and Bastawr inside. He left Coryn and the rest of the morehl on the street.

The shop owner pushed a set of daggers into Garesch's hands, claiming that the weapons were magically enchanted to always keep a keen edge and find the weak spots in armor.

Garesch produced a clear stone from his purse and passed it over the tip of the dagger, which started to rust on the spot. The seer stone did not change color.

Almost every weapon the shop owner tried to sell Garesch failed the test.

In desperation, the shop owner disappeared into the depths of the shop mumbling curses and complaints to the gods. When he came back, he handed Garesch a crescent sword, which he claimed was used by a warrior during the Magestorm Wars.

To Ra'al's surprise, Garesch didn't test the weapon, but paid the full price without negotiations. As soon as they stepped outside, Ra'al asked Garesch, "You didn't test the sword. Why did you accept it as is?"

"I don't have to test it." Garesch caressed the sword as a lover would the hair of his beloved. "It is morehl made. I know this sword as I know my own blood."

"So, it is enchanted?" Ra'al asked him.

"In a way, yes." Garesch sheathed the sword and hooked it to his belt. "This sword has won so many battles that it has a charm of its own, even if not magical."

Ra'al shook his head in confusion and shrugged, but didn't ask more of the morehl prince.

"Here." Garesch held his original sword flat in both hands. "Please accept this as a gift. It is as fine a blade as any, and it has seen its share of battle, and its fair share of victory."

Ra'al knew a bit about morehl and their weapon gifting customs. It was considered as strong as blood bonds for their race. He bowed to the prince. "Gift accepted, thank you." He pulled the sword out of its scabbard to admire it.

"The blade is keen." Garesch smiled. "I have seen you fight with swords, and I know that it will serve you well in battle."

Ra'al bowed his head again and hooked the sword to his belt. After a few steps, the sword felt as much a part of his body as any of his limbs.

Exiting the store, Marnash did a double take at the new weapon upon Ra'al's hip and then spotted the new blade and scabbard Garesch clutched. The blood seemed to drain from his cheeks. "Is… is that…"

Garesch nodded very seriously with a curt bob of his nose.

Coryn raised a brow at the lava elf. "What… What is it?"

"A piece of history," Garesch said. "The vendor did not understand what it was." He deflected further questions and began walking.

They stopped in a dark, musty shop. It was out of the way of commerce, and on the edge of town. The proprietor, unlike the other vendors in most shops they passed, didn't hover over his merchandise, try to push it on customers, or protect it from being stolen.

This shop carried items for those with mystic inclinations. Legend stated that before the stiffening of the arcana veil, artifacts such as focusing rings or sightstones were never needed, and any of Esfah's races could easily harness elemental magic with half the effort required of arcanists now.

The shop owner practically slept in the corner as Bastawr led Coryn and Garesch around. In general, a person's affinity for magic sprouted from his or her race's unique and individual connection to nature. Among the areosa, it was rare to find a powerful magic-user among them. Though all had access to magic, few powerful ones had presented themselves to the world in recent memory. They produced their innate magic through the song of the wind and their bond to it.

Garesch purchased a sightstone for Coryn, in case she ever had need to summon more magic than she could muster.

Ra'al gave Coryn a searching look, but she just shrugged. Ra'al knew that Coryn always preferred her axe to magic, but she did not refuse a gift. Brute force was not always the right answer.

Outside the shop, the party stood for almost an hour distributing the loads among themselves before Bastawr bid them all farewell and departed towards the wilderness.

"I guess we should strike out as well." Coryn gazed at the disappearing Bastawr. She assumed he had some way to cross the bay and reach the mainland of Cyrea from the island nation of Frostshoal.

"No time better than now," Ra'al said and rubbed his massive hands together.

The party knew the *Coral Skip* was due to receive a cargo load and loop across the top of the world and down to Diamantia. They could not use the ship to cross to the mainlands, but luckily, small charters were easy to hire near the port.

Between the six lava eves, one dwarf, and a single frostwing, they easily secured a ferry. The trip from Frostshoal would take two days and the captain promised to take them directly through the Dur'Sona Bay and deposit them on the safest parts of the shoreline east of Kafnysan Mountains. Instead, the ferryman grumbled about weight, speed, and choppy water threatening his boat; he slowed after two days and dropped them on the Cyrean mainland, significantly farther away than promised.

He pointed west. "That's yer path. You should be able to skirt the Big Wet without much goblin interference if you keep yer heads about ya."

"And if we don't?" Ra'al asked.

"Then ye won't have heads to worry about," he cackled as he shoved off and waited for the tide to help his craft turn. "Besides," he called back, "ye got the morehl with ye. They're famous for having an old alliance with the Wet."

The boat soon disappeared behind them without a trace and Garesch muttered, "That old alliance has long since soured."

They marched onwards for two hours before making camp under the cover of darkness.

Passing around soft bread, dried cheese, and fish, the elves advised the others not to start a fire. They were too close to the edge of Big Wet swamplands.

After eating and resting for an evening, the company broke camp with the dawn and started to delve into the forest with the help of the dawn light. Foot trails and animal paths made their way through the trees.

"I think we are lost," Ra'al announced around midday. "This is a no-man's-land. Nothing but an animal trail."

Marnash pressed a hand to the frostwing's cheek as if taking a temperature. He scowled and then stepped back. "Have patience, prince." Marnash clutched one of two stones in his pocket, then knelt on the ground and started to whisper. The grass bent around the morehl and fire shot straight ahead from his locked hands.

The fire scorched a single row of grass blades going directly ahead of them.

"Here you have your road, prince." Marnash winked at Ra'al's hanging jaw.

They resumed their progress slowly as the grasslands soon turned marshy. Sparse forests gave way to thicker foliage after a few days' travel.

"This mud sucks hard on my poor boots." Coryn dragged a squelchy boot after another. "I wish that I wore my sneaking shoes instead of those heavy travel boots."

"You mean your forty stone boots instead of those sixty stone ones?" Ra'al smiled manically. "They are all weapons of mass destruction, dear Coryn."

"My boots have served me well all these years," Coryn grunted as she took another step in the mud.

"I am sure that many enemies fell to them." Ra'al started to laugh. "Come to think of it, your boots have seen as much battle as the dagger Garesch hides on his hip." He laughed even harder.

Coryn frowned. "Ra'al, it is not that funny."

"It is if you look at it in this hazy light." He bent over laughing. "Festrations, you look hilarious in this light." Ra'al fell to the ground and continued to laugh very hard and loud.

"I think the prince could have swamp fever." Garesch looked to Marnash.

"No worries, I suspected as much, earlier. I have a remedy." Marnash pulled something green from his satchel.

As Marnash approached Ra'al, he opened his palm and a vial with green fluorescent fluid swirled sluggishly inside.

Garesch pulled some cloth rags from his pack and gave one to Coryn. "Put this to your nose." Coryn looked stunned. "I would suggest that you do it now," Marnash said and smiled at her.

Coryn looked at him in confusion, but then she noticed all the other morehl covered their noses, so she followed suit.

Marnash tied the rag around his face and grabbed Ra'al's head. He couldn't resist, caught in a fit of laughter. Then Marnash pulled the cork off the vial.

The smell assaulted Coryn's senses and made her wretch instantly. She was at least ten cubits away from Ra'al, and she could only imagine what poor Ra'al had felt.

She soon found out.

Ra'al roared in agony, jumped to his feet, and started gagging furiously.

"Concentrated dragon piss," Garesch said in a low voice to Coryn. "Can chase away most demons of the mind in one whiff."

"Potent stuff." Coryn was still dry-heaving even after the cork was back in the vial.

Marnash tucked it back inside his pockets. "We use it occasionally to combat The Strange, whenever a lava elf succumbs to the same mental affliction."

It took almost five minutes for Ra'al to stop groaning. "What in festration was that?"

"Something that saved your life." Marnash held a water skin for Ra'al to drink. "Drink as much as you need."

The party resumed their journey a few minutes later.

Ra'al raised his head to the wind suddenly. "I smell something wrong."

"It must be that vile odor still lingering in your lungs." Coryn walked happily on the dry batch of grass that allowed her to walk normally for a few steps.

"No, it is a different smell," Ra'al announced. "Wet and rotten, not quite as stinging, though."

"Does it smell of compost and fermented filth, and tingles the back of your throat?" Marnash asked Ra'al.

"As a matter of fact, yes. It has a distinct tingle." Ra'al looked back with surprise at the older morehl.

"Get your weapons on the ready, expect an ambush any minute," Garesch shouted to his men.

A moment of confusion came over Ra'al's face, but he reacted instinctively with a growl and a snarl.

Before the men could ready themselves for battle, a shrill horn sounded through the marsh.

Ra'al unsheathed the sword Garesch gifted him and smiled. Now was as good a time as any to test his new morehl blade.

Coryn readied her axe as the guards pulled out their swords.

The entire party looked right and left, anticipating a coming attack.

No less than fifty goblins burst through the foliage. They fell upon them shrieking and screaming wild, animal battle cries.

The first goblins flung themselves at Marnash. The morehl held his sword point down, waiting for the goblin to close the gap. It lunged forward and Marnash's sword rose and fell. In one fluid motion, the goblin fell with his midsection opened. Before he could reset his sword hand, another flew at him.

Marnash intercepted the trog mid-air, and as he turned to face another, the head of the goblin rolled to his feet.

Ra'al growled and charged two trogs. He blocked the one on the right with his sword as he raked the head of the other with his free hand.

It fell back two steps, allowing Ra'al to dodge and return to the one on the right. He plunged the sword to the hilt and then pulled it free and brought it to bear against the other goblin.

The goblin charged Ra'al from the side, but Ra'al unfurled his wings, knocking the creature ten cubits back.

Coryn swung her axe in low arcs, severing legs and kneecaps, and then she charged at a cluster of goblins.

Ra'al looked furtively at the battlefield. Goblins seemed to come from almost every direction.

The frostwing watched as Coryn blocked one trog hatchet, and then her axe connected with the enemy's stomach. She rushed another and intercepted him before he could attack Garesch's blind side. Coryn's axe severed the trog's left foot, sending him stumbling wide. She continued the arc of the axe and targeted the goblin's neck, killing him instantly.

Ra'al looked at Garesch. His blade was drenched in the foul-smelling, thinly yellow trogs' blood. The enemy paid him the most attention for unknown reasons.

Ra'al charged two goblins that screamed and ran towards Garesch. Ra'al's stroke took one from the back, opening a deep cut across the goblin's back.

The other trog turned and howled at Ra'al. It aimed for him in a frenzy of crude sword jabs and stabs.

Ra'al took a cut in his wing but responded in kind and severed the goblin's sword hand. The wounded fiend backed off, leaving Ra'al close enough to protect Garesch.

The frostwing and lava elf stood back-to-back, as wave after wave of the goblins came at them.

Garesch methodically swiped, blocked, and stabbed. But not all the blood on his body was the yellow of his enemies. Several cuts and nicks leaked steam as his red blood broke the surface. It super-heated when exposed to air. His long tunic turned sickly orange where the two colors of blood mixed.

Ra'al fought ferociously, far stronger than Garesch's faster strokes. He lacked the finesse and speed of the morehl, yet the goblin bodies at his feet matched Garesch's number.

Ra'al's wings took a serious beating from the onslaught of the goblins, but otherwise, he stood untouched. The frostwing started to tire; his style of fighting was effective, but not as efficient. He thought that standing against the next wave of goblin attackers would be a miracle from the gods.

As if the gods answered his wish, the goblins thinned in front of Ra'al and Garesch.

Ra'al stood panting and surveyed the area around them. The number of goblins had thinned only because they found another target; Coryn fought in the middle of the throng.

Ra'al took a deep, ragged breath, beat his wings once, and jumped almost onto Coryn's back. He landed hard, bowling over three goblins in the process.

At least the troggish fighters seemed to stop emerging from the trees. The remaining goblins rushed in one last vicious attack, where the fighters made their stand.

Coryn's axe moved in erratic arcs, which was not what Ra'al expected to see from the well-trained vagha. He noticed his friend drawing upon her last dredges of energy; she would soon fall from tiredness.

Behind them, Garesch's blood seeped from a wound in his shoulder, drenching his sword and shrouding his arm in steam. He rushed to join the vagha and areosa. As his sword rose and fell, his blood dripped and spurted; every move drew him nearer to the realm of darkness and the afterlife the morehl called the Void.

Ra'al's blade weaved, swiped, and connected with enemy flesh. More goblins' blood spurted and splashed in the air. But he grew slower and slower with every stroke. He also started to lose focus and concentration; his defensive posture started to waver, opening him to more of the coming attacks.

One goblin managed to slip under Ra'al's guard and nick his right arm with a stone hatchet. Ra'al snarled in pain and used the claws of his left hand to slice open the face of the goblin who cut him.

Scores of goblins laid dead on the ground, but more appeared.

Coryn strained to keep fighting with long and deep cuts on both arms and her back. Still, she didn't make a sound pronouncing her pain. But her stokes wobbled. Instead of taking a goblin in one strike, it took her multiple blows to catch and kill her enemy.

Garesch fell to his knees, his sword arm went limp beside his swaying form. The prince had bled so much that he couldn't bring his sword arm up to defend himself.

Marnash hurried to his side and stood guard over him. The morehl guards had fought in pairs. Though goblins lay dead around them, half their number had died.

Ra'al shifted his sword to his more rested left arm, and resorted to sheer force in his defense, but his monumental efforts tired him and drained his energy. Like Coryn's, his strokes became erratic and ill-focused.

There were many goblins on the ground, some dead and others wracked by death throes. The air suddenly split as a shrill horn sounded in the distance.

Just as they had come, the goblins disappeared into the long strands of wild growth.

Marnash dropped beside Garesch and pulled out his stones. He helped the prince lay back, as Garesch's breaths were ragged.

"Too many wounds, we need a proper healer," Marnash mumbled under his breath. "But I can stop the bleeding for now."

He finished and called for Ra'al, "Prince, please come."

The older morehl sat on the ground and waited for the others to join him. Marnash had lost almost as much blood as Garesch had. Still, he managed to staunch the bleeding and stabilize the prince, whose eyelids fluttered as he slipped in and out of consciousness.

Silence hung over them for a moment. Their numbers were reduced to five. The others lay dead on the swampy floor.

Marnash took a long breath and stood. "We have to run." He swayed a bit and Ra'al reached for his arm to steady him. "We are familiar with goblin tactics to know that this will not be the last attack."

"Do you mean that another wave is coming?" Garesch found himself lucid and willed himself to remain awake. He looked at the swamp with clenched teeth.

"Yes. They will come, and they will come with fresh vigor and blood lust even more than the first group had. More numbers, too." Marnash shook his head slowly. "We cannot stay in this place."

"We can't turn back either," Ra'al said and shook his head, breathing heavily.

Marnash made calming signs with his hand. "Nobody suggested that. But we have to find shelter, or at least a place that can be defended. It's best if its hidden altogether."

Garesch managed to find his feet. He waved his index in the air to emphasize his point. "A well-defended spot could change the tide of our last stand."

"I can't see any place around here capable of defense." Marnash looked around them. "Only flatlands and marshes as far as the eye can see."

"Then we need asylum somewhere, and I have a place in mind." Coryn sighed. "Even though it is far off the road to Balgavarr, it could be our best chance."

"How far away is it?" Garesch asked her.

"I am not sure. But I feel it close by." Coryn looked at Ra'al. "I think you know where I mean to go."

"I think I do." Ra'al gave her a tired smile.

"We can reach Balgavarr by cutting around the tip of the Big Wet," Coryn said.

"I reckon that this will be a very interesting trip…" Garesch smiled with grim determination. "Provided we can survive it."

Chapter 9

They consulted the map, but knew they could not slow; there was no time for rest. Given they'd each suffered wounds in the trog attacks, they'd all lost much blood. They savaged the packs of their fallen comrades and devoured anything sweet or citrus to try to reinvigorate themselves before launching into a mad dash towards safety. Marnash, the most seasoned of them, insisted they also eat anything salty to prevent deadly dips in blood pressure. They snacked lightly as they moved with as much speed as they could muster. The party started heading to Balgavarr, not typically considered a refuge for morehl.

Ignoring their own wounds, each carried a grim outlook onto the road ahead. They moved along the trails with weapons drawn, ready for any attacks from the trogs at any moment; they knew another raid like the last would end them.

They planned for minimal contact, if possible. There was no shame in running from certain death, and so they ran, darting through wooded trails like foxes with baying hounds at their backs.

Coryn looked at the sky above and then back to the road ahead.

Darkness spread and the clouds filled the night sky, occluding the stars and limiting available light. They could not afford to stop. Neither could they light torches or use any other source of light. The faintest illumination would draw the full attention of the goblins.

The morehl took the lead; elven eyes provided the best night vision, and they paced forward in cautious yet constant advancement through the marshlands.

Fireflies danced near the party. With the occasional bubbling sounds from the swamp at their left and the constant buzz of mosquitos on both sides, the entire landscape formed a surreal atmosphere.

Coryn watched the fireflies dance to a hidden, graceful rhythm. They moved to the beat of the swamp gasses bubbling through the night; the whole world seemed to sing around her.

She smiled, maybe the poet at this party was not Ra'al after all. She always saw magic in nature. She remembered how often Ra'al complained about her perkiness and her constant sense of wonder, but she could never fully explain to him how she saw the world.

Even in battle, she saw the battlefield differently from others. She felt and followed the beat of battle as if it possessed its own music. Combatants dancing to the rhythm of running blood and the rush of her own heart.

Those who attacked yesterday followed a solid rhythm in battle. Though it all appeared as chaos to one who did not see it from her point of view. There was a pattern to the hidden music that led them through a fight; a flow that she felt, but could not explain with words.

She stopped walking. Something was not right. Coryn never knew of goblins to be so organized. She needed to bounce her ideas off Ra'al.

Coryn turned to call for him. "Ra'al, duck!" she screamed instead.

Ra'al looked at her for a moment. Confusion covered his features until he realized something was gravely wrong. He dropped face-first to the mud.

A fireball flew just above Ra'al's shoulder as he fell. The blaze hit a tree beyond him. But the fire burned like black flame— some sort of eldritch fire borne of black magic.

Marnash dipped a hand into his pocket and whispered something under his breath, then a matching fireball flew from his other hand toward the goblin shaman, who hid behind a copse of bracken back on the road.

The fireball hit the bush and the surrounding brush with a loud boom, catching red with Firiel's mystical fire instantly. A blaze raged around the shaman.

Coryn's eyes opened wide with shock. The older morehl was more than a simple healer. He was a magic user and skilled arcanist. Coryn turned her head sharply to the left; she heard a loud scream in the distance and another trog shaman jumped into view and hurled something mixed white and black.

Garesch drew his new sword and slashed at the advancing object. Coryn saw it fly near them. It was a skull painted with evil runes.

Just as Garesch's sword smashed the skull, it exploded, showering him and the area with mystic fire.

The morehl batted the flames away from his clothes and stood unscathed. Lava elves would require, by their nature, a direct hit for flames to damage them. It would be the same for the vagha as well, but that left Ra'al vulnerable.

An arrow flew just past Coryn's right, almost nipping her ear. "Archers!" she screamed.

She drew her axe and stood with her left arm facing the back of the road. She always favored her right arm and a hit to that arm would count her out of the battle.

The morehl sheathed their swords and drew compact, flintlock weapons from their packs. Coryn dove for cover as crude arrows flew straight for her and a cloud of blue-gray smoke erupted nearby.

Ra'al took to the air and rained down a hail of jagged spikes. His leather quiver was growing perilously low on supply.

Coryn watched as Ra'al ravaged the trog archers. Bodies collapsed, spilling out from behind the protective cover of dense foliage. Some bore his jagged quills, others bled from holes caused by musket fire.

Ra'al landed beside her and spotted the trog with a cluster of enchanted skulls. Before the goblin spell caster could concentrate his efforts on him, the frostwing picked up a massive rock, aimed, and hurled it over the outcropping where the creature hid.

Coryn heard a visceral *thunk*. Finally, the shaman goblin fell backward with a ruined, squished face. He died with a throaty gurgle.

"Hurry up." Garesch signaled for them to follow, even as the lava elves reloaded their flintlocks. "More will come soon. These weapons are effective, but they are not quiet."

Coryn ran after the morehl. They had sped far ahead, and she was barely able to follow.

Suddenly, she felt pressure at her waist, then found herself in the air. Ra'al had grabbed her. She heard his labored breathing and felt him wince with every beat of his wings. They weren't ruined, but they were far from decent condition. Still, Ra'al continued to beat at the air and soon glided ahead of the morehl.

Coryn noticed from her high perch that there was another group of goblins straight ahead of the morehl.

"To your left!" she shouted and saw Garesch look up. He understood her directions and waved his arm to signal the elf company should go right.

"We have to land soon, Ra'al…Please, you are not well." She touched the arm that held her tight.

Ra'al kept his silence as his wings beat against the humid, fen air.

She kept one hand on Ra'al's arm. Worry ate at her and she hoped that her friend would heed her advice soon.

"Ra'al …" She tried to warn him again, but he cut her off.

"Coryn, if I land, I can't carry your weight and mine while running." He grit his teeth. "I can't maintain enough speed…except here." He strained as he pronounced every word.

She clung tightly with one hand around his, and patted his other arm, keeping her silence. Coryn looked down and saw no goblins in the distance. She looked behind them, to the left, right, and then back at Ra'al.

"Ra'al, the goblins are far behind us. We can land, now…the elves need to catch up."

Ra'al hummed some tune Coryn couldn't quite recognize. He ignored her requests.

Coryn knew his tune was a bedtime song meant for frostwing kits. His mind had gone to another place, a safer place, as a way to cope with the overwhelming pain.

Ahead, the swamp brush thinned, and the ground flattened, turning to fields of puzzleweed and heather. Ra'al finally angled down to land.

Far behind, the morehl sprinted to close the significant gap. They'd barely been able to keep up, and that had only been because of the wounded flier's reduced speed.

Ra'al touched down upon the ground with a nimble enough landing. As soon as he released Coryn, he collapsed.

"Ra'al!" Coryn screamed.

"Welcome back." Garesch stood over Ra'al. "For a moment, we thought you were beyond our help."

Ra'al winced as he sat. "Frostwings are made of strong mettle, my friend."

Garesch laughed. "I am now certain of that." He touched Ra'al's skin. "You also heal very fast."

Ra'al touched his arm and realized that his entire body was covered in some kind of slimy residue.

"Swamp dung, we call it," Garesch explained. "It's a stagnant water lichen. Crude and disgusting to the touch, but it works miracles with open wounds."

"And for the sinuses as well." Ra'al took a whiff. "It burns all the way down to my bowels."

"Good, then you are in control of your faculties." Garesch smirked. "Can you stand up?"

"I can try." Ra'al placed his hand on the ground and stood, easing himself off the crude travois they'd assembled to drag their large, injured friend. Wounded or not, the party had not been able to stop moving, and an unconscious areosan prince provided no exemption.

As he stood, Ra'al looked around. The party huddled around a fire. The sight and smell of it gave him a pang of worry.

"Where are we?" Ra'al asked Garesch, and urgency bled through his voice.

"At the border of the Big Wet," Garesch said. "You were unconscious for a little more than a day and collapsed just inside the western edge of the troglands."

"We are safe enough, here," Marnash said. "And ready for a much needed rest."

"All we need is to cross the Sareen River and head into the Kafnysan Range. We can seek shelter in Balgavarr," Coryn pleaded. "My father would surely rise to our aid."

"Lady Coryn, *you* can take shelter in Balgavarr, but we cannot." Marnash sighed. "We have not yet formalized any treaty…our lands are still technically at war. Our presence could possibly violate the ceasefire and reignite the old war—we cannot possibly fight both an old war and contend with the undead we both know is coming."

"You have to trust us," Coryn cried. "We will do our best to make this mission succeed."

"We do trust you, lady Coryn." Marnash shook his head. "But forgive me if I doubt that your father would consider rendering aid to a group of morehl." He looked around the tiny circle. Only three of the elves remained.

"This is my father we are talking about." She clenched her fists. "He is a very reasonable dwarf."

"I do trust he is." Garesch's smiled faded. "To other vagha…not to the morehl."

"This is absurd," Coryn argued. "He will help!"

The prince shook his head. "I have to say, again, that I greatly doubt it."

"What is the problem here?" Ra'al looked from Coryn to Marnash. "Why do you both insist on reading a future that is not yet set? The future can only become clear when it becomes the present."

Marnash raised an eyebrow.

Ra'al cocked his head in confusion. "Am I wrong?"

"I first took you for a pampered prince who yearned for the pleasures of his palace. But you've proved to be an adept warrior." Marnash bowed.

"I did?" Ra'al grimaced.

"You've got some wisdom, too," Marnash observed. "And a philosopher's heart."

The frostwing threw his head back and guffawed with laughter. After some moments, Ra'al wiped the tears from his eyes and looked to the party. "Well, my accidental wisdom ends here." He eyed each of them as they looked apprehensively to him, then he sat with a loud sigh. "I don't know how King Dragonsbane will react to the request. None can know for certain. We can only answer so few questions…like what's for dinner?" He leaned closer to the fire and the iron pot upon it, and let the issue drop.

Spending a night in the open so close to Big Wet was a calculated risk. The travelers were too fatigued and injured to travel at a sustained pace without time to recharge. At dawn, the party broke camp and moved out. Ra'al fell into lockstep with Coryn. Ra'al made a tremendous effort not to outpace his diminutive friend.

"So, we are about to introduce our lava elf friends to your father, the great vagha, and formidable war hero." He was silent for a few steps, and when Coryn didn't respond, he turned to face her. "How do you think he will react?"

Coryn pursed her lips, took a deep breath, and exhaled with a whistle. "I am certain that I can sway him to our cause." Coryn looked up the trail for some moments, as if contemplating the road in the distance. "You know, Ra'al, he wanted a trade alliance with the morehl because trade would give them enough skin in the economics game to keep them from waging another leg of this financially ruinous war. But an actual alliance? Maybe I'm delusional about how reasonable he can be where Uruzak is concerned." She held her breath for several seconds, then exhaled. "Maybe he can only remember fighting against them so many years ago. Certainly those memories have to taint a man going forward—even a great man. That war did cause so much death…"

"Who knows, Coryn? Like you said yesterday, your father is the most reasonable vagha you know." Ra'al tripped as he tried to put one foot in front of the other. He was still far from one hundred percent.

"He is. But just as Marnash said, the morehl could be the chink in his armor." Coryn sighed. "Certainly many in the Reaches have not forgotten the horrors of the battle of Balgavarr so easily. It may prove a bridge too far."

"Even in the face of a common enemy?" Ra'al stopped as Coryn did, and he stared at her intently.

"If he listens long enough to understand, and if there is indeed a common enemy, then maybe. But I don't know how common the knowledge of the undead horde is. I know he has seen reports, as has your mother." Coryn pulled a blade of grass viciously from the ground and started to roll it between her fingers. "The real problem is that there was a legion of undead warriors fighting alongside the lava elves in the Battle of Balgavarr. Convincing him that the tide has changed might not be easy; the morehl and bloodless have an alliance as far as Balgavarr is concerned. Even if Garesch is not his father, he still carries King Saugor's face—it may be that no amount of information changes his position."

"He has his father's face. But you have your father's mind." Ra'al smiled. "I trust that you can bring him around." Ra'al held Coryn's shoulders. "If anyone has the sense to make the argument, it is you. You are the emissary of Balgavarr to the frostwings after all." Ra'al laughed.

Coryn smiled. She was chosen by the elders to be an ambassador to the frostwings. Of course, it helped that she was a childhood friend to the next king, but she knew that this was not the only reason they had selected her; they must have thought her capable, too.

A wave of relief washed over Coryn. "Thank you, Ra'al. You always manage to lift me up when I am down."

Ra'al smiled widely. "What are friends for?"

They quickened their gait to catch up to the rest of the group. Coryn's spirits lifted, and she widened her steps to make up for lost ground.

They walked a few more days towards the hidden city. They could reach it in another day, and a decision had to be made.

Garesch and the morehl stopped as the long trail through the forest ended, and they started to make camp with the edge of Balgavarr in sight.

As soon as the camp was erected, Coryn approached the morehl.

"I am sorry that I can't invite you into the city." Coryn stood fidgeting in front of Garesch. "I don't think the guards would act in good faith if they saw morehl approaching."

"We understand." Garesch said and nodded back at his group. "Your father has a legitimate grievance against my people. We will wait here until you get everything sorted."

Coryn thanked him and started to deliberate with Ra'al about their further journey.

Marnash came to sit beside Garesch. "You know, Garesch, I was in the battle of Balgavarr Reaches."

Garesch raised an eyebrow. "I never knew that."

"It is not a memory one can be proud of." Marnash shook his head. "Fleeing and getting captured is not one of my life's highlights. It was long ago, and we captives groveled before your father. This was before he agreed to the selumaris' hefty ransom." He gazed long at the ascending moon far in the heavens. "Ironically, he forgave us. Those who didn't get caught but laid down weapons when the battle was clearly lost were a different story." He watched a night bird fly over their heads, crossing through the middle of the rising moon. "Those he executed for surrendering to the enemy."

"Yes, I remember hearing of his harsh decisions." Garesch turned his head up and filled his eyes with the moon's light. "I wondered for a long time about the sanity of his decisions."

Marnash just bowed and sat silently.

Both morehl gazed at the sky while Werdth, their third remaining elf, began assembling an evening meal. A shooting star flew above their heads.

"A great one will die within the month," Marnash said in a somber voice.

Garesch scoffed. "Superstition, nothing more."

"Some superstitions have a basis in reality." Marnash turned to face the younger elf.

"Maybe, but basing our lives on them is an exercise in futility." Garesch stood suddenly. "I think we should have one last dinner with the dwarf and the frostwing." He cast a sidelong glance to Werdth, who did his best to reconstitute some dried leeks for a traveler's stew.

"I hope it will not be our last." Marnash followed Garesch's footsteps towards the fire.

Garesch kept walking. He hoped they could earn the support of the vagha, not just as allies against the undead, but for Garesch's true designs: to formalize alliances so that he could wrest control of Uruzak from his father. This was what he considered their most important mission, even more important than the secret one involving sages and mist stones.

The lava elves would scarcely survive another decade with the mad king in power. Support from Balgavarr could prove the crucial element that would change the tides of a coming war. He walked slowly and silently. Garesch agreed with his adviser, hoping that this dinner was not about to be his last.

Ra'al and Coryn approached the gates of the city with the sun still in the evening sky. A towering curtain wall formed a half circle around the main gates, which were always guarded by a crew of sentries.

The usual challenge came, and Coryn answered it. The soldiers let them pass. The younger members of the watch whispered to each other, in awe to see the near-likeness of Thrag whose monument all vagha could see upon the neighboring peak.

It had been several years since Ra'al had been to Balgavarr Reaches. To Ra'al's eyes, the city didn't feel that much different from Icehome. After all, the vagha were the ones who expanded the original Icehome, making it into the grand city it was now.

He remembered when he was a small child, watching the vaghan builders. They built the great road to the lands below the mountain. Like all other children, he was fascinated to watch those small people, who barely reached his childhood height, use their machines and magic to shape the very rock of the mountain.

His mother had embraced the new additions to Icehome, especially with the gift of Castle Ice. She was often around, watching, learning, and preparing to teach frostwing builders the ways that the city was built, creating a foundation for the city's future under her rule. Currently, most maintenance was done by mixed company of dwarves and frostwings.

Balgavarr, for a brief moment, caused Ra'al's heart to slow. The mild home sickness he'd experienced when staring into the heavens aboard the *Coral Skip* felt momentarily abated. Calm and warmth welled in his bones.

Coryn followed an older vagha, whom she whispered to as they walked toward the chamber where her father presided. Dragonsbane was still conducting city business.

As they entered the immense room, Geril smiled to Ra'al and Coryn.

Coryn knelt before the throne, and the frostwing followed her example.

"Please stand, daughter," Geril insisted as he stepped down from his throne.

He approached Coryn first. His eyes studied every bit of her, before he opened his arms. She rushed into them gratefully. "You have seen some battle, eh, Coryn?"

"Aye, father," Coryn answered in a muffled voice, pressed against his shoulder.

"And you fared well?" he asked.

"Not at all times, father," she said, still hugging him.

"Then you have fared well for enough of the time. You're here, after all." He released her, smiling warmly.

Ra'al saw the pride in the eyes of the older vagha and wished that he would find the same in his mother's eyes.

"Ra'al, come nearer, my son."

Ra'al walked close enough for the king to hug him. The old vagha had strength, even more than most frostwings. Ra'al thought that Geril could surely beat quite a few of his peers back home in arm wrestling contests.

The king let go of Ra'al. "As much as I love having both of you here, you came unannounced. And you look terrible. Should I assume negotiations with those red-skinned bastards went sour, and that is what brought your return?"

Ra'al respected the directness of Geril. He always had. Yet now, he remained silent. This was the time for Coryn to explain to her father, not for him to throw his own words to the wind. The risks they faced could topple the dwarven civilization, and the daughter and father needed to do this without outside interference. He bowed his head and waited for Coryn to break the news. He hoped that the vaghan king would take it well.

Coryn took a long breath. "No. The undead are rising, as Rashingot feared."

The king looked long into the eyes of his daughter. He took a deep breath, as if trying to breath in a raging sea, then let it out with a long sigh. He held Coryn's shoulders for a moment. "I thought it was about time."

He turned to his aides and said, "Announce a meeting to the council of elders. We have matters of utmost importance to discuss."

"There is more," Coryn said. "I am harboring the lava elf diplomats—not the ones we were supposed to connect with, but *others*. The original meeting never occurred. But these ones…They are different, father."

A dwarven servant brought Ra'al to a huge suite to rest until the frostwing prince could be called on to face the council. He quickly washed and changed his attire, thankful for a bath and a fresh change.

Before he could contemplate a nap, a healer came to his suite on behalf of Geril sa'Ghuren. She was a coral elf, one of several the vagha kept on hand for situations such as these. The selumari healer shared a devotion to the wind goddess, meaning she could summon healing magics that would have a positive effect on Ra'al's body.

Regardless, sleeping was postponed. For the next hour, the healer worked her magic on the frostwing, mending broken skin and bruised bone alike. When she was satisfied by her handiwork, she left.

Ra'al laid in his bed feeling like all his energy had seeped out of his body. He also fancied dried fish for some sudden, unknown reason, even though before his sea trip, he never liked the stuff.

Just as he started drifting towards sleep and dreaming of fish, somebody knocked on the door. A messenger from the council demanded that Ra'al join them.

Ra'al walked behind the messenger for several minutes, following him through long twisting corridors. Vagha stared at him as if it was the first time they'd seen a frostwing. Eventually, the corridor ended at a huge stone door. Beyond it sat the ruling council of the Balgavarr Reaches.

Coryn stood in the middle of the large room, as twelve older vagha sat in a semi-circle around her.

"Prince Ra'al, we receive you with honor." Coryn's father, King Geril, called for the frostwing to join Coryn in the center of the room.

Ra'al bowed and replied, "And with honor, I accept your rule." He recalled the lines his tutors had hammered into him years before.

"Prince Ra'al." A very old vagha shifted in his seat. "We need your testimony about the events of your journey to Balgavarr."

Ra'al bowed and told the gathered dwarves about his and Coryn's journey alongside the morehl, and the events that transpired.

After he finished, the entire hall fell silent.

Then came some questions about the scalder attack, about what happened in the Big Wet, and finally about the party of morehl waiting outside of the city.

Ra'al answered each question with as much detail as he could recall.

"But what about the rising of the undead?" A vagha who wore the classical attire of dwarf wizards wondered aloud.

"We haven't seen any." Ra'al took a long breath. Here came the hard part of the story. "Back in Icehome, the reports of sightings were coming often, and we even heard rumors of sightings while in Frostshoal."

"And the morehl? You claimed that they were on a mission to find new allies. Why would they do that?" Another vagha with a long scar on his face asked him.

"I don't think King Saugor actually seeks alliances." Ra'al shook his head in denial. "But his son, Garesch, who will be the next king, certainly *is*. He believes in a different way of life than his father. He wants the morehl to coexist with the other races in peace. Our original intention of trade alliances to assuage our troublesome neighbors is met in his goals…and then some." Ra'al's eyes darted from the faces watching him, to Coryn. "For what it's worth, I believe that Garesch is honest in his intentions."

"Coryn sa'Geril, what say you about the morehl prince?" the same vagha asked Coryn.

"I concur with Ra'al, Elder Lahmyn. I believe the intentions of the prince are pure and honest." Coryn stood with her head high, gazing at the tapestries on the wall. She knew that Lahmyn acted like a lump of granite in the pumice bin and was the staunchest dissenter on the council.

"Alright, we will convene to decide a course of action," Lahmyn said, and absentmindedly rubbed the scar on his face. "We shall meet again tomorrow morning."

"I am sorry, elder, but time is of the essence, and there is the issue of the maps to the hidden cache," Coryn added in a hurry.

Her father frowned as he looked at her, then shook his head slowly to warn her against speaking further.

Lahmyn asked, "What maps? What cache?"

"Nothing," intervened Geril. "She speaks of a private family matter for my ears only."

Guards escorted Ra'al and Coryn out. They both stood in the long corridor outside the council room.

"Your father didn't look angered about the news," Ra'al said.

"They already knew of the undead rising in the Shadowlands." Coryn shook her head. "I think the situation deep in the Shadowlands is worse than we thought. My father does not share everything with them…Elder Lahmyn especially. He is nothing like his son…"

Ra'al remained silent after hearing Coryn's news. He understood why Coryn blurted the last part about the maps. Maybe it was time to unearth the hidden weapons.

He kept looking at the door of the council, waiting for the elders to call them back. Now, more than ever, the fate of many relied upon the dwarven council. Coryn stood beside him, rubbing her hands together, a sure sign of her current anxiety.

Ra'al found himself lost in thought when the door of the council opened. As they re-entered the hall, the vagha remained standing.

"Coryn Sa'Geril, and Ra'al son of Thrag, we sanction and approve your mission to build a future peace with Uruzak's next leader," Lahmyn announced. His beady eyes narrowed and made his scar shift to contour around his cheekbones.

Coryn bowed to the council. Relief washed over her.

Before they could leave, her father called them back.

They stood waiting as the other dwarves filed out of the room. Once everybody else left, Geril said, "You should have not mentioned the maps, Coryn." He shook his head. "I had to do more lying to cover that up. Gods know I don't like doing that, but Elder Lahmyn is cagey, and oppositional, at best."

"I am sorry, father." Coryn paused for a few moments. "But I think it is time the weapons were taken from their resting place."

"Coryn, I used a single item from that horde and it nearly corrupted me—you might have never been borne had I taken the path it would have led me down...Neither would have this Garesch fellow. I don't want you to face that same temptation." The king's features twisted. "This cache should only be opened when Cyrea faces its darkest hour. Our role is to keep them in trust for the coming Champions of the Gods."

"The darkest hour may be sooner than you think, father." Coryn looked as stony as her father. "I know that you always told me it should only be handed over to the gods' chosen ones, but what if we can't find them? Or the gods never actually chose anybody as their champions? What if they've abandoned us?"

King Geril looked deep into his daughter's eyes, as Ra'al tried to keep silent.

"Your Majesty," Ra'al spoke up, failing. "The goblins are not fighting the way everybody knew them to fight." He knelt to be nearer to the king's ears. "They were calculating and methodical."

"Not only that," Coryn picked up. "They don't care if they attack by daylight or by night. They are motivated now more than ever."

"You think Death has something to do with all of this?" The king looked from Coryn to Ra'al. "You think the final battle of this age might be upon us?"

Ra'al bowed, as Coryn said simply, "Yes, father. If not the end of all, at least the end of the Second Age."

The king sighed and bent his head.

"Alright. I believe you might have a point." The king shook his head. "But for now, the maps are still safe, and they will stay that way until the right time comes to open the caches."

"Father, we have to learn more about Death's connection to the undead in the north. Did the elders reach any conclusion about our next step?" Coryn looked to the king expectantly

"No, but they suggested you consult the selumari. Form our alliance with Garesch. It is only words for the moment, but a quest such as this might form the kind of bonds necessary to solidify a future union." The king pursed his lips. "If he manages to become king at some future date, our actions now may prove vastly important."

She nodded. "We were already planning to make for Tulgesh to report back to Naemyar. She is working with Matrek and city officials to monitor the undead threat."

"Is there anything new to report on that front from my mother?" Ra'al asked, nervous that Icehome would be the first to suffer an attack because of their proximity to the undead movements.

Geril shook his head. "Not that we've heard. The bloodless seem content to roam the frozen wastelands and have not come down so far south as Icehome." He smirked at the thought of the northern city being south of anything.

"Will Balgavarr send troops to her aide?" Coryn asked.

Geril shook his head. "Only a token force, barely more than the courtesy guard that we've already placed there. Until something is formalized with Uruzak and your friend is on the throne, or until the undead attack in earnest, we cannot afford to weaken our southward defenses and leave ourselves vulnerable to attacks. Prince Garesch is a bet placed on the future, but the odds are long."

"But the lava elves would never…"

Geril cut her off. "The council and I have discussed this at length. We cannot afford to take great risks such as dividing our defensive forces." He rubbed her shoulder apologetically, but wore the stern look upon his face that indicated he could not be moved on the matter. "You should go to Naemyar. Ask her if she knows something we don't and send a raven if there is more to report. Her resources are vast, perhaps broader than even King Matrek's. If there is anything to report, she would know ."

Coryn held her hands together. "I guess that is where we must go, then. We head for Tulgesh at sunrise." Coryn sighed, remembering their secondary objective. "Father, there is a ghwereste friend of ours who was supposed to meet us here. He is tigerfolk and his name is Bastawr." She left off the details of his mission to disrupt a plan laid by morehl enemies. She did not want to destabilize all her efforts so far and had to place her faith in Bastawr.

"I shall receive him and guide him to your whereabouts when he comes." The king hugged Coryn. "The gods' blessings be on you, daughter, Coryn sa'Geril. Good luck in Tulgesh… and with your morehl fellows."

"I will." Coryn hugged him fiercely and then let go. "I won't let you down."

"I believe in you. Your generation stands to gain much from a lasting peace with Uruzak. More than mine ever will." The king waved at them and watched the two friends depart in the direction of their quarters.

"You will need lots of luck," Geril whispered a prayer to Mitta, the luck goddess, on their behalf. "I've had my fair share of it already." The king mumbled as Ra'al and Coryn disappeared behind the bend in the corridor.

Chapter 10

After Bastawr left his friends, he skirted the edge of Frostshoal. He clutched a scrap of bedding the morehl had given him from Yarichek's bunk and used it to track the elf. He tied the scrap at his forearm to freshen his nose later.

The trail led him to a small ferry station beyond the border of town. Luckily, another ghwereste operated it; he hoped it could help him negotiate. A lithe houndfolk cocked his head as Bastawr approached and fixed him with his canine eyes.

Bastawr produced the bedding and let the feral sniff it. "You serviced this elf?"

The hound nodded.

"Can you take me to where he went?" Bastawr had decided to leave the corrupt corps of Frostshoal's enforcers, but there had not been time to alert them and turn in his equipment. Bastawr flashed his patch that identified him as a peacekeeper. It bought him an extra dose of helpfulness from the ferryman.

Motioning to his small skiff, the hound agreed to cooperate. By mid-morning, they were skimming across the frigid water and heading north.

"You are not turning to loop closer to Uruzak?" Bastawr asked, surprised.

"He did not go to Uruzak," the hound replied. "He merely crossed, heading due north and into the Shadowlands. We spoke very little."

Bastawr nodded and then continued the journey in patience. He eventually disembarked, paid the ferryman, and then set out into the sparse growth that surrounded the landing. It did not take him long to locate the lava elf's trail.

Ghwereste were especially good at tracking. Bastawr scanned the horizon. Even among the feral folk, he had keen eyes and he could discern movements nearly a league away. But he also had a keen sense of smell. He could distinguish smells as well as most selumari could discern between nuanced hues of colors. His most reliable sense, however, came from Nature herself; the goddess Ghaeial granted him a kind of internal compass. It never failed him.

This was not the first time he'd tracked a lava elf. Morehl were inventive and ingenious when it came to trouble. As an enforcer, he'd hunted his fair share of red elves.

He moved beyond the broken shores where the Wilds of Dur'Sona petered out into a lurch of bracken and sparse bristlebranches, aldens, and ironwoods. He hoped this would be the place he might eventually find the morehl. Bastawr stopped to listen to the forest.

The forest had a kind of heartbeat. It pulsed strong and resonant, but Bastawr detected a faint note of discord in it.

The rising of the bloodless could cause that. Undead were anything but natural. They were an affront to all that Ghaeial represented. The goddess granted eternal rest to the dead; raising them from their slumber disturbed the natural order of existence.

He knelt and kissed the earth, offering a silent prayer and a promise to the goddess that he would do his duty. Then he rose and looked ahead.

Wild growth sprouted all over the place, between the trees, upon the animal trails, and even on the trees themselves. Far in the distance, a bird called for its mate, and a wolverine caught its prey, but he also sensed unrest to the north. Something passed that way which alarmed the inhabitants of the forest.

He smelled the air as he moved deeper still, and among the smell of wildflowers and animal markings, something smelled hot: the spicy odor he associated with morehl. Bastawr found the scent still wafting in the air and moved faster. He was on the right track.

Its fading taint revealed to him that its owner passed this place nearly a day ago, but Bastawr knew the forest better than any morehl. These grounds had been his ancestors' home. He felt every part of it calling out to him. He knew he could catch up to the elf before long.

Bastawr tightened his gear and his pack. He dropped on all fours and started to run, just like his primal ancestors had. When needing to hurry, four feet always outpaced two, and by a wide margin.

Days passed as he pursued and knew he closed the gap a little more each day. It was a wonder, though: either the elf knew he was pursued or he was running towards something with urgent speed. The creature moved with greater haste than he had expected. But it would not be enough.

The cracked and barren landscape turned ever whiter as they pressed north and west across the wasteland. Sheaves of frost clung to broken plates of shale where the earth had heaved them up from its depths. Hazy sky hung gray and pallid, marking everything with a sense of desolation. And always, a trail of footsteps with their spiced, smoky aroma. The next weather system would extinguish if Bastawr did not reach his prey first.

In the Shadowlands, he knew it was unwise to follow a target without caution. A relentless, hostile chase was out of the question. Stealth was required to catch this enemy.

He advanced slower, but as he delved deeper into the twisted land, the smells grew fouler. Bastawr took his time to study the surrounding nature. Everything around had been touched by death. The trees swayed weakly in the wind, dried and hungry apparitions of their sisters. Vile bubbles oozed with spots and weeds rotted around the trees' trunks, submerging them in decay and decorating the landscape with a hellish aroma that lent everything a sickly green light.

Small, furtive creatures scuttled quickly ahead of him. Bastawr could not feel a common kinship with them. They were not living beings connected to Nature; these were sad creatures basking in the shadow of Death.

Crags and fissures dotted the windswept land that once stood proud and flat in these regions. Accompanying his travels were soft wails of Ailuril, the air goddess. They sounded like tortured souls wafting through the air.

But the smell of the morehl grew stronger, stronger than anything he met on the way. He only had to follow it till he found the escaped wretch.

Just as he cleared a mess of swamp growth he happened upon a large clearing, where the land spread in front of him, black and sickly where it was not covered by ice and snow. Nothing grew there. On the far side of it stood the massive Plateau of Langt which contained the Heimdarl Crag: a network of gnarled and twisting canyons.

Bastawr's heart raced. Nature had no presence here; none whatsoever. He knew that he was all alone in this place. *Almost.*

The morehl stood fifty cubits ahead of him with his back turned. A wall of icy stone rose where the mouth of a frozen canyon yawned open upon the plateau. The rift connected to the Heimdarl Crag, a frosty, winding maze that spiraled through a stony plateau in a maddening labyrinth of jagged rock and ice.

Bastawr felt something pulling at his senses—a kind of supernatural wrongness. He focused upon his prey instead. The mission would soon come to a close as he crept along the ruined landscape, darting from broken boulder to boulder.

He removed his pack slowly and pulled his short sword from its scabbard. He inched forward silently, crouching near on the ground and ready to pounce on his prey.

Just before leaping in for the kill, something from his nightmares stepped into the clearing, emerging from the canyon. Bastawr shied back into a safe hiding spot.

A skeletal figure riding upon a rotting and decayed horse approached the morehl. Hooves crunched over ice crystals ominously. The odor of death and rot permeated the air.

The skeleton dismounted, and the morehl bowed low before him.

Bastawr turned his head to hear what went on between the two.

"You have dallied, morehl." The skeletal knight spoke with a stone-scraped voice that echoed over the clearing.

"I had to be sure I was not followed by those I betrayed." The morehl swallowed loudly. "I still have a life to fear for."

"Soon, all meet the embrace of our Lord." The skeleton knight raised his arms to the sky. "Fear for life is illogical."

"This might be your kind's vision, but I hope to live a full life in Malgrimm's service before Lord Death decides I should join him in the dark lands." Yarichek shifted from one foot to the next.

"You will be called upon when your time comes," the skeletal knight laughed, and for a moment, the laughter chilled Bastawr's heart. He winced.

The morehl stepped two steps back from the knight, eyes darting all around.

"Did you get the maps?" The knight took a single step in the direction of the morehl. His armor clanked as his foot crushed gravel and ice shards underneath.

"Yes, I have it here." The morehl removed his pack and rummaged in it, retrieving a rolled parchment.

"Let's have it." The knight's skeletal hand opened and closed with a clicking sound of bone against bone as he beckoned for it.

Yarichek handed it over and then pulled his hand back quickly, as if from a striking serpent.

The knight unrolled it and gazed with his fiery eye sockets. "This is just one of the three pieces. Where are the others?" The knight's eyes glowed blood red, and even Bastawr felt a chill run down his spine.

"This is the only one I found." The morehl stepped back. "I swear by all the gods."

The knight's gaze never left the morehl. "And I expect that you want a reward for only a single piece of map?"

"No, no, my lord." The morehl stepped three steps back. "I only aim to serve."

"Yes. And serve you shall." The knight pounced on the morehl who tried to flee, but the knight buried his sword to the hilt in the lava elf's midsection. Steam and blood poured from the wound.

The fiend pulled the sword free and wiped its edge on the clothes of the dying morehl. He stood beside Yarichek until he breathed his last, then he walked slowly to his rotting horse and opened the flap of his saddlebag.

He removed a vial with something dark and viscous. The knight uncorked it and poured a single drop onto the body of the morehl.

The liquid bubbled and fumed on contact. It smelled of grave scraps and rot. It was a powerful odor, such that Bastawr fought not to gag and give up his location.

The fluid disappeared and the morehl opened his vacant eyes. The newly-made troop stood and faced the knight. He said with a thick and ungainly tongue, "Command me, Lord."

"Much has yet to be done," the skeleton stated. He rode his horse back into the canyon and Yarichek's corpse followed.

Bastawr waited for them to clear the scene before making his move.

The wind suddenly gusted strongly and snow began to fall. Bastawr grabbed his pack and stepped lightly in the direction that the knight and the morehl went.

Every instinct within him told him to flee, to meet his friends in Balgavarr and tell them of this turn of events. He bit his lip and argued with his gut.

Bastawr settled on following this hunt to its end. He had a chance to learn more about the undead's nefarious plans, and he had to take it. This hunt would only end when he held the map…and hopefully Bastawr would still be alive when he did so.

Chapter 11

Ra'al stood at the gate of the city, waiting for Coryn to arrive so they could rejoin their morehl companions.

Just after leaving Geril's sight, she told Ra'al that she had to do something before they left. That had been half an hour ago, and he started to feel awkward as curious dwarven onlookers watched.

"Hey, mate," one of the vagha called to Ra'al. "You are leaving, right?"

"Yes…I intend to." Ra'al finished his words with a nod and stood silently.

"So, why are you still here, then?" The same dwarf craned his neck as he looked up at Ra'al.

"I will leave as soon as Coryn joins me." Ra'al looked over the vagha's head and into the corridor beyond, hoping to spot her approaching.

He and a few others milled about, waiting to watch the frostwing leave. "So, should we go back to our work and come back in an hour or so, maybe?" The annoying vagha looked around with nods of approval from others gathered.

"You don't need to see us off, we can manage on our own. Go back to your work," Ra'al said and flashed him a toothy smile.

"No, no, no. We want to see you fly away and all." The vagha didn't miss a beat, matching Ra'al's gleaming smile with a brown-toothed one. "We will wait." The vagha nodded. "Gods know if you will ever make it back for us to see it again. We don't see enough areosa around here."

Ra'al lost his smile and scowled. What did this vagha think he was? A circus performer?

Just then, Coryn came running down the corridor.

All the vagha cheered.

She panted beside Ra'al. "What did I miss?"

"Oh, nothing much." He shrugged as he eyed the annoying vagha. "Just some well wishes from friends and allies."

As the duo stepped out, the gathered vagha started chanting. *"Fly, fly, fly."*

Ra'al turned back and gave them a deep frown.

"I guess you have to fly a bit, Ra'al." Coryn waved in rhythm to the vagha's chant. "Come on, give the people something to remember."

Ra'al looked down at her for some moments, sighed, and spread his wings. He flexed them once, thankful Dragonsbane kept a resident selumari who could heal Ailuril's children.

He grabbed Coryn from around the waist and leapt into the air.

They cheered.

"Totally worth it, wasn't it?" Coryn yelped as Ra'al climbed higher.

"Yeah, yeah, whatever." Ra'al was tempted to swoop over the vagha. Many gathered in the large balcony atop an access into the city, where they could keep an eye on both the inner courts of Balgavarr and the semi-circle curtain walls that made up the approach's outer court. Ra'al decided that the next few days would be filled with enough excitement that he need not take risks with such low reward.

Soon, they were far from the city and Coryn asked Ra'al to land so they could talk as they traveled. By foot, it would take them most of the day to get back to the lava elf encampment; wings were very fast, but the rushing air made talking difficult.

Ultimately, the road to Tulgesh would take several tendays by foot or hoof; far longer than their previous flight to the selumari city. Coryn had promised she had a plan to shorten that significantly.

"What took you so long back there, anyway?" Ra'al asked.

"I needed to check on the maps." She shrugged. "At least now I am certain that they were not stolen."

"That's good. It gives us proof that Garesch was telling the truth." Ra'al walked beside Coryn, who stayed silent and absently chewed on her lip. "It confirms our trust in him."

Ra'al stopped and looked at Coryn. "You didn't tell me, what did you want to talk about?"

"So, I was thinking." Coryn fidgeted as she looked at her feet. "If we choose to abandon the morehl, this is our last chance to go our separate routes."

Ra'al frowned and touched her shoulder to force her to look him in the eyes. "I thought all that time in the council and the near fight with your father was to seek their blessing for an alliance?"

"Yes, it was." Coryn took a deep breath as Ra'al waited for her to explain. "But I have to ask you something before I must make a harder decision."

Ra'al looked at her in puzzlement for some moments. "What harder decision?"

"It's not the time to discuss it." She sat on a jutting rock waved her hands, as if pushing away the subject. "Just answer my first question. Should we or should we not rejoin the morehl group? We do have an opportunity to make a clean break with them."

"I think they are a good addition to our efforts, plus Garesch is more than just a travel companion." Ra'al shrugged. "He is quite friendly, not quite a friend, but getting there. Besides, there are only the two of us. Without them, we'd be in dire need of additional support."

"Good." She bobbed her head and remained silent.

Ra'al grimaced. "That was it? Really?"

"No, but the next part is going to be even harder." She shook her head. "I wish we had more time…A year or two to build alliances and bridge our differences might be insufficient."

Ra'al found another rock and sat upon it. "I don't quite understand, but you know how intuitive I am. If I can help in your decision, I will, at least as best as I can."

Coryn bowed her head and kept gazing at her hands for another minute. Ra'al waited for her to formulate her words.

"Suppose that the war was upon us." She looked into Ra'al's eyes. "And we have to raise a defense without much preparation. Shouldn't we have all the tools that we can get?"

Ra'al knew what Coryn thought about, and that the logic behind her thoughts was correct. *Why would Geril hide the cache unless there was too much at stake?*

As he mouthed his thought, Coryn shook her head. "I know that my father thought that the temptation of these weapons would be too great for any person to resist, but if the news about the undead is true, then these are dire times and we need to act upon this fact now, not later."

"You would act against the will of your father? I don't think he will forgive you easily." Ra'al pursed his lip and shook his head. "And there are other issues. Who do you give them to? How can you judge who is worthy to wield these weapons?"

"If the undead rise against us, my father will be too busy to be angry with me." Coryn stood and started pacing. "As for who is worthy, none are. If the fate of Cyrea is at stake, we'll have to disperse them quickly and worry about how to get them back after the war. We can hope they wouldn't fall into hands with ill intent."

"I always considered you a logical and reasonable person, but it's like you've thrown all reason and logic into the swamp." Ra'al huffed. "I think we should consult with somebody with better knowledge of what we'd be actually releasing into the world."

Coryn took a deep breath. "Perhaps Naemyar knows an expert on the Magestorm Wars? They can explain to us anything we need to know."

"Then we have to tell the morehl about your intentions." Ra'al stood. "Let's go to them and maybe they will have further input regarding your dilemma."

"Agreed." Coryn fell in step with Ra'al as he started walking.

The walk to the campsite of the morehl didn't take long, and soon they met Garesch. The elf prince was eating the simple stew they'd scraped together. "How did the council rule?"

"Better than we hoped," Coryn said. "We have the support and blessings of the council and my father. They are willing to sanction an alliance provided you can take the throne and implement an indefinite armistice until that time."

"This is good news indeed." Garesch smiled widely and tapped the backs of Ra'al and Coryn.

"Aye," Coryn said in a low voice. "At least we can count on a war at only one front…Though Balgavarr will not mobilize any units until they attack Icehome. Uruzak is well insulated and the council will not deploy more than a token force to the North while King Saugor keeps the throne at the dwarves' back."

The three were silent for some time. Each sipped from steaming cups of tea.

Ra'al nudged Coryn, but she acted as if she felt nothing.

Then he cleared his throat, twice, and again Coryn ignored him.

At last, Ra'al deliberately dumped some hot tea on her leg, which made the dwarf curse and bat at the wet spot.

She looked at Ra'al with narrowed eyes and she clenched her fist before punching him in the ribs.

"I feel that the two of you want to say something." Garesch looked from Ra'al to Coryn and back again.

"No, not really." Coryn gave him a courteous smile.

"Yes, of course, we want to say something." Ra'al winced from the pain in his ribs. "In fact, Coryn has a grand suggestion for you to consider." He leaned back before Coryn could land another blow.

Garesch stared at Coryn, who sat silently for several moments.

"So, what is the suggestion?" Garesch asked.

Coryn kept her face neutral. "It is about the weapon cache. I…I think I can reach it on my own."

Garesch frowned. "Without the maps?"

"Technically, they are not *maps*. More of a riddle, really, but I memorized them, and I have the key as well." Coryn looked down. "But I would burn many bridges, if I went through with it."

"I see." Garesch tapped on the small table that held their cups. "Is it worth it?"

"The cache has items and weapons of immense power." Coryn inhaled and exhaled. "If we can't raise an army in time to face the bloodless ones, it might be our only chance to even the odds." She sighed. "So, I guess it is worth it."

Garesch smiled. "Alright. What do we need to do next to access the cache?"

"You condone her suggestion?" Ra'al raised his eyebrows high. "I mean, these weapons in the wrong hands could be disastrous."

"Exactly, if it was in the wrong hands, like in Death's legions, it definitely would." Garesch waved both hands in the air. "That is a reason to get the weapons in the hands of those who are willing to stand against Death."

Ra'al went silent and fell deep in thought.

"He has a valid point, Ra'al," Coryn said. "They will either end up in our hands, or in Death's."

"What about all your talk about the Champions of the Gods, the chosen ones, or whoever would be worthy of holding the weapons?" Ra'al exploded. "You have been preaching this to me since we were teenagers. What changed?"

"The rising dead, that's what changed," Coryn said in a heated tone. "We might as well be the champions of the gods. Nobody else has presented themselves."

"That borders on blasphemy, Coryn," Ra'al said in a low voice.

"No, it does not." She stared at him with a frown. "The gods could be guiding us through this very discussion. You know that they stopped walking the lands of Esfah ages ago, and who knows how they convey their messages now?"

Ra'al sighed and shook his head. "I think we should first confer with Naemyar before going after the cache."

"She could be the right person to consult on this matter." Garesch bowed in Ra'al's direction. "King Matrek wields more authority, but it is well known that he believes the weapons were destroyed before he ever took the throne. Besides, Naemyar has shown us hospitality and we know Matrek is filled with prejudice. If he took them, those weapons would only end up harming morehl citizens rather than protecting the realm against the undead."

"Then we continue towards Tulgesh in the morning." Coryn looked uncertainly at Ra'al. He merely bobbed his head and wore an expressionless smile.

The road to Tulgesh from Balgavarr could be seen below the travelers as it wound through the mountains and towards the flatlands. Coryn and Ra'al had foregone the journey before and taken flight across the countryside to dramatically clip the travel time. But there was no way Ra'al could carry the four of them, not even well rested and healed.

Garesch and the others set out towards the long road.

Coryn cleared her throat behind them. "Ahem. We're not going that way."

They all turned back to face her, and she flashed a mischievous grin. "I know of another way. Not quite as fast as air travel, but almost as quick." She refused to acknowledge Ra'al's scathing glare. She had been the one to initially send the frostwing guards back to Castle Ice…A place Ra'al very much wished he could be right about now.

Coryn led the way as they traveled west up a slight slope. She refused to give them any other information about their destination except a mysterious, "You'll see."

A regular, rhythmic thumping echoed across the side of the Kafnysan Range and the mechanical kind of sound got louder as they drew closer to the dwarven outpost now visible in the distance. It had a distinctly vaghan shape.. The structure lacked the decorative flair of dwarves, however, and felt more utilitarian. It looked like a warehouse built into the side of a cliff.

Coryn stopped her red-skinned companions. "You'd better stay outside for a moment. I don't know how the boys inside will take to helping lava elves, so we won't tell them that until the last minute…and unless we have to." She opened the door and waved Ra'al through.

Just before the door closed, Garesch heard the frostwing grumble incredulously, "You have *got* to be kidding me…"

Marnash cocked his head and asked their last remaining guard, "Do you hear that, Werdth? Vaghan chain drives."

Garesch and Werdth leaned as far over the steep ledge as they dared.

"Probably steam driven, with the help of counterweights," Marnash surmised.

A huge chain moved up the mountain within a grooved channel, riding a friction smoothed track. Empty pallets with sled feet rode along the chains where they'd been hooked in for an automated ride up the mountain at a leisurely pace.

Garesch gulped, guessing what their crazy dwarf companion had in mind. The loud noise rattled the air as something released a latch and a sled shot out from the station in front of them, dropping a loaded cargo pallet at a nearly vertical angle. It blasted down the chute near the chain drive and quickly left their sight.

The door opened and Ra'al stepped out, chuckling and shaking his head.

"Come on," Coryn insisted. "They will help us and also maintain our secrecy. I've told the workers that this is a confidential mission on behalf of the Council Elders."

Marnash gave the frostwing a skeptical look. "We've guessed what you have in mind. It doesn't terrify you?"

The areosan laughed with genuine mirth. "Oh, no. I'm not riding that thing.. I've still got my wings. I'll follow from above."

Coryn led them through a warehouse filled with goods and sundries, most of them in labeled crates. They emerged from a labyrinth of products awaiting shipment and found the launch station.

A huge hole opened in the floor where a pulley-style lift was used to counterweight the loads they dropped down the vertical shaft.

Four dwarves stood nearby and looked up at them as they entered the main workspace. They had the appearance of journeymen roughnecks who had worked the station for decades. Three of them were busy attaching chairs to one of the sleds. The last one motioned them forward and asked, "How many stones?"

Garesch raised an eyebrow, "Pardon?"

"Your weight?" the dwarf demanded, clutching a piece of chalk. He stood at a large blackboard. The left side of slate listed the day's shipping schedule, shift changes, and an ominous note: *It has been 8 days since the last accident.*

Coryn looked over the trio of elves. "Better hop on that scale over there. It's a pretty exact science."

The workers finished their calculations, set the modified sled into place, and hooked the counterweight into place.

"Have you ever done this before?" Marnash asked the dwarf who made the calculations.

"Nope. But we've all thought about it before, right boys?" The others nodded vigorously, and then worked a massive crank. The four travelers strapped themselves to the chairs hastily riveted to the sled.

"Whatever you do, don't try to free yourselves before the sled stops." The foreman added a number of weights to the four posts on the corners of the sled to keep it balanced and laden enough to gain maximum momentum.

A moment later, the dwarves cranked the counterweight into the air and the pulleys lifted their sled into place. They dangled Coryn, Garesch, Marnash, and Werdth over the hole, facing directly down with the sled lined up over the luge-style chute.

"Ready?"

Coryn clenched her teeth. "You know, on second thought I think I'd rather…"

The counterweight released, and the sled dropped through the shaft with its four screaming passengers riding down the mountain at speeds nearing terminal velocity. Ra'al leapt through the hole, too. He glided overhead and trailed them down the mountainside.

The sled eventually came to a rest, crashing against a buffer in the shipping terminal. A number of vaghan workers and a few others of mixed race gave them incredulous looks. The ride down was equal parts terrifying death-trap and smooth riding.

Wriggling free from their restraints, Ra'al alighted next to them as the workers hurried over to ask them about their ride. The party explained how they came to be there as quickly as they could. Most of the curious onlookers were low and working class vagha and others who needed the inglorious work to survive.

Ra'al looked across the shipping station. Garesch matched his gaze. Only one of the workers didn't hurry over to question the passengers. The worker tried to keep busy and out of sight, but his distinctly areosan form was unmistakable.

The frostwing was neither as tall nor muscular as the prince, and he wore a dark brand on his arm and chest.

"What does that mean?" Garesch asked.

"It is a mark of cowardice," Ra'al sighed, and then turned before making eye contact with the frostwing, letting him save face. "He is an outcast."

Coryn and the others whistled, calling them back. "We've got a heading. It's not far to the channel where we can ride down the Sareen River, which will take us through the shipping lines and straight to Tulgesh."

They fell into lockstep and headed out. Garesch walked alongside Ra'al. "You are not like most frostwings, I think."

Ra'al frowned. "In what way?"

"You are a head taller and almost twice as wide, but you are also still lithe," Garesch said.

"I got that from my father, Thrag. You might have heard of him." Ra'al shrugged.

"Of course, every morehl knows of Thrag Morehl Slayer," Garesch said, and hesitated. "So, you can't use ice magic also because of your heritage?"

"No, my father was a keen wind singer," Ra'al said. "This is what magic users are called by my people." He shook his head. "But I never could attune my heart to the song of the wind, hence, no magic."

"Maybe you are just a warrior, and an exceptional one," Garesch suggested. "I still remember what you did to those faeli at the boat."

"As I recall, you had to save my life." Ra'al laughed. "Not such a good fighter after all."

"No, no, I helped a friend who I know might have managed without me." Garesch waved his hand in negation. "You are a ferocious fighter. I've never seen anyone split a scalder in half with one swipe of the sword; that was impressive."

"I was fueled by anger." Ra'al scoffed. "And I feared for Coryn. Nothing too great about that."

"Who also happens to be a more than capable fighter." Garesch smiled.

"And my little sister in more ways than one." Ra'al smiled and patted Garesch's back. They boarded a small barge with a pointed bow. The smaller barge had some cargo aboard it already, and its pointed bow helped it navigate the unnatural channel that would connect the shallow waterway to the Sareen River.

"Maybe this is the core of your problem." Garesch sat back as the oarsmen put the skiff into motion. "Your fear for Coryn."

"Maybe." Ra'al remained standing between the stacks of boxes.

Garesch stared off into the forest that lined both sides of the waterway, and Ra'al's thoughts sank inward. *What if his unease did connect to Coryn. What if something was to happen to her? Maybe his fears and inability to use magic all came from his worry over her?*

The skiff arrived at a dock the following morning, where the shipping channel spilled into a lagoon that emptied into the Sareen River. Another shipping station sat on the edge of the water where workers unloaded skiffs and hauled cargo onto a larger barge that would ship all the way to Tulgesh.

Two barges were already at the station. One of them, which was nearly filled, bore the markings of Riechus Aqualines. Coryn pointed to it. "Come on! That one belongs to Queen Naemyar. We've got to see the captain right away and get ourselves a berth on that ship.

The party hurried towards the docks and into the staging area for the cargo operation. Coryn left the elves outside the door and entered the office where a few clerical workers and the boat captains lounged. She looked around, but Ra'al had disappeared.

She shrugged and then approached the only selumari there, assuming he was the captain of the barge owned by Naemyar, daughter of Riechus. "Captain," she said. "My small company of travelers is on an urgent errand on behalf of Queen Naemyar and an alliance of kingdoms. We need passage as soon as possible to Tulgesh, so we may see the Queen."

The captain fixed her with a skeptical eye. He nodded slowly, "State the nature of your business and I'll consider it."

Coryn skirted the sensitive details and gave him a short summary, making the barge master stroke his chin and nod along.

Ten minutes later, Coryn and her crew climbed aboard the ship, but still with no Ra'al in sight. Finally, just as the ship pulled into the river, the frostwing landed on the deck boards, carrying a large trunk in each hand.

"Our luggage!" Coryn squealed. It had never arrived in Tulgesh.

"I thought I recognized these trunks," Ra'al said. "At least we have a few supplies and comforts for the journey. It will take us a few days, after all, even with the Sareen's current."

"Comforts. Ha!" Coryn dug in her case and removed two big bottles. "Nectar of the gods, you mean." She brandished the bottles in front of the lava elves and grinned. "It's my supply of Fire Sauce!"

Chapter 12

Of each species that lived upon Esfah, the sentient races that made up its people all obeyed the natural order and respected the reign of Nature above all other life. Even those races whose origins sprang from the Death god had at least some sense of reverence for Nature, the mother goddess, Ghaeial.

Around the planet, a special sense of order rose amid the tumult of life; a thread of sanity that prevented chaos. But that order had a bane, an enemy that worked tirelessly to disrupt; an enemy that cherished anarchy instead of order. Decay instead of birth.

Leisterbane walked slowly through the ranks of the undead. The bloodless ranks made way for him. One by one they shuffled and moaned as he passed through the horde.

A small, crawling insect danced in its panic to avoid Leisterbane's armor shod feet, trying to avoid the imminent end that might catch it at any moment. Even the insects and carrion creatures that frequented the Shadowlands tried to avoid the rift which hid the undead hordes.

Leisterbane looked from the depths of the frosty canyon and up to the sky. He grimaced, promising that one day he would snuff the light of that blasted sun, Soll. One day he would quench the last scrap of life upon Esfah.

He heard the nervous scuttling of the crawler and stopped to inspect the insect as it desperately tried to reach the rocky wall of the rift.

Leisterbane grew quickly bored with the squirming fear that the tiny insect produced. The smell of it was not strong enough to entertain the undead elf. He stepped on it and sneered with what remained of his lips.

Lord Death had gifted him with many boons, least of all was immortality. It was bestowed upon him by his enemy, Melkior, after the eldarim champion fell to the darkness and then dragged the once-proud selumari into it with him.[1] Now fully in the thrall of Melkior's god, Leisterbane appreciated the pleasure he felt as the creature succumbed to the throes of death. He relished the odor of the dying thing's fear. It smelled like exquisite perfume. The scent overpowered the monotony of deathly existence.

He waited anxiously; Leisterbane had been patient now for more than a century. Death had given orders that he could not kill anything bigger than occasional wild animals or stray explorers. But centuries passed like days to the undead general. Soon, he would lead the forces of Death again and snuff thousands of lives with his very hands.

Leisterbane looked at the shuffling troops around him. The ominous, red glow in his hollowed eye sockets shone brighter. Their numbers had grown exponentially over the centuries as his rovers crisscrossed the frozen wastes, locating the bodies of the fallen and reanimating them with Malgrimm's gift: the necralluvium.

His minions were as anxious as he was to overwhelm the living and snap that thread of order that bound chaos to the edges of Nature's control.

When he was alive, Leisterbane had always made sure his soldiers, the legendary Lurneville Guard, were as well trained in the arts of war as they were in the knowledge of Esfah and natural law. He did not need training now. Lord Death taught his own by his very nature. He bound it within the army through the curse of his dread alchemy.

Death's enemies were many, including each of the races of Esfah. That they breathed, and lived, had to be taken away from them as punishment for the war of the sibling gods. That conflict began long before any race walked upon Esfah, even before the dragons. Only the eldarim, in their infancy, had watched it unfold.

---

[1]   See the Esfah Sagas: Ashes of Ailushurai.

Leisterbane watched a new corpse wander into his army. That was not an uncommon sight, and the general continued on his way. He walked deeper under the lip of the rift, into one of the caverns where wild necralluvium dripped and pooled among the frost crystals. Leisterbane walked beside the black bubbling river: a source of Death's power.

One drop of the necralluvium was enough to transform any of the sentient races into an undead minion, and if used in conjunction with magic and infused with the caster's will, a victim could even retain parts of his or her personality and memory. The most powerful undead, like Leisterbane's old master Melkior, kept their autonomy intact. But such minions were also the most difficult to control.

With rivers of necralluvium at his disposal, he needed only corpses to animate.

Leisterbane still remembered the moment he died, and the moment he was reborn to Death. That moment never left his ever-churning mind. He might have lost much of his flesh, and some of his memories had long since withered with time, but he was ten times more able and powerful than he'd ever been as a selumari. He was grateful that Melkior had murdered him and slaughtered the princess and residents of Lurneville. Melkior's genocide of the Teldrim race had been the crucible that made Leisterbane what he was now: powerful. With a thought, he could mobilize a hundred thousand bloodless troops. What warlord desired more?

However, simply washing over the Cyrean continent, and then razing the planet was not the task given to him by Lord Death. His will had been specific. Leisterbane was commanded to break the back of Mother Ghaeial, then destroy the magic of Nature by uprooting the very trees of life that she had planted so long ago.

Leisterbane had already destroyed two of them and weakened the arcana veil. His actions had splintered the ability of Esfahn peoples to draw upon The Source, or magic itself. Because of him, spell crafting became ever more difficult and highly specialized.

He returned to the rift and sat upon the large stone throne. Three of his undead minions rushed to bring him a large, brass plate, upon which a fire burned and crackled.

The undead did not like the fire licking at their decaying flesh. It could strip their vestiges of a past existence from their flesh, and it brought something like pain with it, as much as any undead could still feel. Such was another of Lord Death's gifts. The undead were fearsome warriors, not for their skill, but for their imperviousness to pain and ailments. A skeletal warrior could fight on if it lost both arms and legs, not as efficiently, but they were relentless, and even a disabled creature could eventually be reassembled so long as it could be put back together.

Leisterbane's servants placed the fire plate at the foot of the throne and crawled back to the darkness of the cave. He produced a small vial of necralluvium and flicked a few drops into the crackling fire.

The fire grew to double the height of the undead selumari. Its flames licked at the black liquid and turned the burning tongues to shades of inky gray and green.

Leisterbane knelt and whispered ancient words of power. Few still remembered the old prayers of communion that summoned the will of the Death god: Malgrimm. His power connected the minds of his servants together.

The fire swayed and wavered as Leisterbane whispered to it. With each word, it seemed to quake under the pressure of the magic that passed through the blaze.

Then it settled into a steady rhythm, like the heartbeat of the Death god.

Leisterbane sat back on his throne and waited. The fire sparked once, twice, and three times. He could feel the will of Malgrimm wafting through the fiery vision as it took form.

In the middle of the plate were the shadows of three faces. Two elven ones and one bearded dwarf.

He knew that his loyal minions were thousands of leagues away from him, and many leagues from each other, yet he felt their heartbeats and sensed their fear as if they sat adjacent him.

A voice came from the fire, "Oh, great lord Leisterbane, I bask in your darkness." A groveling voice came from one of the two elven shadows.

Leisterbane laughed. His voice had an echoing quality that mismatched the natural echo of the caves. "You morehl always did have a flair for the dramatic, and you never cease to amuse me. Perhaps this is why I spared you even after so many failures."

"My lord, I strive to do my best, and I always persevere in the face of failure." The lava elf's voice sounded panicked.

Leisterbane relished the flavor of the morehl's fear. It tasted spicy, hot, and was tinged by regret. Leisterbane frowned. Regret was for the feeble.

"Relax, morehl. I still have use of you." Leisterbane spat the words, then he felt the morehl's fear intensify.

"Command us, lord," a voice came from the other elven shadow.

"Selumari, you have been dormant for a long time." Leisterbane shook his head. "I grow impatient with your subtle machinations. My patience is not inexhaustible."

"Soon my lord, my machinations will come to fruition." The selumari said in a weak voice. "You know it is my way—I have taken the Nekarthan path. It is a less direct path to power."

The selumari smelled of fear, but its fear was masked by something else, something Leisterbane could not identify. He ignored the selumari's fear; its flavor was disagreeable to him.

"I hope so, for your sake, I really do," Leisterbane said. "At some point, I will expect results."

The selumari bowed silently.

Leisterbane turned his attention to his third agent. The dwarf had sought out his power only recently.

"What about you, vagha?" Leisterbane decided that the dwarf did not exude enough fear to satisfy him. He sniffed. The vagha's fear was almost non-existent, and this annoyed him to a great extent; such was often the case with those who worship Death for reasons of insanity. "Did you manage to plant the seed?"

"Yes, my liege, and I expect my little weed to sprout soon." The vagha had an odd tone to his voice.

Leisterbane needed the services this pathetic vagha could provide. One day they would prove useful. "That we shall see, vagha," Leisterbane hissed. He vaguely remembered an ancient war, one of many he fought in. He once fought alongside a dwarf. Still, he did not particularly like the species.

The selumari swallowed with an audible noise. "My lord, why did you summon us?"

He never liked the title his agents gave him. Those miserable mortals called him master, lord, and those acolytes beneath this trio of conspirators swooned for him and expected a reward for it. They believed they could earn places of prestige under the reign of Lord Death when the time came for him to claim Esfah. *How foolish could these mortals be?*

But Leisterbane knew the truth: Death only ever granted himself as a reward. And that was what each one would eventually get. He shook his head. *Greed was the worst sin of the living, and it had to be punished accordingly.*

Leisterbane sensed that the selumari hid something from him. "We have a part of the map," Leisterbane said in a gravelly voice. He immediately felt the shiver that ran up the spines of the three mortals.

"A single part, my lord?" The selumari's fear intensified, yet there seemed a hidden gloating beneath the informant's fear. Leisterbane would have smiled, but his frozen remnants of skin were too frigid to move with such subtle movements.

The selumari had hope, but hope for what? Why was this despicable creature feeling hope? Death was all that it could hope for, and Death it will have.

"Yes, one of four." He bent his head towards the fire and the flames crackled higher, forcing the three mortals to step back lest they got burned.

"The rest could be in your hands soon, my lord," the vagha said in a smug voice. "I can help with that."

Leisterbane loathed the smugness in the dwarf's heart, but it could serve the undead's purposes still.

"You can or you will?" Leisterbane felt anger floating from the morehl in waves.

"I will. It is within my ability." The vagha bowed, which Leisterbane noted must have singed his grey beard in the fire. He even felt the man's pain, which didn't taste as satisfying as fear, but for now, it sufficed.

"We shall see vagha, we shall see." Leisterbane crawled from his throne and knelt close by the fire, knowing that all three must feel its heat as he did.

"But what about the cache, my lord?" The selumari's voice brimmed with a hint of expectant lust. *So, this is what the selumari hoped for, the Magestorm weapons.*

"I don't care, either way, selumari, if you can get to them, they are yours." Leisterbane waved his skeletal hand in disgust. "They do not concern the plans of Lord Death, and they never have. The maps to the keys are his plans."

Silence ensued after he uttered his last response.

"I have some reports of a morehl traveling through Cyrea, trying to weave alliances to unify its peoples." Leisterbane concentrated his focus on the lava elf.

"Not for long, my lord." The morehl gnashed on his teeth.

"I consider that a promise, one that I will make you accountable for, morehl." Leisterbane was surprised to feel fear coming from the selumari, not the morehl.

He didn't know why the selumari felt such nuanced fear. The puzzle interested him, and he savored the intrigue for all it was worth.

The general stated, "Remember that Lord Malgrimm sees all."

"I shall consult with my selumari peer and with your spies," the dwarf said. "We shall parley and concoct a plan to secure the remaining maps."

Leisterbane nodded resolutely. He blew a puff of air at the fire and it snuffed immediately. The connection between his minions severed.

Leisterbane stood and walked away from his stony, frozen throne.

A wraith stood waiting at attention. He had been watching the fiery communion.

"Something is afoot," Leisterbane addressed the apparition. "The selumari fears something, but I could not unravel its fear enough to know the cause."

"I shall follow the selumari." The wraith said in a whispering voice that sounded like the moans of the dying.

Leisterbane touched the immaterial body of the wraith. "No. That can wait, shadow the dwarf instead… something about him bothers me. He tastes too much of treachery and ambition for such a new follower of the Black Path. If he makes contact with the elf as he promised, then perhaps you can prove yourself especially useful and unravel both mysteries."

The wraith bowed and disappeared like mist under the morning sun.

Leisterbane moved between the shuffling troops. Some of them succumbed to the long ages spent waiting while decaying. They fell apart slowly over the eons.

Signaling to the death knight who had claimed the map, Leisterbane called him over. The undead general put the map into his bony grasp. "Take the map, Krayell. Locate the first of the stones and destroy it. You will find our northern horde awaiting you in the wastes."

Krayell bowed slightly, honoring the task that had come to him. He climbed his mount and a small crew of lifeless troops followed him north where he could exit the canyon strongholds beyond the plateau and head further towards the magnetic pole.

Leisterbane took out his vial of necralluvium and held it tightly. Leisterbane summoned one of his death crafters, or the magicians who specialized in black arcana, and had the fiend ignite a flame in the center of the Heimdarl Crag's floor. Leisterbane tossed in the necralluvium and watched it burn, filling the canyon with a noxious, oily smoke. The black mist flew lazily and touched each of the decaying troops' bodies, instantly straightening and strengthening them. It reinvigorated the inky strands of black stuff that festered between joints, holding them together.

The general walked back to the cave where the river of darkness bubbled and touched the stream of necralluvium. He communicated with his creator, sending his thoughts: *we are almost ready. The other maps will soon be ours, and another of Ghaeial's trees will burn.*

He finally walked back to the throne and sat. Soon Death would be the only force on Esfah with access to magic… and then the other races would all fall.

Chapter 13

Ra'al watched the sun rise over the Sareen River just as it had done over the glassy ice fields of his home.

The group had ridden the river for a couple days now and this would be the last. It was one of those mornings that forced him to think about Icehome. He didn't know exactly what reminded him of the north. This place was green, too warm, and not a single icicle could be found.

A sparrow flew overhead, weaving between the giant trees of the forest on the north side of the river. Ra'al watched the sparrow for some moments and sighed.

The sunlight hit his thick fur and reflected off it, but he still felt its warmth permeate his heart. Maybe that was why he felt homesick.

Coryn paced the barge deck a few cubits away. She glowered at her boots in her usual posture for deep thought.

Ra'al couldn't envy her. She had plenty on her plate. Still, he yearned for their usual banter and playful jabs. It would have made the journey feel shorter.

At the south side of the river, a road turned from packed dirt to seamlessly interlocking stones. They looked smooth and shiny, as if they were samples of the rare sea-washed stones they used to decorate walls with back at Castle Ice and other wealthy areosan estates.

Ra'al was impressed at the fortune's worth of rare stone pavers.

Garesch followed his gaze and said, "They are smoothed by magic." The morehl pointed to the stones. "They look like washed stones, but they are imitations."

Garesch motioned to Coryn. "She'll tell you how dwarven masons built this road better than my kind ever could."

Ra'al smiled and nodded to the morehl prince. "Thank you, I will ask Coryn." *It would be good to get Coryn talking*, he thought.

He approached her and asked, "How did the vagha build this road?"

"What?" Coryn looked up to him in a distracted manner.

"That road, I heard it was built by the vagha. Is that right?" Ra'al watched Coryn's eyes shine as a smile spread over her face. She did love her people's history.

Coryn launched into an encyclopedic recitation of dwarven infrastructural design. "First, we dig a road to be sure that the base of the road is stable and carry the weight of a dragonkin, mammoths, and the usual other heavy craft…" Coryn went on for the next hour or so.

Ra'al already knew some of the information from watching the Balgavarr's forces build the roads they made for Icehome many years ago, but he didn't interrupt Coryn. He needed to hear her voice, and she needed to think about something other than her potential decision to betray her father's trust.

The journey felt shorter as he listened to Coryn's lectures. They eventually turned to vaghan architecture, both underground and aboveground designs.

Soon, they arrived at Tulgesh's north entry where they disembarked and headed for the city while the ship's captain continued his business. Rickshaw carts of all types rode alongside various people walking the road from all around Cyrea. They came to trade at Tulgesh, or to utilize shipping companies and do business abroad.

The city had been demolished by the morehl a century ago. But a city that size was constantly in the process of renovation.

Ra'al could see the tall towers and domes of the palace and the temples that they'd seen from the air the last time they entered the city.

It was just as beautiful from the ground as it was from the air.

Mother of pearl covered many walls, reflecting the sunlight in a thousand colors, but it especially caught the smoke-like seams of pink where coral had been grown and used to build, contrasting the selumari and vaghan building styles and materials. Huge statues were perched on the city wall which the dwarves had built every fifty cubits.

As they approached the wall, Ra'al could see intricate designs upon the barrier. Engraved images from both the battle of Balgavarr and the war for Tulgesh had been etched by artisans.

Stone reliefs depicted the dragon that Geril Dragonsbane had killed. Another showed coral elves leading a charge against the undead that buffered the invading morehl.

Even frostwings were shown in the huge mural that covered the wall, stretching in both directions. A depiction of Thrag showed him at peace amidst the chaos of battle. The areosa extended a hand for a bird to alight upon a finger.

Ra'al felt smaller as he finally passed beneath the immense gate with its huge arch.

The company felt the eyes of the gate guards linger upon them. Coryn looked at their companions, who merely shrugged off the selumaris' suspicion as they passed through. "This is not uncommon for us in foreign lands," Marnash whispered.

Ra'al did not doubt that they would be followed throughout the entirety of their stay in the city. In a way, he admired the elves for making it seem that they were completely free to roam the city at will while still safeguarding their realm with oversight. Ra'al scoffed. His mother might have been right, after all. Ra'al assessed the politics and strategies of other nations, just like she'd trained him.

He started to laugh at the thought.

Coryn looked at him with a serious frown. "What is wrong with you?"

"I have turned into what my mother wished for me to be all along," he admitted between chuckles.

A few more moments passed, and the seriousness of Coryn's expression forced him back into silence.

They stopped in front of an opalescent-looking house with a grand rosewood door.

Coryn rang the bell, and a servant answered. He recognized the dwarf and frostwing from their last meeting and then escorted the company inside, where the queen's servant came to collect them.

Ra'al noticed the smell of strong spices permeating everything. He could barely smell anything else. The majordomo, who did not appear surprised to see them, seated the group in a large room with a huge window that overlooked the ruler's palatial grounds.

He hoped that their host, Naemyar, would not invite them for a spicy dinner. Whatever the spices were, they disagreed with his nose.

Naemyar entered the room and rushed to salute Coryn with a cordial hug, then she bowed to Ra'al. She offered the tip of her hand for Garesch to kiss.

Politics. Ra'al smiled cordially.

"Thank you, Lotep," she said and dismissed her majordomo. "Please see off our earlier company and tell him we will revisit any business with the vaghan mine iron-leaf dealers the next time we meet."

Ra'al glanced sidelong at Lotep, who hesitated to leave, as if wishing to stay close and eavesdrop. The servant frowned, but departed on her orders.

"Why are you here so soon?" Naemyar stopped smiling and looked around the party with pursed lips. She was clearly worried by what their presence implied. "You couldn't have hardly sailed back from Frostshoal in such little time."

Ra'al sat back in his chair and shook his head. He wasn't certain she'd believe him if he told her about the dwarven shipping luge.

She looked around the room and realized they hesitated to speak. "The area is quite secure," Naemyar promised. "There has been very little business scheduled in my house today, only one other impromptu guest and Lotep is seeing him out now. To be honest, we were not expecting you for some time."

A collective sigh of relief washed over the travelers. They required a great deal of secrecy.

Coryn bit her lip and explained that one of Garesch's lava elves had been involved in some unknown scheme, but that a future truce had been brokered between their people. Rashingot's original mission had been somewhat fulfilled.

"We need to know about the Magestorm Wars." Coryn fidgeted. "Do you know someone you trust who could consult with us? I am faced with a decision, a monumental one, and it would be helpful to know more about the wars before I proceed."

Naemyar nodded slowly. "You may ask *me*," she said. "My father was something of a layperson's expert on them. It was an area of intense interest for him. I may not be a certified expert, but I am already in your confidence, and I'm quite knowledgeable."

The dwarf ground her teeth. Her stomach fluttered as she came closer to the point of decision. "You know that after the Magestorm War, all the gnomish weapons and items of power in Cyrea were collected and hidden?" Coryn asked and licked her lips.

"Yes, I have heard of this myth." Naemyar took a deep breath. "A legendary treasure of items imbued with magical power that was destroyed by your father, so they say."

"They are not a myth, Your Highness," Coryn rushed and shook her head. "In fact, during the events that led to the battle of Balgavarr, my father did find them."

Naemyar raised an eyebrow. "He did? I always believed that was no mere legend…but I was referencing that magic weapons are so very rare. However, they are not as uncommon as one would think. Perhaps they are quite rare in Cyrea because of the efforts to gather and hide them, but such has not been the case all across Esfah, and there is no posted force confiscating such weapons at every Cyrean port. If you stroll through Frostshoal, just a day's ferry ride away, you'll find all manner of them advertised. But I digress." She shifted into a more scholarly tone. "Certainly a large horde of them *had been* sequestered and hidden away by King Walen the True at the advice of Qelekua Magebane."

Coryn raised a brow, impressed. She wasn't sure before, but now felt certain the queen would be knowledgeable enough to help.

Naemyar asked, "Where did Geril find them?"

"They were under the temple of Ailuril, here in Tulgesh," Coryn admitted.

"Were they?" Naemyar sat back in her cushioned chair.

"Yes, but he has since moved them," Coryn continued.

"Hmm." Naemyar bent her head slowly. "These weapons, if they truly exist, could be a formidable tool in the right hands."

"Yes, and that is why I came to *you.*" Coryn swallowed. "You know that there are various reports on the rising of the undead in the north-most parts of Cyrea. When last we spoke, you told me you were on a council assessing this threat."

"It does keep me on edge," Naemyar said and hooked her hands together. "I think another great war might be coming our way. All Esfah could be in danger if the enemy has amassed unchecked, as I fear it has." She frowned, "There is no way to assess the bloodless's number. They are hidden within the Heimdarl Crag and impossible to count. They may be a thousand strong…They may be several hundred times *that* size."

Ra'al gulped against the lump in his throat.

Coryn fidgeted with her hands. "This exactly why I want to unearth the weapon cache. But that would mean I must break the will of my father." She swallowed hard. It barely kept her voice from cracking. "I could lose him forever as a consequence of this."

"I understand the dilemma you are in." Naemyar turned her head from side to side in dismay. "But can you even reach the weapons?"

"I think that I can." Coryn sighed. "I know the location, and I memorized the key to pass the traps laid against anybody trying to reach the treasure."

"Traps? Are there many of them?" Naemyar's forehead creased. "If the location is secret, it hardly seems necessary."

"There are some. It demonstrates just how committed my father is to their safety. I do know that failure to solve the key, a kind of riddle or password, will stop any forward progress." Coryn waved her hands animatedly, and Ra'al could sense how excited she felt about the whole prospect.

"And you know this key?" Naemyar encouraged Coryn to go on.

"Yes, it was a poem of sorts, and not very long. I memorized it in Tulgesh, before we left." Coryn wore a crooked smile aimed at Ra'al. "That was what took me so long."

The smell of spices grew heavier as Coryn and the lady spoke. Ra'al barely held down a powerful sneeze. He wondered on the source of the odor, as he didn't smell any food cooking. Naemyar's servant had delivered only tea and plain sea biscuits; nothing resembling the strong, spicy smell all around him, and only Werdth gave him an askew look regarding the frostwing's nose.

"Could you recite that poem now?" Naemyar asked Coryn.

"Of course." Coryn cleared her throat and started to quote:

"When the shadow creeps on the land, and the night is all
At the moment of your despair when you feel that you will
fall
Seek the foot of the hero whose deeds saved the day
And in the twilight clear all ears for the song of the Jay
The jay's song will play and will tell
How to bring a note from the silent bell
By the sound of this note, the earth will rise
But only if the earth, fire, and air will bond their ties
Walk with light feet in the maze of water flow
The chill and fire should proceed with the earth in tow
In the depth of the darkness, Dragonsbane's blood knows
the key

And through this blood, in the darkness light will be
Put the light in the hand of the chill that lost the wind
For in that hand the time will bend.
As time turned the wheel thus turns
And the fire touched must turn it lest it burns
Look in the ground, your treasure will be
But you must be careful with the broken she
When you have passed the test and done,
Know that what you did cannot be undone.
The earth will open the door to the curse of old
And the prophecy will finally unfold."

Naemyar's face froze. "It's all very cryptic. I don't think I understood any of it."

"I know only the meaning of one part." Coryn danced from side to side on her chair. "Dragonsbane's blood is obviously me."

"Yes, of course, because your father is Dragonsbane." Naemyar pursed her lips for some moments, then smiled again to Coryn. "So, you plan to pursue the cache?"

"I was hoping that you could advise me in that matter…*should* I chase after it?" Coryn asked cautiously.

"Under normal circumstances, I would strongly advise you to forget the weapon cache and to follow the will of your father." Naemyar's forehead creased. "But reports of enemy sightings have been consistent. Their numbers are likely in the worst-case scenario, rather than the better. As we near war with such a deadly enemy, I am not so sure I could make the same recommendation regarding your father."

"And what of my father's reaction?" Coryn's eyes were ringed with worry.

"If you deem it best to take these weapons, I am certain that he will eventually come around. He must understand that you did the inevitable, and he will know that you intended something heroic for all of Esfah." Naemyar reached over and touched Coryn's hand. "He will be angry, but not for long, dear Coryn.

Certainly, it sounds as if he's groomed you all your life to make this exact decision."

Coryn bowed her head and sank silently into her chair cushions.

A moment of silence fell over the party.

Garesch cleared his throat. "There is more to this Cyrean intrigue. My men and I retrieved an artifact, but lost it to a thief in my company."

"Oh?" Naemyar scanned the morehl company. They had numbered many more at the Queen's gala. Now only three remained.

"A few months ago, on our way to Tulgesh, we happened upon a nest of snake people." Garesch sat at the edge of his chair.

"Go on." Naemyar waved with her left hand.

"The sarslayan attacked us and even managed to take one of my men." Garesch looked at his friends for a moment. "But we managed to beat them back and even raided their camp, which they'd obviously taken from another. Inside a chest we found several maps with blood on them. Whoever owned them previously fought hard to keep them from the enemy and died rather than suffer being turned by the waters of Lethial."

"Maps? Maps to what?" Naemyar asked him in a low voice and knelt forward. "Surely it cannot be related to Geril's weapon trove?"

"Yes… and no." Garesch briefly explained the misunderstanding in Frostshoal when Coryn had thought them stolen from her father.

"We are not sure of their exact purpose," Garesch said and shrugged. "They had an ancient sage's symbol for trees on each part, and they were written in old Eldari. I think they may have even come from Yentosh, or at least been copies of ancient ones. I believe their original owner was a sage, and the sarslayan killed them. A newer note in the margin mentioned something called the mist stones."

Garesch omitted mention of the pirate in Frostshoal, and Ra'al wondered why he told that story with the snake people when he dropped the other.

Naemyar took a deep breath. "Was there a symbol of five interlocking circles anywhere on the maps?"

Garesch bobbed his head once. "Yes, on the back of each part."

Naemyar's eyes widened. "I have heard this myth, too, but I never believed it. This one is from an ancient tale."

"Another myth?" Garesch asked.

"Yes." Naemyar cocked her head. "Have you ever heard about the hardening of the arcana veil?"

"Yes," Garesch said. "Long ago, ancient mages forced the veil between our world and the next to solidify. It was intended to weaken the source of magic and limit Lord Death."

"This also caused great difficulty for conjuring magic, except for those with a natural aptitude for it." Naemyar sat upright. "From that moment on, instead of having magic available for all on Esfah, it became something only a few could access. There are many variations on the tale, however; everything from the veil's stiffening caused by the Dragoncrusades, the aloofness of gods after the Second Age began, and the destruction of the Seed of Hope."

"I have heard all those as well." Garesch smiled. "Are you saying the first version was untrue and that the veil was not hardened by Ghaeial's mages, but perhaps something else?"

"The fact that the veil has thickened is verifiably true. But only one of these legends about *why* is factual." Naemyar smiled as if she possessed some secret knowledge. "The gods gave the task of upholding the veil to The Great Trees."

Garesch listened to her with steely black eyes while Ra'al rubbed his nose and tried not to sneeze.

"These Great Trees are hidden by the eternal mists. It is said there is one of these trees in the Shadowlands, unseen by both mortal and undead eyes alike." Naemyar pursed her lips and rubbed her chin for some moments. "The legend states that there were objects of power, created by the sages of old to maintain the mist, always keeping The Great Tree of the north hidden. Those objects were called the mist stones."

Horror crept across Garesch's face. "So, those maps *were* for the location of the stones?"

"I am afraid so." Naemyar touched her hands to her cheeks sympathetically. "You carry a great burden, Prince Garesch. Luckily, if your people have taken the maps, you are in a unique position to reclaim them—along with the throne."

Garesch rubbed his chin. "We already lost one part of the map, and I fear it may have already fallen into the hands of Lord Death."

She stiffened in her chair. "That is dire news, indeed. I trust that you have hidden the other parts somewhere safe?"

Garesch shook his head. "As safe as anything can be. I keep it close. I thought that this would have been the safest way." His eyes flitted to his backpack, which leaned nearby.

"I see." Naemyar sat back in her chair. "There are many reasons one might seek the mist stones, but unless one of you is secretly a sage and tasked with guarding one of the world trees, none of the reasons can be good."

Ra'al suddenly felt the spicy smell lift, and he finally felt he could breathe correctly. He wondered if he'd gone nose blind to the odor, which he suspected may have been a broken bottle of Coryn's fire sauce.

The frostwing sighed, simply happy he could concentrate on the conversation again.

Chapter 14

Bastawr lay motionless on the ground. He kept his breathing shallow and silent lest he be found out.

He knew that the undead could sense the living, but he took refuge in areas where living creatures dwelled. A burrow hosting a nest of crawlers, voles, or other critters would hide his presence from the fiends who could sense a creature's heart pumping.

It had been a tenday since he began tracking the skeletal knight. It had not been a pleasant journey.

The knight delved into the winding canyons of the wastes. He forever moved deeper through the cracked Shadowlands, navigating the rifts and glacial flows. This had proved a more taxing chase than any other Bastawr had done his entire life.

He barely slept, and every time fatigue forced him to recover for a few hours, he had to make up for the lost time by running to catch up and resume the trail of the undead knight and the newly converted undead minion who followed in the canyons below.

To his slightly good fortune, the undead steed didn't charge ahead. The knight led his new minions and set a slower pace. Also, the canyons were not so broad that he could not follow from the plateau above, and Bastawr trailed the travelers from the upper deck of the canyons, leaping the riven openings at their narrows keep pace.

Of greater concern, Bastawr ran out of provisions three nights ago and had to hunt whatever scrawny prey he could find in the Shadowlands, and he had to do it while remaining hidden and without losing his quarry.

Starved rats, misshapen lizards, and larger crawlers were his only source of sustenance these last several nights. Some of them tasted as vile as they sounded; none could be cooked.

Skeletons needed neither food nor rest. Several times in the last few days, hunger and fatigue had driven Bastawr to consider simply jumping the undead, retrieving the map, and being done with it.

But the knight was after something, and Bastawr felt deep in his core that it was crucial to find out what that was. He felt as if the goddess herself had tasked him with pursuing the bloodless mob.

Swamps, craggy terrain, even toxic plants and thorny bushes Bastawr could manage with ease, but the sleep deprivation was something else. All that he thought about for the last five days was getting a full night's sleep. He entered an endless cycle of hunt, eat, run and track, day after day. Bastawr started to feel its toll.

The skeletal knight kept moving towards wherever he headed, thankfully, oblivious to the tigerfolk on his tail. So far, his strategy of always resting among other living things had worked to hide him from the undead.

Suddenly, the skeletal knight changed direction after a momentary pause, as if he got new orders. Bastawr watched as the knight stood and froze in place for some long moments. He wondered if this was it? Had his hunt finished?

Bastawr felt pain and tiredness attack all his joints when the knight started to move again. The hunt was not over. They walked two more nights, and the terrain changed dramatically.

Night fell upon the frozen plain and the undead left the maze of canyons, having only delayed for less than a day, allowing the tigerfolk to rest.

Rocky scree and windswept plains spread open on the far side of the plateau, much like a frozen desert. Bastawr had to stay further back from the bottomless eye sockets of the knight and his minions, lest the enemy spot him. The feral tracker now walked on the same level as his skeletal enemy.

The land in front of him lay completely flat, empty of any kind of cover for Bastawr to take advantage of; it also was void of any life. Nothing remained for him to hunt or hide among.

Adding to his constant lack of sleep, Bastawr felt the pain of hunger at all times. Even scrawny rats and dried earthworms became difficult to find.

Bastawr waited, hidden by a large slab of ice-covered rock, and watched the knight as he disappeared over the horizon.

He waited several minutes to be sure that the knight wouldn't spot him, and then started to trot softly on all fours, as only a feline could.

He trotted for almost an hour before he caught up with the knight again and found a mound of sand to hide behind by lying flat.

As Bastawr focused his vision on the terrain surrounding the skeletal knight, he finally saw where the knight headed. And it was a terrifying scene to behold.

Legions upon legions of the damned filled the flat plains of the frozen land. An army of the dead had gathered so large that Bastawr thought for a moment that it might have been a nightmare induced by his lack of sleep.

But he looked again, and the skeletal figures remained. Ranks of undead stood frozen in tight rows all around the landscape, simply waiting for their commander.

The knight raised his right arm, holding a glowing spear, and the entire army turned and marched with him.

Bastawr struggled between two minds. One insisted that he could never claim the map from this army and that he should begin the long journey back to Balgavarr. It was important to report what he had seen here.

The second argued that too much depended on his surveillance of the enemies' plans in the north…least of all where this army might go next.

As the last of the undead moved beyond view, Bastawr growled and spat. He turned south towards Balgavarr and then turned back and started to follow the black hordes.

Another five nights passed with Bastawr trailing the army. He was able to earn a little extra sleep and spend more time securing food with the horde's slower pace. Their massive swaths of footprints were not difficult to track, even if it snowed.

But even though he felt in better vigor, Bastawr couldn't help a feeling of suffocation. A heavy fog had set in as he tracked the army these last two days. Bastawr could no longer see the teeming line of distant black where the army marched. He could barely see three cubits ahead of him and he relied solely on the flurry of footprints they'd left in their wake.

He had his other senses to help him, however; and the one he used most these last two days was his hearing. Something made noise within the mist; something that Bastawr could not see.

He heard the death knight demand an answer, "Why are you here, lich?" The knight's voice cut through the haze, muffled and distorted.

The tigerfolk's blood ran cold. He'd somehow stumbled close into the ranks of the undead. Their tracks had indicated they'd begun to move more like a column than a disheveled mass, and he must have overshot them in the fog.

Bastawr cursed to himself. He hadn't heard the arrival of the lich. His ears' failure alarmed him. It meant that any of those creatures could stumble onto him and he would not know until it was too late.

"The commander sent me to renew your orders." The lich's voice hurt Bastawr's ears. It sounded like insects crawling within his head.

"And what are the new orders?" The knight's voice sounded amused, as if he belittled the lich.

"You are required to dig up the stone and destroy it," The lich hissed. "Leisterbane thought that my assistance might be required."

"Should I turn the stone after digging, or wait for further commands?" The knight's voice had a hint of disdain. Bastawr didn't know if the undead retained distinct identities. Until now, he had assumed they were mindless drones following a single commander.

"Yes, turn the stone." The discussion ended, and the army proceeded to march again.

Before night fell and cast the mist-shrouded landscape in darkness, the army stopped again. Bastawr maintained a position moving adjacent the army's head whenever possible. He heard the rustling of parchment and guessed that the knight consulted the map he'd taken from the lava elf. Then the dead marched again.

Bastawr gathered some ferns that littered the ground and moved some distance away to reduce the chance of discovery. He covered himself with the fronds and entered a troubled, listless sleep.

After a troublesome night filled with horrible dreams of maggots gnawing on his ears, Bastawr finally woke up near the morning. He started immediately to search for food and checked his ears for worms.

After turning a few stones, he found a frost viper trying to slither away.

He snapped the head of the snake, thanked the gods, and ate his meal for the day before tracking the undead army. The mist became so dense that he almost stumbled into the dead's' numbers. Bastawr stopped barely a hair's breadth away from the column of bloodless marchers. He had to back away quickly, but not so fast to attract them to his whereabouts. Gods knew that living things became so scarce he could barely cover his presence from the undead by hiding near living things.

What surprised him was that they hadn't traveled far during the time he slept.

Bastawr crept nearer as he found a colony of ants traveling to his north, and under their concealing presence, he heard the sounds of distant digging. Whatever the knight and his army were after, they'd found it, and were evidently working hard to unearth it.

Bastawr crept nearer still to better see what the undead army was up to.

When he judged that he was near enough, he found a scraggly bush and squatted behind it. His position was precarious to say the least; he'd left the colony of ants behind, and if any of the undead turned his way, they might sense his presence. He silently prayed to all the gods, begging them to keep his hiding place safe.

The digging continued for most of the afternoon and into the early dusk. Tireless skeletal workers wielded shovels and picks with relentless abandon until finally, the undead stopped altogether.

A cracked voice rang out like iron scraped on ice.

"So, this is the vaunted mist stone," the knight addressed the lich. "It looks like any other slab of rock."

Bastawr squinted, barely able to see the two ominous figures through the gray haze.

"Only because you can't sense the magic coming off it in waves." The lich approached the deep hole in the ground. "There is immense power in that stone, enough power to annihilate even an entire army like yours...If it could be harnessed thusly."

"Do you mean that we can't just overturn it to disable its magic?" The knight peered over the hole.

"One inch more, and the stone will destroy you. Your essence would evaporate. You simply would cease to exist." The lich glowed a sickly purple as he stepped near the hole. "You lost six score of diggers already."

"I understand well enough not to approach the damned stone, stop preaching, heucuva." The knight stepped away from the hole. "Do you have a solution to accomplish the mission?"

"I do." The spell caster laughed. It sounded like a thousand animals screeching in agony to Bastawr. "I need a hundred of your minions. I must consume the remnant of their essence to disable the protection around the marker."

"Take a thousand if you need. We can easily replenish our numbers, and Leisterbane has collected soldiers to his cause for centuries." The knight chuckled with a low growl.

The lich moved away from the hole. "I will also require whatever necralluvium you carry." He glowed again with the same sickly purple.

Bastawr thought it meant the spell caster might be challenging him.

The knight roared at the lich, and for a moment, Bastawr felt the temperature of the air around him drop markedly. But then the knight quieted and a long hiss issued from his rictus grin. Bastawr assumed it was a sigh of sorts. Then he turned over a jar of the black stuff. He raised his arm and a section of the army marched towards the edge of the hole.

"Here are your hundred soldiers." The knight sounded enraged. "Finish your job."

The spell caster bowed formally. His hands glowed yellowish-green as he chanted and waved his arms through the air.

One after one, the dead soldiers fell, and the glow around the lich intensified. His chanting took an otherworldly quality. Some kind of latent power rumbled through the ground.

The surrounding pressure changed and Bastawr felt as if a weight pressed upon his chest, preventing him from breathing. He panted through the pain as the lich continued. Bastawr's vision dimmed, and he started to feel his own impending death loom like a storm on the horizon. He felt an age had passed while he suffered behind the bush, feeling life seeping out from his body, abandoning him.

Then the chanting stopped and Bastawr took his first real breath since it started. He gulped, hungry for air, relieved to know he still lived. He peered at the undead gathered nearest the deep hole. Half of the hundred sacrificial soldiers still stood.

The lich moved among them as if he floated, touching each on the top of the skull as he went. Each soldier the lich touched glowed the same greenish-yellow. Then the fiend held up a flask of turbid glass. He poured the black, viscous contents of the flask into the hole. It crackled and hissed in the pit as it multiplied.

"They may touch the stone now." The lich's voice sounded different, filled with power and darkness.

The knight raised his arm, and the undead scuttled down the pit as one and tromped through the growing mass of inky sludge.

Bastawr wanted to see what they were doing in the hole, but he knew that drawing any nearer would reveal him. He waited behind his cover to see what would happen.

Minutes passed, and nothing happened.

Bastawr dared hope that whatever the lich and the knight tried to do had failed, and that they would be denied their objective. He started to think about his route back to Balgavarr, and how his new friends would work together to prevent whatever the undead were trying to achieve with the buried stone.

But as he counted the minutes for him to make a retreat, an explosion ripped a hole in the ground, followed by a blood-curdling scream that Bastawr felt deep in his bones. It bored its way into his soul.

An eerily green light came from the hole, and even the empowered lich and the knight fell back as light spewed forth from the crevasse.

Bastawr fought to remain awake. The shock of the noise threatened to consume him with psychic blackness. Then, with an equally eerie sigh, the light stopped, and the scream ceased. Oily smoke that smelled of rotten flesh curled from the hole.

The lich and the knight stood and peered over the ledge. "It is done." The lich sounded drained of his ethereal powers, almost like a normal man. "The stone is defiled. The sage's tool no longer works and the spirit bound into the mystic key has been cast away."

The knight raised his arm in silence and sent another section of the army down into the hole.

Bastawr felt tightness clench his heart. Something intrinsic to Nature died this day: something immense and great. He couldn't shake the feeling of anguish.

He held himself in check, lest the urge to weep took control of his body.

Then another boom came from the hole, and another sigh.

Undead soldiers started to crawl out of the hole and returned to their ranks.

"Why is the mist still here?" The knight turned to the lich.

"Patience. It will dissipate." The lich looked and sounded on the verge of crumbling to dust, yet it stood.

Bastawr wondered about the knight's question for some seconds, then his heartbeat quickened.

"Soon, Leisterbane will let us descend upon the filthy homes of the living." The lich laughed his painful laugh. "They will never see it coming and we will devour them utterly."

The mist started to thin. It didn't dissipate completely, but Bastawr looked around with worry. He would soon be visible to the entire army of the undead.

He searched desperately for a better hiding spot, but none were close enough to reach in time.

"The fog is lifting." The knight raised his arms to the heavens. "And now, I can sense the loathed, living things within it again."

"Yes, you are right." The lich turned in the direction of Bastawr. "In fact, there is one right here."

Bastawr jumped from his hiding position just as the undead warriors turned to face him. The tigerfolk drew his sword and looked ahead, then behind him.

The closest of the undead charged towards Bastawr. He sidestepped and decapitated the skeletal warrior as he turned full circle to face the next.

The warrior didn't stand a chance as Bastawr stabbed at his sternum and sheared through the vertebral column of the enemy.

He grimly shook his sword free of clinging, decayed flesh and turned to face the army. Bastawr growled as he faced the wave of undead rushing at him. He prayed the goddess would bless his last moments and he gripped his weapons tightly.

A pang of regret rang through him as he considered his course of action. He knew he would not meet his friends in Balgavarr, except possibly as a corpse under Leisterbane's command. But he could die gloriously and take many of the enemy with him. He smiled wildly as another cadaverous warrior charged at him.

Chapter 15

Naemyar left the group so that she could finish an errand and focus her remaining attention on them for the day. But she insisted they all eat in her absence.

As lunch was served, Ra'al, Coryn, Marnash, Werdth and Garesch discussed their options.

"We have to pursue the missing part of the map." Marnash placed his fork down. "Too much is at risk if my father would use it to reach the mist stone. He is a Death worshiper, and an acolyte of the dark one. I'm sure of it."

"Bastawr already went after Yarichek." Coryn sipped some water. "We must trust that he will apprehend him before he can pass it on."

"Why didn't you tell Naemyar about the meeting with the pirate in Frostshoal?" Ra'al asked Garesch.

"In all truth, we found the first three parts with the snake people, and this caused us to search for the rest of the map." Garesch smiled. "Ry'Ober was simply kind enough to supply the rest. You managed to follow me and uncover our true purpose: to protect the mist stones."

Ra'al chuckled. "Actually, we stumbled *into* you, to be honest."

Garesch grudgingly shook his head. "There is another matter we need to discuss." Garesch looked at Marnash, and the latter gave the strange sign by putting his hand to his chest. "We have hidden some details from you."

"Like what?" Ra'al chewed on a chunk of meat.

"The undead sightings are not limited to the north." Garesch shook his head. "And they are more than mere scout observations. Before we left Uruzak, we heard reports that corpses had been stolen from the graves in many of the smaller villages belonging to our empire." He looked to Marnash silently.

Marnash cleared his throat. "Not only that, but there have been reports of able-bodied men and women sometimes disappearing from their homes. Lord Death is certainly amassing a new army."

Garesch bowed his head. "You see, this is why I am so certain that my father is involved. The dead rise in the north, but there is still some connection to Uruzak and my people…But I fear my people may never throw down such notoriety, if this becomes public. Our reputation could haunt all our kind forever."

Everybody fell silent. Even Ra'al, who gnawed on a leg of lamb, stopped mid-chew.

"Do you have any idea about how big the undead army is, where it is situated, and where it could be heading?" Coryn looked from Garesch to Marnash.

"I don't think they know that much, Coryn." Ra'al placed the lamb leg down. "I think this is why they came in search of alliances. They knew the real war is at everyone's doors. Not a war between Uruzak and the rest of Cyrea, but of Life versus Death."

Garesch raised his hand. "Yes, we knew that the war is coming, but this was not why we came in search of alliances." He shook his head. "You don't understand how the morehl have been swayed by Death's cultists and their lies. Uruzak is victim of a culture war that has waged upon its people from the top down."

"You had to seek help from outside." Coryn put her hands in her lap slowly. "Because you wanted to change the state of affairs in Mount Uruzak…and you are willing to stand against your father?" She took a deep breath and looked deep into Garesch's eyes, empathizing with the notion. "Could you push him from the throne, even knowing it might require extreme prejudice?"

"Yes, lady Coryn. You are right in your conclusion." Marnash nodded. "Prince Garesch is trying to change the morehl, to sway our people away from Death's dominion. And yes, this can only happen if he is powerful enough."

Garesch's eyes were like flint. "And to answer your last question. Yes. If there is no other way to save our people, I will do what must be done regarding my father."

"But lava elves only put trust in power and strength," Ra'al said. "And right now, your father is the most powerful elf in Uruzak. You need more allies than us if you hope to usurp your father's throne."

Garesch fell silent.

"He wants to avert a civil war," Marnash spoke for his friend. "He is trying to serve all of Cyrea by standing against Death. Is this so bad?"

Again, silence enveloped the table.

Ra'al took a long breath. "Your intentions may be pure, and your pursuit of power might be fueled by a wish to stand against Lord Death." He pursed his lips and shook his head. "But you called us friends and shared our journey. You could have been more forthright earlier than this."

"Aye, he could have," Marnash defended. "But would you have accepted us any earlier than this?" Marnash locked hard eyes with Ra'al.

"I don't know," Ra'al sighed, speaking honestly. "Probably not; we would not have trusted you without enduring the trials we shared."

"Well, I understand." Coryn touched Garesch's hand as he kept his silence. "Gods know that I am about to do something akin to what Garesch is planning. I must also stand against my father in the hopes that it will help all of Cyrea."

"So we are set upon opening the cache?" Ra'al looked at Coryn with raised eyebrows.

"Yes, and I mean to do it today." Coryn gnashed her teeth. "And by the gods, I will do whatever is necessary to win this coming war—the real war, not some land dispute over Cyrean soil."

Garesch's mouth thinned in determination. "When do you want to go?"

"As soon as Naemyar returns. We must act fast." Coryn squeezed Ra'al's huge hand and looked him in the eye. "Are you with me, Ra'al?"

Ra'al nodded. "What else can I do? I am with you all the way, little sister."

When Naemyar returned, she found the group already standing at the ready. They'd taken the opportunity to wash and refresh themselves in her absence, and were already ready to once more resume their quest.

In a few words, Ra'al told her how they planned to seek help deciphering the arcane key poem that could let them into the cache.

Naemyar offered any further help, should they require it. They thanked her for her hospitality. And then they left.

Within an hour they had passed beyond the city walls and gathered in the tree grove not far from the main gates.

"Why did you tell Naemyar that we needed help deciphering the words of the poem?" Coryn asked Ra'al.

"For the same reason you led us out of the city, even though you and I both know that the cache is still in Tulgesh." Ra'al laughed. "I don't trust anyone easily, especially people who show too much interest…I think the Queen means well, but she is also a politician. And I do not like the way her majordomo, that Lotep figure, watched us." He shrugged. "Anyway, that spicy smell in her house returned and kept clouding my mind, and I wanted to get out of there."

Garesch looked confused. "What spicy smell?"

"The whole house smelled of a strong, bitter spice." Ra'al noticed that Coryn looked as confused as Garesch. "You all couldn't smell it?"

Marnash touched the immense shoulder of the frostwing prince. "I think you were right… We have been spied upon then."

Everybody looked at Marnash, waiting for an explanation.

"The undead creations of Lord Death can smell the living." He stood as the others circled him. "Frostwings have resisted

Death's power, but their origins are in him, still. By your makeup, you may have a special sense capable of detecting the undead, some of which are guised as apparitions, incorporeal beings. I think that Ra'al has this sense."

Ra'al rubbed his face as he looked at the morehl. "Your origins are similar, but you did not smell it," he argued. "Your makeup is of Firiel and Death."

The typically silent bodyguard, Werdth, sheepishly raised a hand. "I smelled it too, but I did not know what it was. Especially since I find selumari foods and odors so…displeasing."

"So, I guess your theory could be correct." Marnash looked at Ra'al, as if he tried to assess the frostwing's full potential.

"This makes our decision to open the cache tonight even more crucial." Coryn sighed. "We will wait till the traffic at the gate thins out to make our move." She smiled grimly. "We have to get there before twilight, so we may have to use another route into the city. One that only a dwarf can find." She winked to Ra'al.

Chapter 16

As twilight deepened, Coryn led the party round the wall of Tulgesh. But as they reached a part of the mural depicting a vagha pushing a spade into the ground, she stopped.

"See the pinky finger of the vagha?" She pointed to the mural, and all heads followed her. "It is crooked, pointing to somewhere to his left."

"And this is not usual for the vagha?" Ra'al asked, smiling as Coryn gave him a sharp jab.

Coryn passed her hand on the mural in the general direction of the pointing finger, and then suddenly, her hand disappeared in the stonework.

"I knew this would be here." She laughed, then pulled on something within the hidden compartment. They heard a loud grating sound. "It's a rockblanket; a kind of hidden entrance, almost like a very advanced bead curtain."

Ra'al felt the ground vibrate beneath his feet and jumped to one side.

"This is it." Coryn knelt where Ra'al stood. A large, square tile emerged.

The others pitched in and together they moved dirt from the tile, discovering a dark tunnel beneath.

Coryn faced the party. "I will need Ra'al and Garesch to come with me. The rest should stay behind. Only a few should venture within."

"But we are exposed until you return," Marnash argued. Two morehl loitering beyond the wall at midnight would seem suspicious.

"You will have to trust in Firiel's protection, master Marnash," Coryn gently insisted.

Garesch went first, followed by Coryn and trailed by Ra'al.

The tunnel was dark, but short. It ended at a regular wooden door. They opened it and found themselves in a tiny alley that stretched to the royal palace's backyard. It provided King Matrek with an easy escape hatch, if ever needed.

"How did you know this was going to be here?" Garesch patted the dirt from his clothes and looked straight to Coryn.

"I didn't." She shrugged and did the same thing with her clothes. "But vagha are miners, and no miner is going to make a tunnel without an emergency exit, or in our case, an entrance."

They walked out of the tunnel and stole across the emptying streets of the city. The commercial districts were mostly free of traffic. Local buyers and sellers already headed home.

Foreign traders would either be on their way out of the city or heading for the nearest inn by now. Only a few people still walked the streets.

"I never asked, how did you know where the cache's entrance is?" Garesch asked Ra'al as they walked towards their destination.

"When we first came to the city, I noticed a strange carving on the mural," Ra'al said, walking as slow as he could for Coryn's sake. "There was a frostwing holding a jay in his hand, and at first I thought that the bird was some kind of beastfolk."

Ra'al avoided colliding with a merchant holding a bundle over his shoulder. "When Coryn recited the poem key, there it was, twice mentioning the jay."

Garesch nodded and stroked his chin.

Coryn walked ahead, then slowed and fell in with her friends. "Actually, there is one other clue." She pushed through Garesch and Ra'al. "The foot of the hero. There is only one hero in the eyes of my father: the dwarf who single-handedly shifted the tide of the battle for Balgavarr. To Geril, the real hero will always be Thrag, Ra'al's father."

She waved her hands as she explained, "In all of Cyrea, there are only two statues of Thrag. One in Balgavarr, and one here." She laughed. "And my father would never consider putting the cache within the reaches of the most powerful earth magicians in Esfah. He knew they would find it eventually. The cache is still in Tulgesh, and the statue is the key."

"Interesting." Garesch shook his head as he laughed. "Did you decipher more from the verses then?"

"There is one other area I think I found a hidden meaning." Ra'al smiled smugly. *"But only if the earth, fire, and air will bond their ties.* This is the three of us."

"Absolutely right." Coryn bobbed her head. "My father wanted to make sure that the next time the cache was brought out, all the races would be united." She shrugged. "Although, a selumari could have worked in the place of a frostwing."

"Perhaps not," Garesch noted. "Vagha are born of fire and earth and areosa of the air and Death. It is more about dwarves and frostwings."

"And not just any frostwing," Coryn said and swallowed. "I think this meant you in particular, Ra'al. Since you were a kit, you could not feel the song of the wind. You told me yourself, and my father must have known this."

"The chill that lost the wind." Ra'al smiled sadly. "I get it, this verse is about me."

Coryn stopped all of a sudden, and both Ra'al and Garesch stopped alongside her. "The question is, how did my father know that you would be *here?"*

Before any of the other two could answer, she squealed. "The hero's foot, we are here!" She pointed excitedly to a huge statue of a grimacing frostwing.

"This is amazing." Garesch craned his neck as he looked at the head of the statue. "If I didn't know better, I would have said that this statue is *of* Ra'al."

Ra'al looked at the statue with the same awe that Garesch showed. "Many of the frostwings back home say that I look a lot like him."

Coryn left the two mesmerized by the statue and started to search at the clawed toes of Thrag's statue. "I can't find any point to press or to pass my hand through." She stood and looked at the stone feet critically. "This is solid stone."

Ra'al lowered his head and noticed something odd about the statue's attire. "Coryn, you are better versed in vagha runes? If so, can you read this?"

Coryn went to where Ra'al stood and looked at the pants hem of the statue. "It translates to 'the jay sings here'." She looked around her. "Where in festration is a blue jay that sings?"

Garesch looked around just as Coryn and Ra'al did, then he smiled, approached the foot that protruded from those pants, and started to imitate the screeching song of a jay.

Both Coryn and Ra'al looked at him as if he had lost his mind, then Coryn joined him in a different note. Finally, with a loud sigh, Ra'al did as well.

After almost a minute of screeching and in the case of Coryn, flapping her arms like wings, the rock began to move. It sounded like stone grating against stone, and it hurt their ears.

They stopped screeching at once and ran to where the sound came from.

At the back of the statue, a tile on the ground moved, covered by the grass and the growth of many decades. Darkness could be seen under it from the corner.

Garesch and Ra'al grabbed the tile and lifted it back, revealing a staircase that descended into the darkness.

Coryn tore a part of her axe dress, the one she insisted was to protect the axe's edge from rust, pulled out her dagger, and wrapped the cloth around it. She doused it in oil, then struck her flint to the cloth and held her makeshift torch high before descending the stairs.

The stairs ended in a narrow passage that looked like it had been molded from the surrounding earth. Ra'al had to stoop, half-bent; the ceiling was too low for his height, and they all had to file one after another. The passage only allowed for one person at a time.

The three walked twenty cubits down the narrow passage until they came to a dead end. Coryn raised her torch to see the wall better.

It was a marble slab, not unlike the one the statue of Thrag was made of, and on it was engraved a huge bell.

"The silent bell." Garesch touched the engraved bell, then withdrew his hand fast. "It's cold."

"You think we should screech horribly at this slab as well?" Ra'al suggested to the other two.

Coryn shrugged. "I guess we could try."

After a few minutes of dissonant screeching, the three realized it was not working.

"All right, I think the jay means something different here." Garesch rubbed his throat. "Besides, if we screech one more time, I think I will go mute."

"The jay's song will play and will tell, how to bring a note from the silent bell," Coryn repeated the lines quietly, trying to fathom their meaning.

Ra'al stood silent, breathing on the heads of Garesch and Coryn as they each repeated the verse.

Out of boredom, he blew a hard and long breath, and it caused the flames on Coryn's makeshift torch to waver for a moment.

"Did you see that?" Garesch cried out.

"What? What was it?" Coryn looked at him with confusion.

Garesch took the torch and rested it against the stone wall so that the slab was bathed in darkness. "This." Garesch pointed to the many phosphorescent images displayed on the door and the wall. They slowly darkened by the moment. The markings had absorbed a tiny amount of light, which were now slowly fading.

Ra'al reached out and touched the drawing of a jay at the upper corner of the bell.

The stone gave way under his touch, so he pressed harder, until the wall started to crumble.

All three stepped back as the wall succumbed, collapsing into a fine dust.

"I should have suspected that this was a compressed dust wall," Coryn said smiled in appreciation. "The ancient dwarves used to build these in front of temples and let them down on special celebrations."

"But was it necessary to find the jay? Couldn't we just push on the wall at any spot?" Ra'al still held his hand to his nose and eyes as the dust filled the narrow and tight passage.

"Actually, yes." Coryn waved her hands around the passage and at the now gaping hole, clearing away some of the dust. "Only one single spot is made of rarified dust. When this part is moved, the air penetrates the rest of the compressed dust, quickly toppling the whole structure."

Coryn retrieved her makeshift torch.

Ra'al and Garesch both gazed with wide eyes at the clever craftsmanship of the vagha and followed Coryn into the descending corridor. It ended in a massive room sprawled maybe fifty cubits by one hundred.

In the middle of the room, a glass case stood holding various gems. At each corner of the room, a glass pedestal was posted with a small groove upon its flat surface.

The room was lit from several glowing mushrooms that grew where the floor met the walls. All three looked around and then headed to the case.

Ra'al looked to Coryn. "What now?"

"I guess this room has to do with the fire, earth, and air ties." She turned each of the stones in her hands. "These are all different in weight and type, and each is a precious or semi-precious stone."

"I know that some of those are bound to certain elements." Garesch picked one up. "This agate, for example, is bound to fire. It is my family's charm stone."

Ra'al pointed to the corner pedestals. "I think they go on there."

"Okay: ruby for fire, amber for the earth, and sapphire for air." She picked the three stones and handed Ra'al and Garesch each a stone guessing at the symbolism in their colors. "Let's put them in the pedestals."

Each ran to a corner and put one of the stones on a pedestal. Nothing happened.

"I think we should place them in the same moment," Garesch suggested.

"Or each has a specific pedestal," Ra'al said.

Coryn turned around, looking for more clues. "This leaves the last pedestal without a stone."

She suddenly stopped. "The jay will tell." She cried out. "The jay was in the upper right corner. This is where we should start."

She ran to the far-right corner of the room and placed the obsidian. "Garesch, I think you should place yours in the far right corner, and Ra'al, place yours in the lower left."

Ra'al and Garesch did as instructed, and still, nothing happened.

"I have another idea." Ra'al ran back to the pedestal. "We need stones that represent earth and fire and air, all in one."

"But none exist." Coryn followed him. "Only a few represent two elements at the same time, never all three."

"We could try a version of that with stones that each represent two elements. That might be the key," Garesch suggested.

"Agate represents Earth and fire," Ra'al said, picking up the agate.

"And tourmaline represents Earth and Air." Coryn hastily grabbed the tourmaline.

"Finally, pietersite for Air and Fire." Garesch picked up the final, (description) gem.

The three ran to each corner and placed down their stones.

The three pedestals descended into the ground with a loud grating noise, while the fourth rose to the ceiling and hit it hard. Its boom was followed by a torrent of sand falling into the room.

The three watched in horror as the room began to fill with it, threatening to bury the occupants.

But then, the room jolted and started to drop.

The opening to the outside quickly slid up, and even though the sand stopped falling, the room plunged into the unknown. It jarred Ra'al, who was more comfortable in the open air than underground.

As suddenly as it had started to move, the room stopped.

"We have something like this in Balgavarr," Coryn said in a low voice. "Only ours is barely two by two cubits and carries only a single person at a time. The elders use it to access the archives of the city."

Neither Ra'al nor Garesch responded. Both scanned their new surroundings.

"Coryn, what was the next verse?" Garesch called to the dwarf, who inspected the pedestals that had disappeared into the ground.

"Walk with light feet in the maze of water flow, the chill and fire should proceed with the earth in tow," Coryn repeated the verse. She knelt at the circular holes of the pedestals and pushed her hand into the soft mud there.

"Garesch, Ra'al, come here," Coryn called for the two.

As they arrived where she knelt, she looked up. "I think this room is the next piece of the puzzle."

Ra'al knelt by her side. "How?"

"This mud, it pushes down with pressure, but comes back up when I release it." She pressed again with her hand to show them. "I think there are trigger pads below them."

"So, we press on them?" Garesch asked her.

She bobbed her head once. "In the sequence of air, fire, and earth."

"But which is which?" Ra'al asked her.

"I don't think it matters."

"So, we step on them?" Ra'al asked.

"Yes, step with light feet." Coryn winked at Ra'al and Garesch as she went forward.

Garesch went to the far side and stepped on the mud. "I guess we follow the same order as the gems then."

Ra'al smiled at her and stepped on the near right spot where the opening used to be, and Coryn went to the last one.

As the three stood, they heard the sound of stone grating under their feet, followed by the rush of running water.

Water started to flow into the room and soon, they stood in a growing puddle.

"You think the room might go down again?" Ra'al asked Coryn.

"I honestly don't know." She shook her head as the cold water started to numb her feet.

It reached the level of Coryn's knees fast. "This is getting scary. I am not much of a swimmer. We vagha are earth and dirt types, not water. Not at all."

Nobody answered her as the water continued to rise.

The water soon reached Coryn's waist and she cried out. "I can't feel my legs, this water is freezing!"

Ra'al didn't suffer. His body was normally quite cold, and Garesch's hot body helped insulate him.

"I think it will be over soon, Coryn," Ra'al said in a soft voice. "I don't know if the puzzle will break or not, but if the water rises any more, I am coming to you."

A few minutes later, the water reached Coryn's neck. She started to sob.

"Hold still, I am here, Coryn." Ra'al took large strides to Coryn and pulled her to his shoulder height.

Coryn continued sobbing. "I brought us here." She hugged Ra'al and cried. "We will die a horrible death because I broke the will of my father."

The water kept rising, even after Ra'al and Coryn left their spot. The level rose above the height of the elf, who paddled to keep his head above the water.

"Ra'al, it was an honor knowing you." Garesch swam towards Ra'al. "And Coryn, it was a pleasure adventuring by your side."

Coryn continued to cry and whispered, "I am sorry, I am so sorry. This was all my fault."

The water reached just above Ra'al's chin and lapped at his nose. He lifted Coryn even higher.

"Ra'al," Coryn whispered. "You are just postponing the inevitable, you don't have to lift me any higher. Just…Just let me drown."

Garesch looked up to meet the swollen eyes of Coryn, and then he noticed the ceiling. Where water splashed at the walls, the wet stone changed color. He splashed the ceiling, and it changed color, too. "Look up!" he shouted.

In the middle of the ceiling, a diamond-shaped tile of about five cubits did not change when splashed.

Ra'al unfolded his wings and flapped them against the water, splashing gallons at the ceiling. He repeated this two times, three times, and on the fourth round, the tile started to disintegrate.

"Garesch, follow me." Ra'al walked on his tiptoes, sinking now and then as he slipped under the water.

As Garesch followed, Ra'al extended his arm up towards the hole in the ceiling. "Use my arm as a boost to reach up and pull Coryn from there."

Garesch did as ordered and found himself in another corridor. He knelt down, opening his legs to use as an anchor against the opening of the hole, and reached for Coryn.

"What about you, Ra'al?" Coryn cried out as Garesch pulled her arm.

"I will float, don't worry." Ra'al jumped up and down to avoid sinking beneath the rising waters. "I will follow shortly."

Coryn climbed up Garesch's body, then pulled him up.

Both watched as Ra'al tried to stay afloat, but it was evident he was failing. The frostwing had too much gear on his body.

"Unfold your wings, Ra'al!" Garesch suddenly shouted.

Ra'al bubbled and spread his wings. It created a larger surface area that allowed him to rise above the water level, if only just a little.

They all waited on bated breath as the water carried Ra'al towards the opening, giving both Garesch and Coryn time to pull him up. He shook like a wet dog, drying himself as much as possible.

Together, they stood in a very dark corridor. The only source of light came from the submerged mushrooms in the watery room below. They joined in a burst of laughter, slightly hysterical at having survived.

"What is the next verse? Let's face our new trial." Garesch smiled to Coryn.

Coryn smiled back. *"In the depth of the darkness, Dragonsbane's blood knows the key, and through this blood, in the darkness light will be,"* she said "This one is clearly about me since I am of Dragonsbane's blood."

The corridor ended at the north side and continued deep into darkness as it turned to the south.

Several dents lined both sides of the walls.

Ra'al ran his hand along the wall's grooves. "Ouch, they bite." He looked at the blood leaking from his hand.

Coryn pushed a breath out. "I think the blood thing is literal, then." She placed her hand on the dents.

Whatever was inside cut her as it did Ra'al.

Moments passed, then the sound of machinery around them whirred to life. Light flooded the corridor coming from the wall's indentation.

"This is blood magic mixed with science." Coryn looked around with wide eyes. "I wonder if these lights can detach."

Coryn reached for one of the inset lights and found they were actually globes. She pulled her hand away fast. "It is freezing."

"This explains the next verse," Ra'al said and took an orb in his hand, seemingly unaffected. *"Put the light in the hand of chill that lost the wind."*

They smiled and proceeded to the south end of the corridor.

At the end, they faced another wall. On it, they found a large sand hourglass.

Garesch bowed and flourished to Coryn to move forward and solve the next puzzle.

She approached the hourglass and touched it. "It can be overturned, but what do you think this will trigger?" She looked apprehensively to Ra'al and Garesch.

"What is the next verse?" Ra'al asked her.

"For in that hand, the time will bend, as time turned the wheel thus turns." Coryn looked at the hourglass for some moments. "Honestly, this verse is the most cryptic of them all."

Ra'al and Garesch stood silently as Coryn turned the hourglass up and down to no effect.

Then, Ra'al reached with the light orb to the hourglass. Just as he touched it, pictures swam in front of his eyes.

"Keep it horizontal, Ra'al," Coryn urged Ra'al.

As he adjusted the hourglass, images started to play on the right-side wall.

It was Geril, Coryn's father. He stood with four other vagha, conversing with them. Geril looked in the direction of the three adventurers and smiled. He walked to a notch unseen in the wall, pointed his hand to it, and made turning motions.

"Huh." Ra'al laughed. "Very impressive."

"Very impressive indeed." Garesch watched the pictures as they projected in a loop. "These moving pictures are a piece of strong fire magic. Vagha share that devotion to Firiel."

Coryn walked to the notch that her father pointed to and put her hand inside it. She withdrew it instantly. "So, I think I got a frostbite and a burn to match. There is a very hot round thing inside."

"I guess this brings the next verse into light." Garesch exhaled a long breath. *"And the fire touched must turn it lest it burns."*

Garesch walked to Coryn and put his hand inside the notch. "Not that hot, maybe a bit, but it is tolerable." He started to make turning motions inside. "It is a wheel of sorts."

As Garesch turned the wheel, water flowed in from the hole where they'd escaped. It rose more quickly than before. "The water is going to fill this corridor." He stopped turning the wheel. "I think I should stop."

But when he stopped, the water flow doubled.

"Garesch, I think you should continue." Coryn pointed to the water bubbling from the hole.

Garesch grit his teeth and turned the wheel. This slowed the water advance a bit, but not enough.

The wheel was not smooth, and it had several tiny dents and snags. The friction from Garesch's grip scratched and welted his hands.

Ra'al looked at the water already covering Coryn's boots. "I think you must do it faster."

Garesch smiled through tight lips and cranked the wheel faster. The wheel shredded his flesh, but he didn't show pain to Ra'al and Coryn. Instead, he sucked in his breath and continued his agonizing duty.

The wall nearest the notch and wheel started to raise, but as Garesch slowed down, it started to fall.

Garesch clenched his teeth and reached into his pocket with his free hand. He withdrew a sightstone. He activated it so that it glowed slightly.

Blood started to drip back on his sleeve, drenching his arm and making his grip on the wheel slippery.

Garesch groaned and turned the device faster, clenching hard on the hot wheel. Inch by inch the wall raised up, siphoning the water into the next room.

When the wall rose high enough, Garesch shouted, "Go through, both of you! I will follow."

Ra'al grabbed Coryn, who was about to say something, and dove with her into the next room.

The wall fell quickly as Garesch abandoned the wheel. Closing the open gap, he dove inside just before the wall fell, sealing them shut.

Coryn touched the surrounding walls, and something bit her in the darkness. "Festration," she cursed.

Light flooded the room, radiating from all four walls, and giving shape to the chamber. The room was immense, at least two hundred cubits on all sides, and formed a perfect square.

But it was completely empty.

Coryn turned round and noticed the blood dripping from Garesch's hand. "By the gods, you should have said something." She pulled his hand to assess the extent of the damage.

Ra'al approached them and looked on as Coryn pulled cut a ribbon of cloth from her tunic and used it to dress Garesch's wounded hand.

"You must ask Marnash to tend this the moment we get out of here." She bit her lip. "You are no use without your fighting hand."

The morehl smiled and bowed to her.

Ra'al walked around the room, wondering where the cache could be, when he noticed a raised ridge on an alcove inset at the far wall. Three large wheels on long poles protruded from it.

"What is that?" He pointed to the raised ridge.

"I would say that is a lift, most probably to the outside," Coryn said.

"But where is the cache?" Garesch turned slowly around the room. "There is nothing here."

"*In the ground, your treasure will be, but be careful with the broken she,*" Coryn said, softly. "The cache is under our feet, but how can we reach it? And who is the broken she in the poem?"

"Maybe we can dig the ground and pull it out?" Ra'al looked around. "Although, I don't see any digging tools here."

"I think we need to use earth magic to uncover the cache." Garesch knelt and touched the ground. "I can sense the magic items under here."

"Can you do that? I mean, can you uncover the cache?" Ra'al asked Garesch.

"No, not really." Garesch shook his fist. "I feel a large variety of magics. But we can only use fire and death magic. It would take a vagha to do this."

Ra'al and Garesch looked to Coryn.

"Don't look at me." She stepped back. "I was never inducted. I might have the spark, but I don't know how to craft spells."

"What, then?" Ra'al asked her.

"Harol is in Tulgesh." Coryn pursed her lips, remembering the ambassador. "He should at least know what spell to use, or possibly he knows enough vaghan casters in Tulgesh."

Garesch stood. "Can we trust him?"

"I think we can…I hope we can." Coryn chewed her lower lip. "If the vagha council trusted him enough to represent their local interests, we should be able to trust him, too."

"So, we just leave?" Ra'al looked at her with a mad smile. "After all the hell we just went through to reach this far?"

"I think once we use the lift, a door will open on the other side directly to this room." Coryn let her breath out her mouth. "It even said so in the poem: '*When you have passed the test and done, know that what you did cannot be undone*'."

"All right, let's find master Harol, then." Garesch walked fast to the ridge. "Let's not lose this night."

Ra'al pulled one of the cold light orbs and followed Garesch. Coryn followed soon after.

The three turned the three wheels, and the ridge started to raise, inch by inch.

They went through level after level of corridors that they couldn't otherwise access. Finally, the lift raised to a level where the ceiling was right above them.

Ra'al pointed his light at the ceiling and they could clearly see the frame of a door.

"Lift me up, Ra'al," Garesch said and signaled towards the door.

Ra'al lifted Garesch, who pushed as hard as he could against the barrier. He beat against it over and over to no effect.

The door finally budged with a loud *clang*. Chunks of rock and dirt fell down on them, and the three huddled away from the overhead passage until the onslaught of dirt stopped.

Before they could climb up, an unseen gruff vaghan voice called out to them. "Who goes there?"

The mystery door led them into the residence of the vaghan embassy in Tulgesh. A thin veneer of stone had obscured the secret passage, like the shell that formed upon gargoyles when they slept. From the inside, the adventurers crumbled the material and opened the passage to find Harol standing in the hallway of the dwarven embassy.

It would have never been discovered from the other side, as the structure was a historic landmark of vaghan construction. There was virtually no chance it would ever be torn apart or opened during a renovation.

Ra'al clambered to safety last and immediately wrinkled his nose. "Something nearby smells terrible." He caught Garesch and Coryn's eyes and shook his head to alleviate any suspicions that it was the same odor detected at Naemyar's.

His friends wrinkled their noses, too. The pungent smell was noticed by all.

Harol flashed him a grin. "Apologies, areosan prince. Your nose might be more sensitive than others." He motioned toward a nearby door at the end of the hall. "My chef is experimenting with dry-aging cuts of meat. It rots the outer layer, which will be cut off in a few days when the steaks are served, though it has a certain, unpleasant aroma during the creation process. That is why we use this out-of-the-way storage room to prepare it."

"Delicacy or not, I think I will skip that meal," Ra'al breathed through his mouth.

Harol shrugged. "That is what brought me down this hallway. I came to check on it when I heard all the commotion within my wall. But surely you must be curious. Would you like to see the process?" His hand reached for the doorknob for the barrier holding back the worst of the smell.

"No! No, that is quite alright," Ra'al insisted, not wanting a more potent dose of the odor. He shook his head. Between rotted meat, swamp gases, and dragon's piss, he'd experienced more foul odors these last few months than the rest of his life combined.

"Very well then," Harol said and peered down the shaft. "You must tell me what is down there."

"We will," Coryn promised. "And soon—tonight if possible – but first can you send a man for our remaining companions?"

Harol looked into her eyes and nodded. "And certainly you'd like towels and a fresh set of clothes…perhaps something to eat?"

They nodded vigorously.

"Just not any of your fancy meats, please." Ra'al wrinkled his nose.

Harol nodded and led them to the main part of the facility.

As the three adventurers got cleaned, dried, and fed, they sent a messenger to retrieve Marnash and Werdth. The servant informed their companions that the three were alright and that they were at Harol's house.

It was very late, with only a few selumari guards walking the evening streets. Most of them stopped and watched the three suspiciously, before returning to their patrols after they'd safely passed.

The walk to Balgavarr's embassy didn't take long. Nevertheless, the three traveled in silence, doing their best to minimize any interest in the fact that morehl walked the Tulgesh streets.

While Harol went to prepare refreshments, Coryn leaned against Ra'al. She was still enchanted by the amount of thought her father had put into those obstacles which barred the entry to the final chamber. "He knew all along that I would be the one to find the cache. With traps such as those, he must have suspected I might have been put under duress to retrieve them," she mused. "Traps such as those might have allowed some hypothetical version of me to get the better of an enemy agent."

Ra'al grinned. "Don't forget that he knew I would be present as well."

Coryn nudged him more gently than usual. "He always liked you—never had a doubt that you'd be with me to the end."

Harol rejoined the crew and welcomed them, escorting the rest of their party in.

Over the reheated remnants of the embassy's supper, Coryn told Harol about everything they'd gone through before reaching their exit into the vagha embassy.

"You were absolutely correct to come find me." Harol patted Coryn's back. "This has to be kept a secret. People should never know that the entrance to the Magestorm cache is right under the dwarven embassy."

"A problem still remains; I need to know how to open the earth and extract the cache." Coryn shivered. "I can't just leave it accessible to anybody."

"I'm not sure how to help." Harol shook his head slowly. "I don't think any single wizard could melt the earth and force the cache out. Trying to dig for it would require scores of workers and would certainly attract unwanted attention to the cache."

"Then what would you suggest we do?" Garesch sat at the edge of his chair.

"The only course of action I can see is to return to Balgavarr. Enlist several wizards for the task and return with them to extract the items," Harol said. "I think you need no less than four wizards to perform this feat." He looked at Coryn, his head tilted askew. "Certainly your father will lend them to you?"

She bit her lip, confirming Harol's suspicions.

"Alright, then," he promised. "We will keep it secret and keep it safe. You should be able to convince a few to join you if you motivate them properly and privately. Your father need not be told."

Coryn nodded. "Then that is what we will do." She stood and addressed her companions. "We have to leave immediately."

"Now? In the depth of night?" Harol stared at her with wide eyes. "Please, spend the night here and go in the morning."

"No. We can't," Ra'al said in a rough voice. "We need every moment we can spare. The trip is too long as it is. But perhaps, since we are dealing with spell casters, we can have them return us more quickly with a Path spell. That would cut the return voyage from days to mere minutes."

Quick goodbyes were traded, and the travelers headed into the darkened Tulgesh streets.

Chapter 17

"We have no time to dally," Garesch said and strapped his pack onto his back. "Fly with Coryn to Balgavarr. We will meet you at the same place we camped before, unless you can act swiftly—then you can collect us along the main road we observed from the Sareen River."

Ra'al nodded. They did not know how long it would take to quietly secure the necessary thaumaturgists to recover the cache.

"No." Coryn stood with her face red, tight lips, and a grim demeanor. "You will meet us at the gates of Balgavarr."

Garesch stopped cold. "Are you sure that is wise?"

"I think what *could* be done and what *should* be done has long become unimportant." Coryn strapped her gear on as Ra'al grabbed her. He started to take to the air as she called, "We will meet you at the gates, if not sooner."

After they were airborne, Coryn said, "There is no doubt that the undead have already penetrated Tulgesh." She clutched Ra'al's collar as he gained still more altitude. "The smell of spices in Naemyar's house confirmed it. I think they might be watching the moves of all influential people in the city; we are lucky our ambassador has escaped their notice, so far."

Ra'al shouted against the wind, "I think your father could shed more light on the matter." He flapped his wings, determined to make record speed. "We should disclose everything to him."

Coryn fell silent and stayed that way for a long while. To tell Geril meant admitting she violated his wishes. Though Ra'al was certain that she had heard him, he added, "This entire thing has spun out of control. We can no longer accomplish our task without the help of others."

"Aye," Coryn finally said; though her voice cracked with sorrow. She tried to keep the wind from making her eyes water and convinced herself that was the reason for her tears, and not that she would have to face her father. "We may need to come clean."

The morehl would journey along the Sareen Road, which ran mostly adjacent to the river. Their trip was three hundred leagues to Balgavarr and made a four tenday journey by foot at a brisk pace. They'd likely stop to purchase mounts and cut that in half. Bypassing the road and flying direct cut that distance considerably; the added speed that ignored elevation meant Ra'al could make the trip in only a few days.

Their trip went as quickly as possible. They stopped to rest as needed, but moved with purpose enough that they made great speed. Soon, the dwarven home was in sight.

Ra'al landed in front of the gates of Balgavarr Reaches and let Coryn down from his arms. They entered the city with haste and pushed their way through the city's busy marketplace. Light streamed in through the opening further up the slope where the lookout balcony was and illuminated the traders' square.

An attaché of a councilman bumped into Coryn as she led Ra'al through.

"Coryn Sa'Geril, welcome home." The elder vagha smiled through his creased face's folds.

Coryn recognized him as a member of House Kiyh, like Harol and his father Lahmyn. They were one of Balgavarr's older families and owned a large operation that harvested iron leaf, the weighty folioles that fell from the ironwood trees and which sprang up around the Kafnysan Mountains. Historically, they were a rival family that tried to discredit her father when she was young, but aside from Harol's appointment, she had not heard much of them in years. Besides them being political sticks-in-the-mud.

She assumed that either they had buried the axe during her last fifteen years in Icehome or else Harol had turned out considerably different than the rest of his house in order to gain the appointed post in Tulgesh. The latter made more sense, she decided, since Harol had only mentioned House Kiyh once in the entire time she'd known him; he hadn't depended on his family's name to make something of himself.

Coryn smiled politely. "Thank you, sir."

"So, what brings you home?" the elder asked slyly.

"I came to seek a meeting with my father." Coryn looked past the elder's shoulder, trying to disengage from him. "It is an emergency and I must find him straight away."

"All right," he said slowly. "And I see you have brought your frostwing guard along."

Ra'al smiled widely, making sure to catch the light of the lamps against his shiny fangs. He growled as if he was a simpleton. "We eat. We Coryn friend. We fight." He felt certain the dwarf did not understand his sarcasm.

The elder took three steps back. "Coryn, keep your frostwing at bay. I think it wants to harm me."

"Sorry, they are very hungry." Coryn stifled a laugh and kept a straight face. "And they consider older creatures to have the highest nutrition value."

The elder gave them a final look, pulled the hem of his robe above his knee, and started hurrying in another direction.

Coryn and Ra'al laughed as he hustled all the way towards the throne room. The humor only momentarily distracted Coryn from the twisting knot in her gut. She had to own up to her actions before her father sooner than she had prepared.

They arrived at the heart of Balgavarr and paused at the doors. Geril was in deep conversation with his five armored guards.

Coryn took a deep breath and then approached him.

Geril caught sight of her in his peripheral. He finished his whispered orders and the armored dwarves departed. Geril rushed and took Coryn in his arms. Before he could welcome her, Coryn started to cry.

She mumbled through her tears and sobbed something unintelligible into his shoulder.

"Coryn." He held her at arm's length. "What is wrong?"

She cried for some moments as Ra'al tried to avoid the searching eyes of the vaghan king, who he'd long considered an uncle. Ra'al felt the same guilt as Coryn, and then some; he was older than Coryn, after all, and was supposed to be wiser.

"Father, I passed the Tulgesh maze and reached the Magestorm cache." Coryn sniffled.

Waves of different expressions traveled across Geril's face. "You already reclaimed it from the earth?"

"No, father." She sniffled some more. "We couldn't reach it; I did not have the foresight to bring casters capable of transmuting the stone to mud."

"Did you leave enough guards at the entrance, then?" Geril's voice wavered.

"We notified the vaghan emissary in town, and he told us he would guard the exit and keep it secret. We were not seen entering the dungeon." Coryn finally took a handkerchief and dried her eyes.

"Not the wisest move, daughter." Geril shook his head as he tightened his lips. "But at least Ty'Rassal sa'Melluhn has a wise enough head to handle the situation. He might even bury the exit altogether to prevent access along the simplest route."

"Rassal?" Coryn stopped drying her nose. "That is not the emissary."

Geril trembled as he squeezed each of Coryn's shoulders tightly. "There is no other ambassador to Tulgesh! Coryn, who did you disclose the location of the cache to?"

Coryn looked at her father with wide eyes and quivering lips. Ra'al wore almost the same expression; a sinking feeling lodged in the pit of his stomach.

"I left it in the care of Harol Sa'Lahmyn," Coryn said with a trembling voice. "He said he was our emissary to Tulgesh?"

Geril choked on her words. He grabbed Coryn's arm and started running with her, and Ra'al followed after. Geril dragged Coryn through countless corridors until they ended up in the king's quarters.

He dropped Coryn's arm, and she rubbed it in silence. Geril sucked deep, ragged breaths in an attempt to calm himself.

Coryn and Ra'al stood in silence until the older vagha composed himself.

"Listen, daughter, I would have accepted your choice to access the cache," Geril said and took a long breath. "I could even have accepted it if you'd left it unguarded, but in secrecy."

Geril exhaled with a grunt. "But handing the location to Ki'Harol sa'Lahmyn whose family plotted and planned against us for years is a grave error."

Geril balled his hands to fists, and then he dropped them in exasperation. "What were you thinking? That a vagha of House Kiyh would keep his promise? That he would ignore the opportunity to obtain the most powerful items on Esfah for his own?"

"But Harol is not like his father, Lahmyn. He is a scholar, an esteemed member of the community." Coryn's fingers knotted and released repeatedly. "He is not like the rest of them."

"Of course, he isn't," Geril spat the words. "He is *far worse* than all of them. He was banished for dabbling in Death magic. Harol Sa'Lahmyn is a traitor to his own kind, worse still, he could be an agent of Death himself and we've long suspected he is an Acolyte—one who has forsaken the gods of his heritage in order to worship another."

Coryn stepped back in the face of Geril's rage. Her eyes widened as she realized the gravity of her mistake. *Harol had set her up from their first meeting.*

"And who told you that Harol was the emissary?" Geril paced the length of his apartment.

"He was present in the gala at Naemyar's. He introduced himself as the emissary to Tulgesh." Coryn swallowed. "Everybody in the gala seemed to recognize him."

Geril halted. "What gala?"

He shuffled towards his desk, a place where Geril did far more to advance Balgavarr's causes than the throne room. Coryn explained the socialite queen's party as her father found a stack of papers: communications sent between Tulgesh and the vaghan crown. Geril scowled as he sorted through an older letter and then a newer one..

"The foul wizard may have done far more damage in that gala," Geril sighed and dropped the two letters. "At some point in the last several months, Rassal's signature has changed; I should have noticed. We will discuss this later, Coryn. Right now, we must hurry back to secure the cache."

"I am sorry," Ra'al said softly. "But how come it was not announced that Harol was a traitor and a possible agent of Death?"

The older vagha sighed heavily and shook his head. "My dear Ra'al, sometimes the world of house politics is filled with traitorous negotiations and clandestine cover-ups." He leaned heavily on his desk. "I made a wrong call back then; I should have publicly exposed him ten years ago when we first discovered traitors in House Kiyh. Gods know, I've still got one of them seated on the council, festering like a cancer, just waiting for an opportunity…Harol's father," he mumbled.

Geril rubbed his forehead and then raked out his beard. "Now, I regret not exposing that evil dwarf for what he is, and because of that, he might be already in possession of the weapons."

"What should we do, then?" asked Ra'al. "We came originally seeking to borrow vaghan magicians for a transmutation spell." Ra'al exhaled hard. "We didn't expect any of this."

"You will have your wizards. And I am joining you as well." The king stood to his full height. "It is high time I left my desk and letters behind and took up my father's weapon again. This time, if I find Harol, you can believe he'll feel the edge of my axe."

They followed Geril as he stormed out of his apartment and into a long hall where items were hung in memorial to the vaghan heroes of old.

Geril sa'Ghuren snatched the weapon mounted in a place of honor. "Rest assured, this time it won't be merely trog or dragon blood that Thunderfist's axe draws."

Geril sent for two of his most talented wizards and three of his closest guards. He also summoned Warlord Kile, the military commander of Balgavarr's home defenses and the dwarf who had held the line as Geril and the other vagha, frostwings, and ghwereste pressed the attack during the old war.

Kile raised an eyebrow when he recognized Geril's royal armor peeking out from beneath the loose-fitting travelers' cloak. His eyes flitted only briefly to Old Thunder. The nickname dwarves had given the axe wielded by Zephras Thunderfist, a weapon that had killed at least two dragons in its history. Warlord Kile said nothing, but his eyes glistened with understanding that a grave situation had developed.

Geril and Kile had formed a deep trust in the aftermath of the battle and Kile had become one of Geril's most trusted peers. He swore the warlord to secrecy and appointed him as his steward until he returned.

Together, with Coryn and Ra'al, they left the city without announcing anything to the public. They hoped that nothing would go amiss while Kile managed Geril's affairs.

Coryn remained silent the entire time. Ra'al didn't want to intrude on her dour mood. After all, he felt much the same way. His mind replayed the facts. Why had they not gone to Naemyar for counsel instead of Harol? He'd had his suspicions of Harol since their first meeting—especially after the way he'd met with Lotep, who Ra'al suspected may have been a spy.

He walked bent for most of the way back to the road towards Tulgesh. Ra'al feared returning to find the cache gone, and he feared the consequences of the coming war. He was only certain of the cold and coming wind; even if he couldn't hear its song, he could feel it in his bones.

Ra'al and the others moved through the shadows as much as possible, taking back alleys, hallways, and moving in general secrecy. He noticed that the magicians had, at some point, abandoned them.

By the time they were outside, the magicians arrived beyond Balgavarr's gates. Their path spell emerged from the ground like an eggshell being forced up from the soil. The sphere of thin stone broke as those inside the path spell arrived. Geril's vaghan casters had done the math to calculate where along the Sareen Road the morehl would be. The casters had gone south and retrieved them.

Garesch threw his arms into the air after Coryn informed them of Harol's treachery. "So, we went through all of this for nothing? The only advantage we had in this war has now fallen into the hands of the enemy."

"We are not certain that Harol has claimed the cache yet." Geril let out a slow breath. "We can only hope that he hasn't gathered the magical skills needed to unearth the cache."

"What if his accomplices have those skills?" Garesch paced anxiously.

"We can be certain that he is part of some death cabal." Geril scoffed. "Gods know they have plenty of foolish people to spare." He scowled. "Acolytes find their own: those who change their allegiance from one nature to worship another and forswear the gods they were born to. If he has Death acolytes, we know they cannot cast magic that will soften the earth for him."

They all fell silent for some minutes. It should have been good news, but Harol's aptitude for black magic did not encourage them.

"King Geril." Garesch looked at the others as if taking permission. "Tell us what to do and we will do it."

"Our only path ends in war, and it starts in Tulgesh," Geril stated with cryptic words.

Ra'al had a thought. "Pardon, King Geril," he asked. "We forgot to ask about our friend, Bastawr. He should have arrived at Balgavarr some days ago." The frostwing briefly explained Bastawr's mission.

"I am sorry, Ra'al, he never showed up." Geril shook his head sadly. "But he is a ghwereste, I am certain he will be fine. My only concern right now is these artifacts—if there is army ready to use them, then all the more reason we must act swiftly."

Ra'al nodded, but he was entirely convinced that simply being beastfolk would not spare Bastawr whatever hardships had befallen him.

The dwarven spell casters clutched their sightstones and summoned all their energies as the travelers clustered together. "Focus on the path, and on Eldurim's grace," said the lead crafter to all who were vagha. They had to maximize their arcane energies to summon a path for a group their size.

Bubbles of stone enveloped them and they could feel the inertial shift as they shuttled through the ground by the grace of the earth god, Eldurim. The feeling of movement eventually petered out, and they came to a stop. In groups of three and four, the travelers broke free from the spherical pods that had transported them.

The walls of Tulgesh rose only a little ways' back.

A few hundred cubits beyond, another stony sphere arose to the side of the road. Coryn's father did a brief head count after the bubbles had each ruptured to account for each of their party members.

Geril clutched his axe and approached the sphere, unsure what it might contain; the entire party had arrived alongside him. His guards walked with him, weapons readied.

The dwarf smashed the shell and broke it open to reveal the form of a half-starved tigerfolk. Ra'al thought it looked a lot like Bastawr, only this ghwereste was much scrawnier and had earned many wounds.

Upon seeing Ra'al, the tigerfolk smiled. "Thank you," he declared wearily. "I had no idea how to escape this bubble."

It was Bastawr. The thought ran through Ra'al's mind. *This couldn't be just a mere coincidence; it must be a miracle arranged by the gods.*

Ra'al, Coryn, and Garesch rushed to the tigerfolk.

"Is this your friend?" Geril asked his daughter, who checked over the wounds on Bastawr's body and head.

Coryn nodded.

"My pardon," Bastawr said. "I must have just missed you. I found Warlord Kile who had a caster send me to Tulgesh…I've not had rest or a meal for more than a tenday."

"Sheron," Geril called to one of the wizards. "Can you heal the ghwereste?"

The wizard nodded and moved between the frostwing and the tigerfolk. "Please, clear a space for me to tend to his wounds."

Some ten minutes later, the wizard stood. "I did all I could. He will retain a scar or two. What he needs more than anything is a night's rest and a heavy meal with plenty of meat."

Bastawr laid panting on the ground, but Ra'al noticed that tigerfolk already looked far better than he first did.

"I have horrible news." Bastawr gripped Ra'al's embrace and pulled himself up. "We don't have much time."

"Did Yarichek give the map to my father?" Garesch stood beside Ra'al as he asked the tigerfolk.

"No. He gave it to an undead knight." Bastawr looked around him. "They have a huge army. They dug something up… something they called the mist stones."

"The gods spare us." Coryn held her hand to her mouth. "They dug up a mist stone?"

"But that is not what I risked my life to warn you about," Bastawr cut off Coryn. "They have an immense army. The undead have been plotting for centuries—the war for Balgavarr was merely a blip in their numbers. I think they plan to attack any day."

Everybody looked at Bastawr for several seconds. Dark silence fell over them.

"Do you have any idea if they have mobilized?" Geril asked the tigerfolk. "And if they've mobilized, then where to?"

"I am not sure." Bastawr shook his head. "I lost them at the edge of the mist after attacking their leaders. I did not stop till I reached Balgavarr Reaches." He took a deep breath.

"Praise the gods." Coryn bowed for a moment.

"Accompany us into Tulgesh," Garesch suggested and looked to the others for approval.

Geril extended his hand to Bastawr. "Welcome aboard, Bastawr. I fought alongside your grandfather."

They approached the gates to the Cyrea's premiere coral city. The travelers broke into smaller clusters and headed towards the gate.

"You are king of Balgavarr," Coryn told her father. "Why can you not simply enter as royalty—surely King Matrek will speed our efforts?"

Geril frowned. "You said the undead have at least some presence in the city." He walked in the shadow of the bastion walls. "We don't want to attract attention before the time is right."

A bubble of stone emerged before their eyes. One very confused frostwing crawled out from the soil, gasping for air as he clawed his way out from the egg-like shell. He clambered from the magic vessel and hurried to Ra'al's side like a scared pup.

The frostwing bowed to the prince, and they spoke in their native tongue.

Ra'al's face changed color, and he turned to face Geril. "My mother wanted this message to reach your ears." He took a ragged breath. "Hordes of undead are marching across the Tundra and mustering for war between Balgavarr and Icehome."

Ra'al started to unfold his wings.

"What are you doing?" Geril shouted at him.

"I have to go back my people." Ra'al clenched his hands. "I can't leave them to face the undead alone."

Geril held Ra'al's arm gently. "We have to get to the cache, Ra'al, and we have to seek the aid of the selumari on Icehome's behalf. Nobody has the authority to do that like you do."

"But…" Ra'al tried to object.

"We will leave Tulgesh before daybreak." Geril held Ra'al's arm. "I promise you, we will reach Icehome in time, if there *is* still time."

"So, our objective in Tulgesh becomes more difficult, yet again," Coryn stated flatly. She asked, "Are adventures always this challenging, father?"

Geril nodded and exhaled a long-held breath. "Yes," he admitted. "And war is calling all of us back together, and again we face impossible odds."

Chapter 18

The city streets became considerably more crowded as the secret travelers entered Tulgesh.

Geril looked at the familiar structures with pride. His people helped rebuild them after the war with Uruzak. But he didn't pause to show the others as they passed through; they were on a mission, and that did not include sightseeing.

He led the party through the streets of Tulgesh. Not far into the city, movement through the streets became nearly impossible. An angry mob of local dwarves shouted and waved their axes.

The leading dwarf screamed at a selumari guard. "You are doing nothing! Don't mock me with your worthless words, elf. We demand action!"

"This is guard business. Disperse now and leave us to our duty." The guard shook his spear at him. "We are going to catch the culprit, just keep out of our way."

"It is a bloody massacre, that's what it is." The dwarf continued rousing the crowd. "Vaghan wizards must be called. They are the only ones capable of finding this killer. The council and the King Dragonsbane must be notified."

"Our own wizards are more than capable of handling this, and they are on the way, if you will back up and allow them to reach the embassy." The guard banged the butt of his spear repeatedly against the cobblestone at the feet of the vagha. "And your king will be notified, but this is not our business. This is a matter for the authorities."

The dwarf did not take lightly to the veiled threat from the selumari and his spear. He snarled and clanged his axe against the shaft of his weapon, pushing the guard backward.

Recoiling, the guard aimed the tip of his polearm at the dwarf's head. "If you don't disperse right this instant, we will have to expel all vagha from the city—on the tips of our spears if necessary!"

The mob cried even louder and axes swung through the air; the sound of crossbows locking quarrels into place clicked ominously. Coral elf guards issued a readying shout and lowered the visors of their helmets as they aimed their spears to a ready position against the vaghan mob.

Geril's face twisted with dismay. The situation had gotten out of hand, and any bloodshed could be cause for more discord between Balgavarr and Tulgesh. Right now, they needed unity more than ever.

Casting off his cloak and revealing his royal armor, Geril pushed his way through the mob until he reached the forefront where the vagha and selumari guards squared off.

Geril raised his voice. "Put your axes down!" he commanded his citizens.

The dwarves recognized Geril the moment they saw him. Some cheered; many lowered their axes. They were perhaps the stubbornest race on Esfah, and even a command from their king could barely restrain those yearning to fight.

"Here comes Dragonsbane," a dwarf shouted.

Another yelled, "King Geril will handle this matter!"

A host of other insults flew at the selumari enforcers, aimed by instigators emboldened by Geril's presence.

"What is going on here?" Geril looked from the guards to the vaghan mob.

The dwarf leading the uprising spoke up, "A massacre, King Geril! More dwarves killed in a single night than in the war for Balgavarr."

Geril had been in that war. He knew that was hardly possible and detected exaggeration in the speaker's voice.

"Balgavarr's embassy was attacked in the dark of night. It must have been the coral elves! They never liked us anyway." One vagha waved his axe as spittle flew from his mouth. "Our brothers were slaughtered and they won't even let us see our kin."

The captain of the elven guard bent to whisper to the king. "There was a break-in at the embassy and the residents were all killed. We've not had time to investigate." The guard spoke in a desperate tone, "But Your Majesty, I assure you that we will find the culprit, whoever they might be and of whatever race they are." He stopped short when the vagha pressed forward and waved their axes.

Geril nodded and stretched his lips tight. He turned and addressed the crowd, "I am here now. I will get to the bottom of this. We will find the culprits and avenge the fallen," he shouted . "Go back to your lives; return to your trades. I will handle this personally."

Faces in the mob looked at Geril. One by one they nodded, rapped their fists to their chests, and then slowly filed away. Only the loudest instigator at the front remained. He bowed.

"King Geril, I am your humble servant, Fargan." He pointed to his chest. "My brother-in-law worked in the embassy as a guard."

He paused and pulled off his helmet to show a few remaining strands of hair that had not yet gone grey. "He was a good kid; he didn't deserve to die like that. Done for like a dog." The dwarf took a deep breath and continued in a ragged voice, "he just wanted to serve his people, Your Highness-ship."

Fargan stopped for some moments as he searched Geril's eyes. "Please, do avenge him for the sake of my grieving sister." He bowed deeply, then he left.

Coryn rushed to her father's side as Fargan left. She whispered, "surely this is the work of Harol?"

Geril held her shoulder by both arms and stared hard into her eyes. "Run to his house and check if he is there." Geril then turned to Garesch. "We need Naemyar to be present. Can you send one of your men to call her to the embassy?"

"Aye, Your Majesty." Garesch turned, called Werdth, and sent him running.

Then Geril called one of his guards, pulled a parchment and a quill from his pack, and scribbled something quickly. He rolled it and placed it in the hand of the guard. "Take this to King Matrek on my behalf, we might be running out of time."

With Ra'al and the rest of his party in tow, Geril marched to the embassy, followed all the way through by the selumari guards from the altercation.

The embassy looked normal from the outside, except there were no vaghan sentries posted at the entry. The lack of guards at the door spoke volumes to Geril; there was supposed to be a minimum of two posts at all times.

A coral elf inspector from their marshal's office met them and followed them in.

Passing through the threshold, Ra'al sneezed.

Geril shot him an askew look.

"The spicy smell… It is here. Marnash thinks it is a sign of an undead spy." Ra'al sniffled and then knotted his forehead. "It is ten times stronger here than in any other place I've been."

Geril nodded grimly.

From the entrance, they walked to the main reception chamber, which doubled as the meeting room for gentries. Inside, six vagha lay in pools of blood that spread macabre entrails along grout lines of the tiled floor.

Geril advanced alone with the rest standing by the door. He walked between the bodies slowly, staring at the faces of each one of them, as if memorizing their features. He finally knelt beside one of them; the dead dwarf looked older than most vagha, even older than the elders back in Balgavarr.

The king let out a sigh and held the deceased's hand for some moments, nodding to nobody present.

"They were killed more than half a day ago." Geril stood, clenching his fists. "He is completely stiff." He turned to the guard. "I assume that these other dwarves were killed more recently. Their stiffness hasn't set into their bodies yet."

A coral elf inspector looked apprehensive as he nodded to Geril.

Geril pointed to the wounds on the body of the dead vagha. "These were done by an axe." He puffed the air out of his chest. "And from the look of it, whoever killed him, had the same height." He pointed to the angle of the wound and to where it started.

The guard nodded again, and Geril assumed that the guard concurred.

"There is no sign of Ambassador Rassal?" the king asked.

Gulping, the coral elf in charge nodded and led the way to the back of the estate, where a long hallway terminated in a busted wall and a closed storage room. His face blanched as he swung the door open to reveal the dismembered, rotting corpse of the dwarven ambassador.

Ra'al plugged his nose with his fingers and muttered something about dry aging.

Coryn found them, panting; she'd done a quick search of the building. "No sign of Harol, or any of his servants." She paused and panted a bit more. "They've even taken the furniture from a few rooms."

"This is odd," Garesch commented. "Not even furniture?"

"Not so odd," Marnash stated. "I've heard rumors of wizards who can track a person by sniffing their belongings. Some are so accurate, they say they can tell you where in Esfah they are and what they are wearing."

"He's likely heard the same tales and hatched this plan the moment you told him," Geril spoke to Coryn, but did not meet her eyes.

Someone cried out in the front of the house, "Gods, have mercy on us!"

They found Naemyar in the reception area accompanied by Werdth and two of the queen's own guards. She wore an ashen face and averted her eyes from the blood. "Who could have done this?" She shook with both rage and fear.

"Ki'Harol Sa'Lahmyn," Geril said. He gave her a stiff bow and acknowledged her position. "It has been long since we've seen each other."

"King Geril," Naemyar curtsied. "It has been indeed."

"I am sure you are aware that my daughter led an expedition to find the weapon depository from the Magestorm Wars." Geril talked as he led the group towards the sublevel. He put up a hand to leave all the other selumari guards behind. "This is Balgavarr's jurisdiction."

The guard stretched his lips thinly across his face, but bowed and ordered his men back.

Only Naemyar followed with the rest. "I am aware of the story and of Coryn's wish to unearth the weapons, but she did not disclose the location of the fabled cache." Naemyar walked slowly beside the dwarven king.

"Well, they found it. It was under our very feet…until recently." Geril reached the door in the long hall. One of his personal guards walked a little further onward and closed the door to shut off the stench emanating from what remained of Rassal's body.

A twisting stair began a few cubits below a steep drop where it was hidden in the wall. "Coryn and her team couldn't unearth the weapons at the end of the maze, and so they went to Harol, assuming that he could help them with the earth magic required."

One of the wizards produced a light ball and let it float above their heads as they accessed the dark sub-levels. Three more bodies lay slain at the lip of the lift; they each looked like earth-crafters, dwarves who specialized in Eldurim's magic.

Geril approached one of the bodies and solemnly closed the dwarf's open eyes. At the base of the steps were the lift controls.

"The lift can't carry all of us in one go." Geril pointed to the trapdoor in the ground. "I will go with one wizard, Coryn, and Ra'al, then I will send it back for the rest." He paused for a moment. "That is, if anything remains."

Coryn, Geril, and Ra'al operated the wheels to take the lift downward. Just as the lift stopped, the wizard created another globe of light and let it float into the massive chamber.

In the center of the room, a gaping hole yawned open. It still dripped with muddy vestiges of the transmutation.

Geril walked slowly towards it and stood gazing into the abyss. "Is there anything left?" He looked to the wizard who nodded, knelt, and placed his hand on the lip of the hole. "I sense some magic there, yet."

They descended into a large room; five times bigger than the one they came from. They delved further into the pit and found broken strongboxes and crates.

Geril remembered the racks of magic arrows, blades, and larger weapons stored in closet-like rooms which contained deactivated blade golems, magic carpets, and other extremely rare artifacts.

"There is a single room that was not disturbed." The wizard took Geril's hand and stood. "I can open into it if you wish."

"Please do." Geril rubbed his eyes and sighed. "Let's see what Harol left us, shall we?"

Coryn and Ra'al stood stock still, as silent as could be.

Over the next minutes, the wizard concentrated on a point southeast of the original hole, laying both his hands flat on the ground.

Then, the earth started to change form; the ground melted and boiled.

The liquid ground parted and slowly formed a narrow staircase that descended into the darkness.

When he finished, the wizard took Geril's hand once more to steady himself. He straightened and called the ball of light to precede them down the steps.

Around the perimeter of the room, lockers stood waiting, untouched by the hands of mortals for nearly a dozen centuries.

Geril went to the first locker, opened it, and found some leather-bound manuscripts. "These are volumes from the original

Book of The Land, priceless, but worthless to the likes of Harol." Geril spat on the ground.

He pointed to the rest of the people who went down with him. "Open the other lockers and check what is inside."

Ra'al and Coryn rushed to the locker, evidently glad to have something to do.

The party found that most of the lockers contained little but dust. The rest contained books, some of them the wizard caressed with a smile. "Those are books from the library of Yentosh, priceless tomes of knowledge lost to Esfah decades ago."

Coryn pulled another huge book and read the title aloud, *"Drakyntatsu's Sphere?"* She opened it to pages containing maps and directions to several parts of Esfah, plus several strange astrological maps as well.

The wizard almost ran to take the book from her hands. He looked at the binding, then flipped to the last page, where his smile widened. "This is the second edition copy." He hugged the book along with the others he amassed in his arms. "Another priceless find, although the first edition would have been even better. It contained a map to the Eternal Lands, which the author claimed to have visited by Tarvanehl's power. Most copies have been destroyed."

The search continued.

Ra'al produced some strange items. The wizard touched them and searched his senses. Finally, he declared that they were not magical.

The frostwing prince found and fidgeted with a cube of interlocking plates that bore intricate designs. He shrugged and then set it down, assuming it was some kind of child's toy that had been left with the rest. Coryn picked it up to inspect it, trying to find a way to open the puzzle cube.

Geril opened a locker that contained a warhammer and an armor set sized for a vagha. He piled them at the end of the room near the stairs. Another locker contained an assortment of daggers, which Coryn added to the pile started by her father.

Yet another locker had an assortment of pendants and rings. The wizard rushed to scoop them up. "All of these items will amplify a sorcerer's power far more than a sightstone."

The wizard held one up to inspect it. "This one would double the casting abilities of most magic-users," he said and pocketed it.

Geril collected the rest of the gnome-made jewelry and placed them in his pockets. He shook his head at the cleverness of the gremmlobahnd, who had crafted such items in the First Age…damned weapons that had nearly split Esfah open during the legendary Magestorm Wars. He cast an eye across the room, remembering how much more there had been when he'd first buried it all those years ago, hoping to prevent these items from falling into the wrong hands.

The last locker contained three swords, an axe, and a bow, all of which were made from a strange green material, and all had a subtle glow. Ra'al piled those with the other weapons at the pile near the stairs.

After all the lockers were opened, Geril called the wizard. "Are any other rooms around us that remain sealed?"

The wizard shook his head. "I am sorry, King Geril, this is all that remained."

Geril nodded and sighed. "Let us return, then," he said and began to load the lift with the others.

When they had finished stacking everything, they ascended and unloaded the lift.

"So, the treasure is intact?" Naemyar looked from Coryn to Geril.

Geril shook his head. "Sadly, no. This is all we found. The rest of it, nearly a hundred times this amount, is gone."

Naemyar put her hand to her mouth and caught her breath. "I knew when I couldn't locate Rashmar this morning that something was awry."

"Who is Rashmar?" Coryn asked her.

"He was a dwarf introduced to me by Ambassa…by Harol." Naemyar shook her head and corrected, subtly reminding the others that she, too, had been duped. "Rashmar claimed to be a scholar researching the Magestorm Histories." She drew in a ragged breath. "He gained much knowledge from me, though I should have thought the timing suspicious."

"Your Highness, do not blame yourself." Coryn touched her arm. "That traitor Harol fooled us all."

Garesch approached Geril quietly. "King Geril." He cleared his throat. "What do you plan to do with these weapons?"

"I will give them away." Geril looked at the pile of weapons. "But they should go to the front of the battle at Icehome. This task has been thrust on me, twice." Geril looked at the weapons as if they were a pile of snakes, then he shook his head and turned his back on them, wanting nothing more to do with them.

As Naemyar approached the mound, a trumpet echoed outside the embassy building.

Selumari guards filed into the embassy soon after, followed by King Matrek.

The coral elf king bent his head to acknowledge Geril. "So, this is a fabled treasure of the Magestorm Wars?" He walked around the pile for several moments. He scowled, "I find it quite modest."

Geril bent his head to the same degree and sighed. He'd intentionally kept the treasure from Matrek for decades, fearing the zealous coral elf would use them to advance Tulgesh at his neighbor's expense. "This is what is left of the treasure; the rest has been stolen."

The selumari stiffened. "King Geril, we need to talk," he said with a tight jaw.

Geril nodded. "Aye, King Matrek, we do, and formalities be damned. Now would be favorable as time is of the essence."

Chapter 19

The wind hit Harol's face with the salty sting of the sea.

Seagulls croaked their usual calls as they circled his ship, the ocean pulling beyond the harbor.

Twelve horses gave their lives for him to make last night's harbor run; he'd worked the beasts to death. But it was worth it. What was the value of stupid animals compared to the worth of the treasure stowed in the belly of a ship?

Harol laughed, recalling the stupidity of Geril's daughter. She had practically handed him the treasure without his ever having to ask for it.

He knew that he didn't have much time and the moment she left his house with her ragtag team of misfits, he sprang into action. Harol sent a message to the secret Death cabal in Tulgesh, and the rest was history. He'd also had to trick more than a few vaghan spell crafters and swear them to secrecy on the premise they were "doing the king's business." He personally killed each one of them by the end. Only the dead kept secrets with any efficiency, though his axe arm still felt sore from all the effort.

The ship rocked and a splash of seawater sprayed Harol's beard. He cursed and swore against the clumsiness of Ry'Ober. She might have been the most resourceful privateer in the sea, but she did not take a care for the comfort of her guests. People were merely cargo to her.

Still, Harol smiled. The lady pirate carried a lot of unsavory qualities, but her ship was the fastest, and because of that, they were already tens of leagues beyond Tulgesh.

He anticipated the look on Leisterbane's dead face when he dropped this treasure in his lap. Harol stopped smiling and contemplated the lack of facial expression on the undead lord. But the smile crept again on his face. He could now demand the eternal life promised to the most favored of Lord Death's servants.

Harol savored the name of Lord Death, *Malgrimm.* For others, the name was a curse that should not be spoken, but to him, it was his hope for something more than a mortal existence.

A wave rocked the ship mightily. Harol cried, "Bring it on, Nature! I fear you not."

Ry'Ober approached the elated Harol and cleared her throat. "Ki'Harol Sa'Lahmyn."

"What do you want of me?" Harol turned with glaring eyes.

"You are certain of your destination? It is a barren and desolate bay." Ry'Ober looked at him. "You know they suspect your trove has great value, and to throw it away by dumping it on the shore does not sit well with..."

Harol strung a chain of colorful words. "The destination is correct."

"You are sure?" Ry'Ober repeated her question. "The crew is considering leaving you to die in the barrens. Abandoning a priceless treasure upon the north shores is insanity."

"I know what I asked for, Ry'Ober." Harol raked the salt from his beard. "Your sailors were paid well for this mission, but if they need further convincing, you may return to our first drop point where we will leave half the treasure. Feel free to take it then, but only *after* you have ferried me and the second half to Dereh'Liandor."

Ry'Ober fixed Harol with a stern look. Finally, she nodded. "I believe that will assuage their concerns."

"I know my business and where I am going, and your crew should not mention it again." Harol pointed to his ears. "The wind has ears."

Ry'Ober nodded and left Harol to stand by the rail laughing to himself like a mad man. A single thought circled in his mind. They will never know; they will never find out.

He laughed so loud that the sailor stationed at the top of the mast peered down to look at him.

Still, Harol chuckled until he could hardly breathe.

"All right, Geril, what is going on?" Matrek paced the room adjacent the dwarf king and his mixed company. They met in the upper floor of the vaghan embassy, where they were far enough removed that the stench of death did not reach them.

Geril puffed a blast of hot air through his nose. "It's exactly what it looks like: a massacre and the theft of the Magestorm weapon cache."

"Listen to me, Geril," Matrek said and waved his stiffened index finger. "I have tolerated much from your vagha over the years." Matrek's eyes creased into crows' feet. "Your builders changed as you saw fit, you placed this embassy in front of the palace, and you've denied me access to this cursed cache even when we needed it most—and that fact has been a thorn between us for decades and it has cost selumari lives, vaghan ones too, over our lifetimes."

Geril set his jaw. "It all boils down to that, doesn't it, Matrek? You hold an old grudge because of this weapon cache, even though you knew how dangerous it could be."

"You hid them so well that even I believed them destroyed, as you told me they were, so how in festration was it stolen?" Matrek shouted. "And by whom?" He took a long breath. "Did you let your secret slip in some drunken squabble as you Balgavarrians are known for in my city?"

"You know Matrek, under different circumstances, I might take the dwarven army and level your whole wretched city, but I need you. And you need me." Geril faced Matrek and slumped his shoulders. "The undead are coming—they were not all destroyed on the slopes of Balgavarr when Morguus Ebraxus fell. Death's forces are at our door."

"What kind of nonsense are you spewing?" Matrek threw his hands in the air. "The sightings of the undead are sporadic and inconsequential. I receive regular briefings from my advisers on the issue."

"Geril speaks the truth," Ra'al said after his long silence. "My mother, Queen Rashingot, sent a messenger to tell us that the undead are emerging from the wastes and gathering upon the tundra."

Behind him, the only other frostwing in the room nodded with grave agreement.

Matrek stared at Ra'al for some moments; something like recognition flashed in his eyes. "You are Thrag's son, are you not?"

"I am," Ra'al spoke with a voice like iron. He returned an equally hard stare to the coral elf ruler.

Matrek stared at Ra'al for a moment, then turned back to Geril. "Who took the cache?" He narrowed eyes.

"We assume it was an acolyte of Death." Geril sighed. "A banished dwarf named Ki'Harol Sa'Lahmyn."

"Harol, your ex-emissary?" Matrek's eyes widened in surprise.

"He never was one. Harol is a skilled liar and his falsehoods cultivated a position in your society. He used that fake position to glean details from my daughter and access the cache." Geril grit his teeth. "He is nothing more than a traitor and a menace."

Matrek looked down. Resignation set in. "Can we retrieve what he took?"

"Maybe. I don't know if we have the time to pursue him." Geril released a ragged breath. "We have to ready ourselves for war."

"What do you need to retrieve them?" Matrek insisted, still more concerned with magic weapons than the northern battlefront.

"Matrek, we have far more pressing matters here. The dead will arrive, and soon," Geril said, his shoulders stiffening . "If you are not willing to help, then we must go. We are needed in Balgavarr, and even more so in Icehome."

Matrek snorted. "*I will help*," his voice dripped with condescension. "I have no other choice, right?" His mouth twisted with melancholy. "Just like the old times, eh Geril?"

Geril smiled back. "Hell on Esfah and death at the doorstep."

"Except we are not fighting the morehl this time." Matrek raised an eyebrow towards Garesch.

The lava elf prince nodded back, hoping the selumari king was right.

"All right." Matrek stood. "Arrive at the palace within an hour. We will take an airship and my enchanters to summon the winds. It will be significantly faster even than your speediest frostwing." He shot Ra'al a look, and the areosan prince did not dispute him.

Geril and Coryn, Ra'al, Bastawr, and Garesch stood with their full crew atop the palace's air dock. It was still early and despite the grisly scenes the day had brought so far, Ra'al's stomach rumbled; he'd skipped breakfast and lunch was still an hour away.

An airship descended gracefully and hovered ten cubits from the dock. Coral Elf sailors dropped a rope that the ground crew pulled, bringing the airship down the last few cubits.

Matrek stood with a troop of his warriors. For some minutes he talked in whispers to their commander.

Finally, Matrek nodded and headed for Geril's party. "The airship can reach Balgavarr within the day."

He pointed to the soldiers in their full armor standing at attention. "This troop will join you; let it not be said that Tulgesh did not act with its allies. If the undead are sighted in the vicinity of Balgavarr Reaches by the time you arrive, send a message and I will lead the greater army to your aid."

Ra'al's mouth twisted, but he kept silent. If the undead had reached the Kafnysan Mountains, or even the Wilds of Dur'Sona, it would mean that Icehome had likely fallen.

"I suggest that you prepare immediately," Geril told him.

"Are you certain that I need to mobilize the army?" Matrek stared hard at Geril.

"Aye. It sounds as if it is no mere skirmish—and a small battle would mean the undead are up to far fouler things than a mere assault upon the living," Geril said.

"Fine. But we get our own pick of the cache once it is found." Matrek gave him a hard stare. "The weapons have been released into the wild, and there are many you cannot use. Tulgesh will have its due."

Geril nodded reservedly. "A share of them is expected," he confirmed the deal.

"That is all we want." Matrek turned and waved the soldiers aboard. They advanced in regimented step and loaded onto the airship.

"Farewell, old comrade." Matrek nodded to Geril and then departed.

Minutes later, the airship rose upon its inflated air bladder and steered towards Balgavarr. It did not seem to move at the king's promised speed. Ra'al grumbled to himself as he stood next to the unusually sullen Coryn. Ra'al had half a mind to grab her and fly on ahead to Balgavarr and make advanced preparations.

Then a cry went up from the sailors and they traded commands, releasing knots and unfurling side sails that extended like wings. The frostwing watched the process. *Not wings... more like a fish's fins.*

As the coral elf sky sailors deflated and tied down the air bladder, the ship lurched forward with greater speed, no longer inhibited by the balloon's drag or buoyancy. Strong winds arose behind them, directed by selumari enchanters, and the air ship careened through the sky at twice the speed of the fastest flier in Icehome.

Ra'al finally relaxed. Maybe they had enough time to reach Balgavarr and Icehome before any battles would begin. Better still, maybe the battle would not happen for some tendays; that would give them more than enough time to prepare and muster troops for the coming war.

Better yet, as long as I'm dreaming, maybe there will be no *battle and the undead will simply walk into the sea and drown...Can the undead survive the deep?* he wondered

Ra'al slumped by the rails, still daydreaming about ensuring the safety of his home, and then finding Harol and taking the weapon cache back.

He gazed around. Geril was in deep discussion with Captain Taerlon, who helmed the ship before planning with the selumari troop commanders. Coryn fiddled with a metallic cube, which Ra'al recognized from the vault of the cache. Marnash spoke heatedly with the two vaghan wizards, but Garesch slumped against the rails just as Ra'al had.

Ra'al nodded to Garesch. "Daydreaming?"

"Not really." Garesch shook his head. "Anticipating the battle is more than daydreaming."

"Maybe we are mistaken," Ra'al said in a hopeful tone. "Maybe we'll have much time to prepare."

"I seriously doubt that," Garesch said and stiffened. "I feel Harol's blasphemy in the embassy is only the beginning." He wrung his hands as he tried to explain. "Agents of Death are usually keep hidden, working from below or inserted within society to undermine life. Harol's act is a declaration. He has announced war."

The frostwing glanced away and his eyes caught sight of the shuffling masses dotting the landscape below. He stood and surveyed the valley-like approach to Balgavarr Reaches where Geril had slain a black dragon decades ago and his heart plunged into his stomach. Regimented phalanxes of bloodless warriors stood in neat groups, dull armor hanging to expose bleached white bones and rusted blades.

A dead commander seated upon a corptic steed with stands of rotting flesh hanging off it looked up. His blazing eyes locked upon the sky ship.

Ra'al's jaw tightened. "The undead." Ra'al choked on the words. "They are here."

Chapter 20

The coral airship came in sight of the Balgavarr Reaches. Currently, the main entrance remained hidden behind a massive wall of rock that formed a semi-circle to protect it. But dwarves were skilled earth-crafters and with a couple days' notice, they could reroute the internal tunnels to the mountain, open a new doorway somewhere else in the slopes, and collapse the old one. They'd done it countless times over the eons to frustrate their enemies. But now, they needed time to act, and the dwarves were not inside. Hidden or not, it had been decades since they'd last shifted the location of the main gates, and so it would not take any great skill to follow the roads and find the entrance—not if an enemy was already on the correct path.

Rank upon rank of the undead crawled across the vale where Morguus Ebraxus met his end for the second time. Geril paced upon the decks of Captain Taerlon's airship and cursed. They slowed as the mages re-inflated the air bladder, hovering.

Even the light was dying in Balgavarr. With the Soll descending below the mountains at their west, Ra'al identified all manner of bloodless warriors. The majority were skeletons; thousands of the foot soldiers formed clusters grouped around the mountain where they'd cut off the road, and more continued coming, streaming south from the Wilds of Dur'sona.

Ra'al identified at least two spell casters. Gaunt, with drawn faces, they exuded power as if they had been proud nobility in life,. Other underlings grouped around them, likely lesser magicians lending their potency to their betters.

At the lowest spectrum of his vision, ethereal forms flickered barely within sight, like eternal wisps. Those Ra'al assumed were wraiths and ghosts, invisible to the naked eye, and seen only by magic users and those with Ra'al and Werdth's particular gift. Some said the incorporeal fiends were dead elemental spirits, others claimed them special products of Death magic. They *did* know that some could sap the life force of the living like lampreys on fish.

Behind the vaghan wall and up the mountain, stood two trebuchets loaded with heavy stones. But nobody manned the war engines. Between the parapets, only a handful of archers stood at the ready with crossbows locked into place.

The gates of Balgavarr remained open and ten dwarves ran into the wall's inner courtyard. They cast spell upon spell and summoned sheaves of stone to fill the gap in the wall, completely encasing it. It otherwise had no gate or portcullis to slow an enemy. It was now a solid, impenetrable wall with no footholds or door that could be breached.

"That'll never be enough," Marnash mumbled beside Ra'al.

The frostwing hadn't even realized the morehl stood beside him.

"Any army worth their salt can bust that down within a few days' time, or simply scale it," Marnash continued.

Coryn stood at Ra'al's other side. "Why are they hiding in the city?" Coryn's voice cracked. "If they don't whittle that army down, they'll face the full strength of it."

"Gods know who gave the order to close the city," Geril shouted. "Certainly not Warlord Kile. The fools will bring about the end of Balgavarr!" He muttered below his breath, "Lahmyn and his faction of elders."

"This is what Tulgesh tried in the last war," Captain Taerlon said in a low voice. "They relied on defense when they had the opportunity to strike first. We lost the city to the morehl and their allied undead because of it."

Geril grumbled something unintelligible, followed by, "I know. I was there and had to retreat alone after my company was massacred by the reds...That was when I met Thrag."

Ra'al looked to the horizon, hoping to see his people coming to the rescue of Balgavarr, but no frostwings appeared in the sky. With a heavy heart, he muttered, "If the undead are *here*... They must have come past my home. It means...it means..."

Coryn put a hand on his arm. "I'm sure your mother is okay. She is a very crafty frostwing—and maybe the enemy divided its forces, deciding to siege us both at once, rather than in sequence."

Ra'al frowned, hoping she was right.

The ship angled towards the mountain peak, skirting the edges of the skeletal vanguard.

"I would think they would have shot at us by now," Captain Taerlon said, meeting the vacant eyes that turned up to them. "We've certainly gotten the fiends' attention."

Bastawr shook his head. "I scarcely saw a working bow among them. Bow parts are more subject to decay; a blade may rust or chip and remain usable, but bowstrings do not weather time so well."

The clustered black magicians pointed and sneered at the ship. The blood of those on deck ran cold.

Ra'al snorted, almost like a sneeze, and then whirled, drawing his blade.

"I smell it, too!" Werdth yelled, pointing, but not acting as quickly as the frostwing.

Ra'al stabbed the air. His blade sizzled and flashed brilliant and violet. The shape of a tall man flickered and then broke apart like a dashed puzzle. A wave of extreme cold rolled over those nearby, and then dissipated as the demon's blade materialized and clattered to the deck boards loudly, reminding them that even the incorporeal enemies could kill them.

"That was a wraith," Marnash said with a shiver in his voice. "This is worse than I thought. They are not common."

Taerlon narrowed his eyes at Ra'al. "How did you know it was there?"

Coryn piped up, "He can smell them. Him, too." She bobbed her head towards Werdth.

"We discovered that fact in Tulgesh," Ra'al said and looked at his sword. It still shimmered faintly with the monster's afterglow, is if it bled something altogether different. He looked to Garesch silently, and the morehl nodded his approval.

The coral elf in the lookout howled, "Incoming," and pointed towards the horizon. Elven bowmen nocked arrows as flying figures streaked towards them.

"No! It is my kinsmen," cried the areosan messenger.

"He's right," cried Ra'al. "Messengers! News from Castle Ice…"

Four frostwings glided for them, angling towards the airship. Black bolts reached out from the liches and their minions like crossbow quarrels that bled smoky trails after them. Three of the frostwings took direct hits; they curled their wings and tumbled, falling to the dirt where the dead ripped them to shreds.

Dodging the black missiles, the fourth grabbed a hold of the rail and sank his claws into the edge. "Prince Ra'al! News from home—the undead have… oh, Prince Ra'al—your mother is…"

His eyes suddenly rolled back, and he pitched backwards, releasing his grip. The messenger plummeted to the depths, stone dead. A black trail of vapor traced back to the lich below, who sneered with a rictus grin.

Ra'al howled, denied any solid intelligence from the north—denied reports on his mother's fate.

Bastawr's eyes ringed with worry as he paced the deck anxiously. "No support from Icehome can be expected." He cast his eyes across the massive army. It grew larger as the dead poured forward from the trees. "We cannot fight that alone."

"It'll be two days at minimum for King Matrek to arrive," said Captain Taerlon. "And that's if we send a message right now."

Geril tightened his jaw. "Send a bird, then. The dwarves will have to hold until that long."

"I must go," said Bastawr. He stood upon the rail of the ship, wondering how he might escape.

"I did not guess you for a coward," Taerlon groused.

Bastawr shook his head. "There are always ghwereste in the wild. Perhaps I can rouse some aid, such as it may be."

Taerlon nodded an apology and signaled one of his elven air crafters. "She will guide you…Jump."

Bastawr took one last look at his friends, wished them success in battle, and then leapt overboard. The elf magician summoned winds to guide him to a shaky, but survivable, landing on the side of the mountain, well away from the undead and their black, deadly missiles. The tigerfolk disappeared into the trees as soon as he landed.

The captain shook his head resolutely. "A fool's errand," he muttered. "But he may be the only one of us to survive the coming night…If he is wise enough not to return."

"We have to land in the city," Geril barked to Taerlon. "We must rally the vagha or the battle will be lost before it even begins."

"Can we land there?" Coryn asked, raising a brow and looking at the tight landscape below.

"I think we can," Marnash answered slowly. "There will be wind shears against the mountainside, but the air bladder should help the ship land safely."

"Captain, have your pilot land us inside those walls, between the trebuchet's." Geril growled his suspicions beneath his breath, "Warlord Kile must have been usurped in my short absence."

The airship started its descent towards the walls of Balgavarr.

As the vessel almost docked, Geril turned to Ra'al. "Fly us over to the balcony."

Ra'al nodded and grabbed the vaghan king around the waist and unfurled his wings. Two beats carried him beyond the airship, then he thrust through the air and descended onto the balcony, where the dwarves' defensive lookout could also watch over the central market of the city.

There was not even a lookout at his post in the stony perch. The market was a flurry of motion below as the dwarves hurried to make changes to the mountain's layout—a task that would take days to complete.

"People of Balgavarr, listen to me," Geril shouted. His voice rang through the curved undercroft and penetrated the hubbub of bustling dwarves. "There is no time! Death's forces already have the location of the city and they are at our door."

The crowd stilled and gave him their attention.

Geril howled, "We must face them on the field of battle if we hope to push them back. Your families—everything you have—is at stake!"

"Elder Lahmyn says there is time," one dwarf shouted. "Many will die if we go outside!"

A line in the crowd dispersed, making way for six elders. One of them clutched a long staff, which he used to propel himself towards Geril.

Grabbing the edge of a vertical steel ladder, Geril slid down the rails and landed within Balgavarr.

Ra'al looked back and watched the crew tie the airship down. In a few minutes, they would also arrive in the city proper.

"What are trying to do, Geril?" the elder statesman shouted. Spittle flecked at the corners of his mouth. "Are you trying to undermine the entire council and their decisions?"

"Elder Lahmyn, I knew it would be you." Geril bared his teeth. He raised his voice for all to hear. "Listen Balgavarr, I have just returned from Tulgesh, where the residents of our embassy were slaughtered by vaghan blades."

A murmur rose in the crowd.

Ra'al took another glimpse back and the army of the dead began approaching up the slopes. Time was running out.

"This is a lunacy," Lahmyn screamed. "If our people were slaughtered, then bring their murderer to the council for justice. Besides, there is no time for this! The council has already overruled Warlord Kile's decision to throw vaghan lives away in needless battle."

Only the unanimous decision of the council could overrule the king. But, by law, a simple majority could take control from his appointed steward.

The ship's crew emerged at the edge of the crowd. One of the wizards howled, "It is true! I am Sheron sa'Bahr, and I saw the slaughtered. The culprit could not be captured because we had to come to aid of our city in its darkest hour."

"You are a liar, Sheron," Lahmyn shouted. "Long have you been a friend of the king. You must bring proof of these deeds."

"What matters now, Lahmyn, is that the culprit was your son." Sheron took a long breath and projected an orb of light above the crowd. Everyone gasped as they saw Harol Sa'Lahmyn strike down the ambassador with his axe.

It was only Sheron's interpretation of the events as he imagined them and was far from evidence, but the crowd screamed their rage nonetheless. Images greatly swayed public opinion and the mob turned unruly, specifically fixing their attention on Elder Lahmyn.

Lahmyn took one last look at Geril as the other elders faded away, ceding back control to King Geril. "You will pay dearly for this Geril sa'Ghuren," he hissed for the king's ears only. "Remember this moment. Freeze it solid in your mind." He growled low, "I'll knock you off the throne for this—*permanently.*" Then he, too, slipped into the crowd.

Geril ignored him and shouted at the mob, "Sound the trumpets of war and call our army to the gate!" Geril drew his axe. He led the first column of archers and shield bearers into the gate to take their positions. Spear carriers and the footmen hurried to close the ranks, and Sheron and his wizard corps brought up the rear.

In the midst of all the chaos, the trio of lava elves grabbed the frostwing messenger who had reached them in Tulgesh and dragged him down a tunnel, locating the first open chamber they could find. Garesch pulled off his pack and withdrew the scroll cases. He opened them to show the guard three coiled scrolls stuffed within his pack. "What is your name, frostwing?"

"Hennedy, sir."

Garesch put the haversack into Hennedy's hands. "On your life, Hennedy, protect these. If I fall in battle, the undead must not have them—they belong to the Sages, but it is better that they are destroyed if I cannot deliver them." The morehl prince pointed around the room, "Only surrender them to one of us three—if we all die here, then give them only to lady Coryn or to Ra'al. Barring that, hand them to King Geril" He swallowed. "If we have all perished, destroy them."

Hennedy nearly trembled with the responsibility thrust upon him. "And if the dead breach the city and come for them?"

Garesch pointed towards the clay fireplace. "Get that thing started as soon as we leave. If the skeletons breach your door, incinerate them and then die in glorious battle."

Hennedy nodded and rapped a hand against his chest, in what he knew to be the lava elf salute.

Garesch and his crew dashed from the room and headed for the battlefront just as the selumari archers joined the dwarves on the parapets and nocked arrows at the ready.

The morehl took their place beside Ra'al and Coryn as the clanking footsteps of approaching skeletons shook the air.

Geril shouted his final call to arms, "Show them how the vagha fight!" Geril raised his axe high over his head and waved it in a circle.

Arrows and crossbow bolts slowed the skeletal hordes, felling hundreds of them in the first sweep. But thousands still came rushing and clamoring towards the wall. They carried no battering rams or siege weapons to bust it down. They formed a wedge and hit the wall like a hammer.

Ignoring the missiles that the dwarves hurled at them, they built a ramp of corpses, both animated and collapsed. They poured over the wall, onto the parapets, and into the courtyard. Only a few hundred cubits of open space and vaghan soldiers barred their entry to Balgavarr.

Dwarven spears pierced the undead, breaking rotten ribs, crushing skulls and crunching bones. The enemy hurried up the slopes, forming wild footpaths that circumvented the walls and poured into the bowl of chaos within. The skeletons that collapsed one moment stitched themselves back together as inky tendrils of necralluvium stretched out like black spider silk. The undead reformed if the fiends' heads were not removed.

Ra'al felt Coryn rush by, swinging her axe and cleaving skeletons. She forged a path of destruction. Geril did the same, several cubits away.

The frostwing rushed and met his first undead. He pushed it back and hacked cleanly through neck and chest. He advanced at the next enemy, snarling as Garesch ran past him, systematically hacking and parrying.

Screams of fallen dwarves echoed louder than their battle cries, signaling the shift in the pitch of battle. *The dwarves were losing.*

A loud crack and boom shook the ground as huge segments of the wall fell away. Carrion worms tunneled huge furrows below the barrier, destabilizing its foundation, and the dead threw grappling hooks over its edges. They dragged sections of it down, tipping them outward.

The defenses fell, but it also let the forces of Balgavarr advance into the open air. They were no longer penned up against the city's entrance.

Several selumari ran beside Ra'al as he covered the now empty distance.

He hacked several skeletons apart, and glanced to his left, watching the trio of warriors from Tulgesh hack, block, and cleave through the enemy with the grace of ocean waves.

One of them suddenly collapsed dead, clutching his heart, even though he'd taken no wounds.

Ra'al smelled it: the intense odor of bitter spice. He turned to find an ethereal shape lunging for its next victim. Ra'al swung his sword and hit something invisible, just as if his blade had struck a solid object. The familiar hiss of striking that accompanied a wraith's collapse was followed by the flash of purple light.

He turned a circle. The battle was far from over. Ra'al unfolded his wings and took to the air. He swooped an arc around the battlefield and snatched a pair of skeletons, jabbing his talons into their eye sockets and plucking them from the battlefield. Ra'al beat his wings mightily and dragged them into the sky before finding his targets.

From high overhead, Ra'al dropped the bodies into the cluster of dead magicians. They smashed into the ground, breaking apart and dashing one of the liches to pieces.

Ra'al roared a challenge.

The dead answered immediately. Three black balls of pulsating energy flew at him.

Before Ra'al could evade the vile magic, they smashed him fully in the chest. He found himself suddenly falling, like in the dreams he'd had as a kit, before becoming as skilled in the air as he was on land. Ra'al could feel his essence slipping away and the afterlife calling his spirit towards the void.

His mind played images, like he'd seen in the dungeons below Tulgesh. Some were of the father he barely remembered.

Thrag spoke in the native areosan tongue—he'd been known to have a poor command of the common one. "Ra'al, my son, remember what you must do to learn the song of the wind. You must surrender yourself to it." His father smiled gently. "My father taught me this. I will teach this to you." The memory was a real one, Ra'al was certain of it—they were his father's final words to him before leaving with Geril for their final battle. Ra'al had been very young.

Ra'al hit the ground hard and his chest smoked, but his senses caught up to him quickly, reminding him of his present reality. He pulled himself up and found he was buried deep behind enemy lines. The dead closed in on him fast.

Death would find him soon, whether from by the skeletons' blades, the injuries from his fall, or the pulsating smoke rising from his chest.

Ra'al took a deep, long breath, then let it out again. *I am ready. Let them come.*

A strange sensation ran through his entire body, from wingtip to wingtip; from his tufted hair to his toe-claws. He felt lifted in a wave of sound. *The song of the wind.*

As he exhaled, steam formed in front of his face. Ra'al looked at his hands and frost formed between his claws.

Ra'al took another breath and roared a torrent of ice shards. They devastated everything in its path. Ra'al felt the wounds mending at his chest as a layer of ice frosted over it.

He turned and roared at another group of skeletal warriors coming his way before unfolding his wings and taking to the air. Ra'al clenched his fists and opened them. Ice crystallized spears within each hand.

The frostwing reached behind his back and snatched the leather quiver where he held his short javelins. Yanking it off, the leather strap broke and he cast it aside.

Clutching an icy spear in either hand, he hurled them below, knowing in his frosty blood that he now followed in his father's wind wake.

Ra'al smiled grimly, finally in tune with the song of the wind. His only lament was that it came on the likely day of his death.

His spears shattered the corpses below and rained frozen hell down upon them. *Only another ten thousand to go if we are to win this war.*

Chapter 21

Coryn wiped her brow with a sleeve. Grime and grave dust covered her from head to toe, intermixing with the blood splatters of her comrades and clotted sprays of filth from the gore of hacked apart zombie flesh.

She spotted distinct spears of ice exploding far inside the enemy lines. Coryn looked up and found Ra'al hurling one ice spear after another. She smiled; the child who had lost the wind had finally found it.

Coryn brought her axe to bear and intercepted the sword of an undead warrior. She kicked him with her steel boot and he busted apart. Before she could locate her next prey, those bones began to rattle as the black gunk at the joints crawled towards each other, trying to rebind the bloodless creature.

Coryn threw her axe down on its skull, smashing it to bits. The black goo at the base of the fiend's skull hissed with a pop, like a sutured boil. It emitted a grey puff of smoke and then the creature fell still. The cursed skeletons only stopped moving when the light in their eyes went out, and that happened only when their skulls took a direct hit or were removed from their body.

Dwarves around her employed similar methods to take down the enemy, cutting them down to size and then smashing their skulls. Bone dust and shards flew all around her, but so did vaghan blood.

Balgavarr's forces fought valiantly, but the numbers of the undead were far larger than they could handle. Despite their best efforts, they would still lose this battle.

Coryn gnashed her teeth and tasted blood in her mouth. *They could not lose this battle. All Balgavarr was at stake!*

Rage filled her, and she resumed her attacks, taking one skeletal warrior at a time. *Break the legs, then crush the skull.* She and her peers were all that stood between the undead and open gates to Balgavarr Reaches.

Geril's daughter howled an ululating battle cry and rushed towards the fiendish warriors with a vengeance. Another female footman caught her cry and took it up, charging after her.

Coryn grinned as she crushed another skull, and then another. They were not alone. Several beardless dwarven warriors wielded hammer, axe, and blade. The women of Balgavarr would help protect it.

Marnash watched as the cadaverous casters hurled arcane missiles at Ra'al. The lava elf pulled one of his many sightstones and attempted to counter the spell from across the battlefield.

The great frostwing took the hits squarely and fell. Marnash felt a tightness in his chest. Garesch was like a surrogate child to him, and Ra'al had been growing on the wizened lava elf like any other orphan boy in need of a father.

Marnash dropped the stone back in his pocket and grabbed another, the red one. He knew a spell, one he had cast often under Emperor Saugor's orders, but he'd never used it to his full capacity before. Now was the time to do so. It was a desperate move; Ra'al had fallen, but he might be able to save Garesch from impending doom.

As he began chanting the horrible spell, Ra'al rose into the air and started to hurl spears of ice upon the liches and the undead. Marnash's heart took courage, seeing the prince had not been killed, and that he remembered the areosa had some measure of magic resistance.

He hastened his spell before the arcanists could recover and strike the frostwing again. Marnash summoned a white-hot ball of energy. It grew larger than his hand and continued increasing as he chanted, crackling with orange fire.

A dwarven wizard came beside him and added his fire-magic to it, tripling the size of the burning orb. As the ball sizzled and crackled with the captured energy, it continued to grow until they both hurled it towards the lich and his company.

The ball burned skeletons as it passed, eventually exploding when it touched down near the death-crafters. It erupted with a booming sound and the explosion tore open a crater, casting rock shards and bone splinters a hundred cubits in every direction. Hot flames washed over any creatures near the fiery caldera and torched them to ash. The flames lit the battlefield with a burning flash, reminding the defenders of how late the hour was.

But even with the other nine wizards, Marnash knew that the chances of winning were still too slim; close combat was not a wizard's game and the hordes had crept right up to the gates. Marnash's mind turned over and over as he compared the numbers. They were still too few, and he felt convinced this army was only a fraction of those gathered in the Shadowland Wastes—they still hadn't seen the ancient selumari who led the evil hordes.

Marnash bit his lip. *Hennedy will have to burn those maps in the end.* He turned and nodded to the vaghan wizards at his side. "Sons and daughters of Firiel, let's make this battlefield wild with the goddess's fire."

The eldest dwarf caster grinned with a broad, toothless smile. "As if I needed your permission," he laughed. "Come on, morehl, show us what you got."

Marnash smiled as he clutched his sightstone and amplified his magic. He intended to show the vagha exactly what he could do.

Garesch could barely see in front of him. Bone chips covered him from head to toe. The prince knew Marnash crafted magic with the fire casters on the far side of the dwarven vanguard, but Werdth stood alongside him. The lava elf guard had proved his worth countless times since they'd first set out from Saugor's domain.

The prince hacked and chopped alongside Werdth as if in a choreographed dance; they likely learned their skills from the same instructors in Uruzak. They didn't have a chance to even wipe the grime from their faces.

The sword Garesch had purchased in Frostshoal sliced through bone and rotted tendon as if through butter, severing skulls and quenching the ominous red light that glowed within their eye sockets.

He moved among the undead slowly in widening circles, expanding the sword dance. Werdth mirrored his actions. Block, dodge, swipe, then thrust.

Garesch looked back through the hazy, low light that burned in the deep of night, bathing the scene in ominous tones. He saw the vagha advancing slowly upon the field.

A surge of skeletal forces rushed around him and Werdth, and they whirled among the undead's rusty blades. The elves severed arms and hands while spinning back to take their heads. The prince yelped when a zombie thrust a blade into his thigh on his blindside.

Garesch turned with surprise; Werdth should have destroyed that creature. Garesch heard his dance partner's death gasp. Garesch staggered back and turned his eyes to find a bloodless fiend twisting a dagger into Werdth's lung. Steamy and brightly pink oxygenated blood spurted from the wound.

Werdth collapsed with a death gurgle and his eyes glistened stony and lifeless.

The prince cleared the area quickly, taking any heads within reach of his sword. Then he bent momentarily and brushed his fingers across his loyal servant's face, closing his eyelids against the crows that would eventually come after the battle had long ended. Garesch grew suddenly aware that he had pressed too deeply into the enemy line. Undead hordes collapsed the wide, defensive circle and threatened to overwhelm him. There was no path back to safety.

Suddenly, ice spears rained down upon those enemies closest to him. A frostwing hurled icy destruction into the surrounding battlefield. He recognized Ra'al who cleared a path just big enough for Garesch to retreat to the vaghan lines.

Finally back among the dwarves, he wiped his eyes and face clear of debris.

The numbers were impossible to beat. Unless the vagha put weapons in the hands of their untrained, the elderly, and the children, they were outnumbered by a large score, and even that wouldn't prove helpful.

Garesch traded a knowing glance with the warriors at his side. Coryn stood adjacent him and recognized the same desperate situation. They nodded to each other slowly, then Garesch raised his blade to his lips.

"Today might be the day I die, but I will not go quietly to the Abyss. I will embrace my end with glory and valor…then let the old master try to bend me to his will, for he will fail!" He wiped his blade clean across a scrap of cloth.

His words sparked inspiration in the dwarven troops near his side, bolstering their fervor. They shouted wordless battle-cries, and together they advanced.

Geril's heart sank as he watched another vaghan general limp off the field.

Out of the forty selumari soldiers and their airship captain, only twenty-five remained standing. A similar outcome had arrived for the vagha warriors. Around a third were already out of the battle, including Warlord Kile, who had to be carried to the infirmary.

The endless flow of the undead wore upon Geril. A brilliant light caught his eye, and he watched the explosion of the fiery energy ball annihilate those undead imbued with eldritch power. It gave him some hope. *If anybody could even the odds, it was the wizards.*

Geril's heart quickened, and he roared at the top of his lungs. "For Balgavarr, Cyrea, and all of Esfah!"

The battle cry carried down the lines of the fighting warriors, igniting a second wave of vigor. The vagha and the selumari started again to press on the advancing undead.

Step by step, they gained ground. Geril spotted a death knight seated upon a skeletal steed. The thing locked its burning eyes upon him.

Rage boiled in Geril's soul. He suspected that if the leader were to fall, the entire undead army might be cast into disarray, finally giving Balgavarr a chance.

"To me." He shouted as he advanced towards the fiend, desperate to end this uneven battle.

Suddenly, snarling dogs with pale yellow eyes rushed towards the dwarves. Bestial pack animals the size of bears charged at him.

Geril's flank faltered under the monsters' charge, and by the time he looked up, the enemy commander had moved deeper into the protection of his own kind.

"Damn it!" Geril squeezed his grip around Old Thunder's haft.

Vagha fell all around him, and Geril felt the pain of each one of them as they collapsed to blade, and scythe, and tooth and claw.

"Retreat!" he shouted before he even realized it. He led the forces back towards the safety of Balgavarr, lest he lose all of them, praying that the bird had arrived already in Tulgesh and that they could hold out until Matrek could render aide.

Geril feared it would come down to a skirmish in the streets of the Reaches, and only the selumari's arrival would save them. But they would have to survive a couple days, still, for even that.

As the fenhouds dashed past his minions and snapped at the oncoming vagha, the undead commander steered his mount deeper into the midst of his forces.

Finally, I will make Leisterbane proud. The death knight sat upon the back of his skeletal steed and watched the battle unfold. Beside him stood the messenger who had delivered him the mist stone map. *Yarichek, that was your name once…before beginning your eternity.*

The morehl revenant's flesh had already begun to peel away from its body in blistering patches, exposing the bone of his jaw and exuding the stench of meat rot. The death knight kept his minion close so that he could siphon knowledge off him. His morehl peers held the rest of the maps.

We could overwhelm the city if we are not careful. These vain little things think they stand a chance against Lord Death. They cannot see past their puny lives: that a far grander game is at play.

He watched the lava elf prince and his servant cut swaths through the mindless forces of his bloodless. And then Garesch's friend fell. "Werdth." The knight cocked his head as he pulled the name from Yarichek's memory.

"Heucuva!" the knight called for one of his mystics.

A spell casting skeleton wearing grave shrouds approached. Its bones were engraved with black runes and sigils, and it looked up at the knight. "Command me?"

The knight pointed to the fallen lava elf. "Werdth. And none other. They must not suspect a thing." He reached into his cloak and produced a vial of necralluvium, which he gave to the heucuva.

The fiend bowed and then dashed into the skeletal fray. It eventually fell upon the red-skinned cadaver and located the elf's chest wound. Unstopping the container, he poured a single drop of the inky fluid into the opening, imbuing it with certain permissions and autonomy. This zombie had to retain his memories and a certain amount of free will for his master's purposes.

Werdth's eyes shot open, and he stared into the night sky though glassy, obsidian eyes that had dulled to a slate gray; void of the life's spark.

"Arise," the heucuva ordered. "Your master has a task. You know what you must do."

Zombie Werdth stood to his feet, picked up his blade, and then staggered back towards the dwarven lines. The wound on his chest had stopped steaming when the necralluvium hit his blood, and he appeared as if any other wounded warrior would.

As Werdth reached the dwarven vanguard, he turned and began to battle skeletons, beating them back until a trio of dwarves rushed to his side and helped him retreat. Through the creature's link to the undead, both the heucuva and death knight knew the vagha recognized him and understood he was wounded. "This way, morehl—through the main doors…You need a physician."

Werdth nodded slowly and then limped his way past the battle lines and inside the main gates of Balgavarr.

Chapter 22

The selumari airship captain, Taerlon, led his few remaining men behind King Geril. Many undead fell around the retreating vagha as they plowed their way through the ranks, intent on retreating to safety.

When Geril called for warriors to follow him into the thick of the battle, Taerlon didn't hesitate. He'd hoped that following a legendary war hero, even into the thickest part of the battle, meant he'd stand the best chance at surviving.

Now, Taerlon looked at the retreating dwarves and thought that the lot of them might be slaughtered before they reached safety.

Their retreat was haphazard and coordinated. They had just abandoned land to the enemy and fled with their backs turned.

"Troop, form a retreat shield," Geril shouted to his men. They immediately formed up on his position. The team moved towards safety with methodical, precision.

Five of Taerlon's warriors fell in the intensifying fray, and he started to think of his beautiful wife. *She would not know that he died on the battlefield for at least another tenday.*

He knew he would die here, and that death would come soon. But he would not let it have him easily. Taerlon roared and urged his men to hasten towards the city; its people would need defending as long as possible. *Perhaps one of them will tell my wife of my valor?*

Taerlon grimaced in the face of Death, and a ray of light caught his eye as it peeked past the statue of Thrag on the nearby Kafnysan peak. Perhaps some vagha would honor them with a statue like that someday. He grit his teeth against the fatigue in his sword arm and swung his blade as if he hoped to be counted worthy of it. He wanted his death to make a difference.

Then he heard some new kind of cry in the distance. Taerlon's blood ran cold and his gut twisted with fear that it might be a black dragon summoned by the army of the dead, drawing upon wyrmcraft to affect a coup de grâce.

Something leaped above his head, flashing past like a striking hawk. It growled as it landed, crushing three skeletal warriors beneath its girth and smashing their skulls under malleted hands.

The bear-like thing stood tall upon its rear legs and gripped a jagged stone blade. It gave him a wink before rushing forward and mowing down a horde of the dead, leaving Taerlon and the badly battered defenders behind. They finally had room to breathe.

Against all odds, the ghwereste had arrived.

Taerlon fell to the ground, injured and more tired than he'd ever been in his life.

He gazed to the furthest edges of the battle and spotted men with long beards and women with wrapped braids. They rode horses and rushed to fill the ranks of the fallen selumari and vagha. Taerlon smiled. Bastawr had managed to even find a few amazons.

"Down that hallway," a dwarf said and pointed. "That's where you'll find the medics." The corridor led to a makeshift triage ward set up and staffed by dwarven healers. The helpful vagha put a hand on Werdth's shoulder and steered him, mistaking the animated corpse's movements for signs of shell shock. Regardless of the species, those symptoms were almost universal.

"Can you manage?" the dwarf asked.

Werdth nodded and staggered in the appointed direction. As soon as the soldier turned his back, Werdth veered off the set course and headed down a familiar hallway where he opened a very specific door and entered.

Hennedy stood when he recognized him. The frostwing looked him over hesitantly. "You…You are wounded?"

Werdth grimaced but waved him off. "I have endured worse before," he lied with a slight lisp.

"The battle? Is it won?" Hennedy asked.

The zombie shook his head, doing his best to mimic the lava elf's mannerisms. "No. We are losing, and badly. Prince Garesch commanded me to retrieve the maps and meet him at the city gate. The morehl have no choice but to flee if we are to save them."

Hennedy handed over the pack, albeit reluctantly. "I will accompany you. You are injured, after all."

"No. I will be fine as soon as I return; Marnash will tend my wounds. Prince Ra'al wants you to remain here for further instruction." Werdth shouldered the knapsack, feeling the weight of the scroll cases at his back, and then left.

Hennedy stared at Werdth's back as he left, wondering at the stout creature's tolerance for pain. He'd shouldered the burden without so much as a grimace, despite a nasty wound that had ruined the fighter's tunic.

The door closed behind him, leaving Hennedy to wait in silence for the areosan prince.

As soon as Werdth cleared the exit door, he turned and made for the winding footpaths that wended around the Kafnysan peak, and then exited out the north side. As soon as he had enough height, he searched the battlefield and spotted the death knight.

The commander locked dead eyes with him, nodded subtly as the rays of morning light began to crest above the distant horizon. The snarls of newly arrived feral folk rang through the morning mist.

Werdth turned north and headed for Leisterbane and the Heimdarl Crag, borne by untiring legs.

Bastawr led the ghwereste towards Balgavarr. He'd managed to summon many of his kind, crying out to them in the wild. Even a cluster of humans, far from Seshara, had answered his call and joined them.

When they arrived at the slope, they were stunned at the number of fallen warriors. Hundreds of vagha lay on the ground, injured, dying, or dead. Spalts of blue pocked the deathscape where thirty-odd selumari bodies laid among their allies. Flashes of light erupted as wizards hurled eldritch blasts at the hordes of skeletons and zombies.

Bastawr's blood boiled hot. He roared across the battlefield and threw himself towards the front line, not considering their superior numbers. He'd rallied perhaps a thousand to Balgavarr's aide, but he would have needed five times that number to evenly match the enemy. The other feral folk followed Bastawr into battle, regardless of the odds, and the amazons charged towards the edge of the battle, picking off stragglers and harrying the flanks.

To his left, five amazons fell upon a nearby lich, shredding the wretched creature limb from limb. Its desiccated skin burst like a paper wasp hive.

The beastfolk each charged two or three of the bloodless warriors at a time. Immediately, the pitch of the battle shifted and the army even began to retreat from its rear-most clusters. They turned back to the north and shambled back the way they had come, back towards the Shadowlands.

As the battlefield started to clear, those skeletal warriors closest to the fray charged blindly. They reacted as if by impulse, no longer controlled. They hacked and slashed whatever living things drew close enough to become a viable target.

Once the last of the skeletal warriors fell, an eerie silence fell across the fledgling dawn. Those humans with magic skill spread through the battlefield, searching out the wounded to heal or ease the pain of those too far gone to save. Beastfolk shamans followed suit.

Bastawr searched the heavens for Ra'al, but couldn't find the massive frostwing. He half expected to see the areosan prince chasing down the enemy army, beating them all the way back to Castle Ice and casting them out of his home.

He couldn't find Ra'al, but stumbled upon Coryn, who laid on her back as a shaman removed an arrow from her left leg. She grimaced as the healer administered magic to staunch the blood.

She smiled at him through the pain. "I'll be dancing again in no time."

Bastawr did not understand her joke.

Garesch stood next to Marnash, who healed his cuts. They looked as if he'd been thrashed by a mob, but both had survived. King Geril knelt upon the ground, closing the eyes of a dead vagha. He scowled and clutched the handle of his axe.

But Ra'al was nowhere to be found.

"Ra'al." Bastawr cried aloud.

"I am here," a voice called.

The frostwing emerged from near the airship. Taerlon leaned near him where they assessed the vehicle's ability to travel safely. Ra'al insisted on returning to Icehome as soon as feasible.

Coryn winced and limped nearby. "So, you can hear the song of the wind now, eh snow-head?"

Ra'al smiled widely. "Aye, and what a pleasant tune it is."

Geril finally found them. The older vagha looked to have been made from steel, but his eyes told a different story. He carried the weight of the mountain on his mind. He bled from many wounds but ignored them all. Two physicians hovering behind him, trying to administer aid as they could, but he kept moving away from them. "Thank you, Bastawr. If you didn't warn us about the undead army, we would have never arrived in time. The folk in the mountain would all be dead by now."

Bastawr's eyebrows knotted, and he bowed, accepting the king's affirmation, but the quickness with which the enemy had retreated bothered him. "This was far too easy, though."

Ra'al scowled. "Perhaps they were needed to reinforce a siege against Castle Ice?" A hint of hopefulness entered his voice.

"Let us hope that the frostwing city endures," Bastawr agreed, and the party staggered their way back inside the mountain halls. He turned to Geril as they entered. "I have other concerns as well. I think we should talk."

Chapter 23

Geril sat with evident pain. He'd summoned the council and his military advisers to the war room.

Bastawr sat uncomfortably in the vagha sized chair, and Ra'al looked to him from across the chamber and shrugged. He knew exactly how the tigerfolk felt.

Taerlon slouched in his chair, barely managing to stay awake. Garesch and Marnash sat adjacent to Coryn, who sat beside her father and the grouchy Warlord Kile. He sported fresh pink skin that formed a scar on one side of his face. He fidgeted with it, mumbling something about how it ruined the lines of his magnificent beard.

In a long row down the table, twelve of the thirteen dwarves from the council had responded to the summons. The twelfth, Councilman Lahmyn, had refused to respond. Many of the other council members wore sheepish looks for their earlier actions and refusal to heed the king's appointed steward. For his part, Warlord Kile glared daggers across the table at them.

Once everybody settled in their chairs, Geril cleared his throat. "Please, Bastawr, repeat what you told me after the battle."

Bastawr shifted from his left thigh to his right, trying to find a comfortable position in the chair. Finally, he stood. Bastawr said, "I told you about the conversation I overheard between two dead commanders while hidden in the mists. They were looking for something called a mist stone and they'd already claimed one map that led them to the first of four. Further, this army, large as it was, was only a fraction of their forces, most of which are hidden in the Heimdarl Crag...Everything about the siege of Balgavarr feels like a diversion, and at the center of it are these mystic stones."

Coryn's eyes bulged and Ra'al's jaw tightened. Garesch leaned towards Marnash and whispered with animated hand motions.

"Thank you, Bastawr." Geril raised his voice enough for all to take notice. "I was hoping that this was over." He struck the table with his fist. "But by festration, I think this is only the beginning. It worries me that this might be a mere ploy to divert us from some grander scheme…But what?"

"With all the casualties we had?" Coryn's eyes looked skeptical. "We lost more than one-third of our fighting forces, and this was a mere diversion?"

"I am afraid so, daughter," Geril said and put a hand over hers.

Silence fell over the room. Finally, Garesch raised his voice, "But if this was the diversion, then where is the real army headed?"

Geril scoffed. "We can only assume they seek a far bigger target than Balgavarr Reaches. Bastawr, do you think they might be headed for these stones?"

Bastawr nodded. "I do. And they know the location…"

Marnash and Garesch traded a surprised look with each other. They had not yet told anyone their secret: that the maps had been stolen.

Bastawr took a long breath and continued. "A death knight and the lich unearthed and deactivated one of the mist stones, and the eldritch haze dissipated in the area we stood. It was a kind of magic fog they could not penetrate. I believe it hides something. But the mist did not lift completely. The location, I think, is geographically fixed, but inaccessible by Death's forces with the mist in effect." He fidgeted momentarily. "I think the map was more of a key to deactivation than a map, at least by our understanding."

The tigerfolk averted his eyes with a tinge of shame creeping across his face. "When I was discovered, my impulse was to fight to the death in the Shadowland wastes, but I turned and fled instead. I deemed it most important to return and deliver a warning to Coryn and Ra'al who were expecting me, but found the Warlord instead."

Kile nodded, fumbling with his uneven whiskers.

"They pursued me for a time, but they had no archers, so I was able to escape," Bastawr said.

Ra'al cocked his head. "Did you escape, or did they let you go?"

Coryn looked with wide eyes to Ra'al. "What do you mean?"

"I think they let Bastawr flee to warn us. They made him a part of the diversion."

"That has one flaw, though," Marnash interjected. "They were not attempting to get at *you*…They wanted *what we carried*. What Yarichek stole from us in Frostshoal."

All eyes fixed upon the morehl. Garesch nodded. "In our efforts to form new alliances, we stumbled upon a cache of arcane maps that unlocked the mist stones. We sought to return them to a sage if ever we found one. Yarichek delivered one of these to the undead who learned about our task from the traitor who knew our plans."

"And how does Harol's theft of the Magestorm cache fit into this?" Geril asked.

"Maybe Harol was acting on his own," Coryn suggested.

Garesch shook his head. "If he did, where did he find helpers to kill the vagha at the embassy? I have long been familiar with inner workings of Death worshipers. As far as I know, his agents do not move without their master's approval."

Geril leaned back. "Let's consider that the agents of Death do not all see eye to eye. Perhaps some have their own agendas…perhaps multiple agendas? Maybe Harol is vying against the other agents?"

Ra'al nodded hopefully. "Then perhaps all this means an attack against Icehome was also not in earnest. Maybe that was also a mere diversion."

Coryn looked at him, hoping he was right.

"We have another serious matter, aside from the coming war, the Magestorm cache, and Harol," Garesch said. "The remaining three maps to the mist stones have been stolen. The enemy killed my soldier, Werdth, and reanimated him, using his body and knowledge to sneak them away. Once they were secure, the army retreated. They got what they truly wanted and then left us just as they'd come. That is the true reason they left as they did."

Geril Dragonsbane flashed the morehl prince a grave look. "We must make plans immediately. Death's plans must be thwarted." He looked from face to face. "I fear we are merely in the eye of the storm."

Epilogue

Ki'Harol sa'Lahmyn stood on the transom of the *Chariot's Wake,* Ry'Ober's ship. He felt keenly aware of the sidelong glances her crew of pirates cast in his direction, and back at the pile of loot they'd helped dump a hundred cubits inland from the high-water mark. They left it abandoned to the elements.

Harol knew how badly they wanted to simply kill him and steal the weapons for their own. They might have done it, too, had the dwarf not promised them further payment only after his arrival at Dereh'Liandor.

A salty wind arose, frigid and terrible as it pushed the vessel south and away from the cache they'd unceremoniously dumped upon the frosty scree. He smiled and watched the shores disappear across the horizon.

He was ruthless, calculating, and patient. Harol had promised Leisterbane he could deliver, and he'd done exactly that—though the size of the artifact horde had never been disclosed.

The cagey dwarf played multiple shell games, and all at once. Soon, he would arrive in Dereh'Liandor where his contacts assured him he could earn a position of *true* power.

Harol was no fool. His heart was black and given over fully to Malgrimm and the Death God's power, but he took a more nuanced approach. The undead were not the only path to curry favor with the Dark One.

He finally turned back and looked to the horizon he headed. Harol knew his future looked promising. Leisterbane had been a means to an end, and he had not completely outlived his service to the fiend. That shell had not yet been overturned and there was much left in this game.

He grinned again. All his life, Harol's father, Lahmyn, had pushed him to achieve power. And now, it lay just at the base of his fingertips.

Lahmyn sat across from the others at the table and set down two more mugs of ale.

"I said, is it true, about your son?"

Lahmyn curled his upper lip. "True? What is true…We still cannot know that without testimony or concrete evidence, Elder Trinean. My son has been a fool most of his life, but he is blood. *Geril,* though. He has taken the council for granted for decades and rules as an emperor when his true duty should be to execute the will of the elders."

He spoke passionately and the five other dwarves at his table rapped their mugs against the timbers. "And what do you have planned?" Trinean asked.

Lahmyn scowled into the foam atop his mug. "Plans have been set into motion. Some on the other side of the council table have been bought. Others I have acquired leverage over." He shot conspiratorial looks to those seated around his table. "I have heard that Geril and his forces will be headed for the Shadowlands as soon as they can be made ready. As soon as he leaves for Icehome, we will act."

Trinean wiped froth from his whiskered upper lip. "Aye. I've heard those rumors too; he intends to leave Warlord Kile behind again, and this time the people will uphold Geril's desire for Kile's stewardship. We can't go against him again."

Lahmyn stood and walked a slow circle around them, retrieving an ornate, wooden box from his buffet table. "Gentleman, this has all been pure conjecture up until now." He met each one's eyes with a flinty glare. "If you've not the stomach to act in the hard times, then ye best be heading for that door. Once I open this box, you lose your plausible deniability and become a conspirator."

He completed his circle around the room and returned to his seat. "Very well, then. The cabal is formed. We have moved beyond mere talk." He placed the box before him and opened it. A bolt of purple silk had been wrapped around a hard object. Lahmyn unwound the silk and let it drop, placing the object onto the table with an ominous thud.

All eyes fixed upon the handheld musket. "What is it?" Trinean asked.

"One of the legendary Karaktoan flintlocks. A product of madcap gnomish engineering. They are very rare in this era and as such are the weapon of morehl royalty." Lahmyn slid the weapon further into the middle for further examination. "It would certainly be unfortunate if Warlord Kile had an accident…and I know of a certain member of lava elf royalty who have been granted unfettered access to Balgavarr. He is just the sort of person who could possess such a weapon."

Dark chuckles circulated the table and Lahmyn sat back in his chair, steepling his fingers. He muttered below his breath, "I told you Geril sa'Ghuren…You would regret crossing me."

Ra'al stood adjacent to Taerlon. The selumari had barely enough troops to operate the airship, and it would take a little more than a day to reach Icehome at top speed. The remaining magicians would be hard taxed to summon enough winds to guide the craft at the necessary speeds, but they desperately needed to reach Icehome. Ra'al needed to discover Rashingot's fate before making the voyage back to Tulgesh and consulting with Matrek about the mist stones, and Cyrea's next move.

Geril had already made arrangements with his chain of command for an absence of unknown length. He did, however, shoot glances up the balcony aperture where Lahmyn stood glaring daggers at him. But Geril had every faith in Warlord Kile.

Bastawr knelt before a ghwereste elder, a weaselfolk, and accepted his blessing. The tigerfolk had nearly eaten his weight in meat since arriving on the previous morning. His bulk had started to fill in again, but it would take some time to return to full health after his earlier voyage through the wastes.

Coryn sat against the rail and held the toy cube in her hands. She fiddled with it, practically ignoring everything else.

Ra'al finished his discussion with the Hennedy and Taerlon. They had assured Taerlon that the wind crafters of Icehome would be up to the task of helping them on their return voyage, especially as the selumari enchanters would be too fatigued to continue. He walked near Coryn. "Why are you still obsessing about this cube?"

"I don't know. It takes my mind off what's coming." Coryn shrugged, still fiddling with the cube. "It is a puzzle, and you know how much I like a good puzzle. Who knows? Maybe there is an item of power inside. We did find it in the Magestorm cache, after all."

"I don't think so." Ra'al shook his and smiled. "The wizards would have confiscated it if they thought it was anything important."

Coryn scoffed and kicked her steel boots out from beneath her, sitting upon the deck boards like a stubborn child. "I am a hero of the second battle of Balgavarr and daughter to King Geril; *twice* the hero of Balgavarr. Who dares take it from me?"

"What is this all about?" Garesch asked, walking past.

"Nothing much, addictions and obsessions mostly." Ra'al shrugged. "Oh, also self-worship and hubris."

Garesch looked at them and then shrugged. "I have to go check on my men. Marnash was able to find fifteen loyalists posted on the border area, where I believe you were supposed to meet Uruzak's delegation months ago?"

Coryn flashed him a sheepish smile. "Oops. We ran into a little trouble. Something to do with my fire sauce supply."

He merely grinned and then went off in search of his forces.

Ra'al began talking with Hennedy again, hooting and growling in their native tongue. Coryn left him to it and meandered the ship, fiddling with the cube absentmindedly as she checked over the supplies and calculated the kind of provisions they might need for the trip. It seemed overladen to her. The trip was only planned for a few days.

Exploring the ship was mildly exciting, especially when the floor shuddered slightly. The air bladder lifted the vessel and began its rise. She spun to return above deck and watch the liftoff when the cube clicked in her hands.

Coryn couldn't contain her awe as she opened the box.

A wild, gold light poured from inside and washed over her. It flashed with a heavy pulse and a whiff of ozone.

Coryn tried to scream but nothing came as she felt her body ripped apart, sucked inside the cube, and stitched back together within.

The cube clattered to the floor with a sharp thud. It locked tightly again, just as it had been for the centuries previous.

Ra'al searched the airship for Coryn, but she was nowhere to be found. He proceeded through it deck by deck, walking through the corridors, inspecting supply rooms and the nooks beneath stairs and ladders.

He walked in mounting frustration when he hit something hard with his foot.

The frostwing bent over and picked up the gold-tinted cube, recognizing it as the one Coryn acquired from the cache. *Where was Coryn?* A pang of worry shot through his chest.

Ra'al called aloud, "Coryn? Coryn, where are you?" But she was nowhere to be found.

The End

278

Appendices

The Shadowlands
Icehome
Frostshoal
Gyrea
Briney Main
Kafnyian Mountains
Balgavari
Wildwood
Dur Sona
Deep River
Tulgesh
Thurisa
Plains of Sesham
Uruzak Mountains
Plaguelands

Glossary of Terms

Abyss - the home of the Void, a realm where silence reigns aside from pockets of terror and chaos where unknown gods reign. This is a similar concept to Greek myths of an underworld.

Ailuril - the second born of the Esfahan gods. She is represented by the color blue and has power over the air elements.

Aguarehl - the fourth born of the Esfahan gods. He is represented by the color green and has power over the water elements.

Amazon - the race of mankind said to have been deposited whole upon Esfah as one of the few races created by Tarvanehl himself. Amazons are the warrior caste of human race.

Areosa - commonly known as the frostwings, a frigid felinoid, winged race with magic resistance.

Bloodless - another common name for the undead.

Deadzone – synonym for the Abyss, except from the point of view of the trogs or morehl. Within their respective religions, versions of the afterlife differ wildly and as often as they align in geopolitical goals, neither could imagine spending an eternal afterlife in the company of the other.

Death - the half-brother god who is the child of Nature and Void.

Dragons – these beasts come in two forms: Drake and Wyrm. Drakes have wings, and wyrms do not. Though the dragonkin are a kind of subspecies, they are not the same thing, no matter how similar they are. They used to live hidden across Esfah, but were nearly eradicated in the Dragoncrusades. Dragons have eternal spirits and when they die, they return to the plane where they now dwell. Dragonmagic came in two forms and it summons them from this realm or from nearby (the older form of this magic which has now been forgotten since these mythic beasts have largely gone out from Esfah.)

Drakufreet - the dragonkin come from the same realm as dragons and appear as a type of draconic hybrid race.

Eldarim – a human-like race that emerged over eons from Esfah's primordial soup and predated the gods-made races. The eldarim are versatile and have proven the capacity to breed with many of Esfah's races. They are called eldarim, meaning "from the earth."

Eldurim - the firstborn of the Esfahan gods. He is represented by the color gold and has power over the earth elements.

Efflorah - the race of treefolk.

Esfah - the world and one of two planets revolving around Soll.

Empyrea - known commonly as the firewalkers, a war-loving mercenary race.

Faeli - commonly known as scalders or steam dancers. These creatures are fickle and capricious and were once captured and tormented by Death.

Festration - a kind of location so tainted by evil activity that the very land itself has become corrupt and avails itself to wickedness.

Firiel - the third born of the Esfahan gods. She is represented by the color red and has power over the fire elements.

First Age - everything from the beginning of creation to the year 863.

Frehlasuhl - also called the Forsaken or Mudbloods. They are the offspring of selumari and morehl unions. They cannot breed with each other to have children, only with one or the other race, but they are rejected wholesale by both.

Ghaeial - the mother goddess known more commonly as Nature.

Ghwereste - called the "feral folk." These are a hybrid of animal and man created at the dawn of the Second Age.

Kreethaln - there are three of these mystical artifacts made of an unknown metal. Little is known about them except that they each possess some kind of arcane power. Their names are Life-bringer, Wisdom-giver, and Spell-crafter.

Leguin - a sister planet to Esfah that also orbits Sol; it can often be seen in the night sky appearing above the horizon like a bright star.

Lich - a powerful undead spell caster. Lichs often possess necromantic capabilities, though their created undead are maintained by force of will, rather than by other means, such as the Necralluvium.

Morehl - commonly called lava elves. They have red skin in addition to their elf-like features and their blood is said to smoke when exposed to air.

Necralluvium - a kind of magical potion with a seeming life of its own. This black filth can kill the living. The dead that are exposed to it become animated.

Rhaudian - the name of the moon. It circulates Esfah twice in a daily cycle.

Sarslayan - commonly known as swamp stalkers. These snake-men emerged in the Second Age as a result of Death using magic to twist the creations of his half-brother Aguarehl. They create more of their kind through magic conversion rather than by reproduction.

Second Age - everything after year 863 of the First Age. This began when Ghaeial walked the face of Esfah and surveyed the damages of the myriad of wars. The 864th year is year 1 of the Second Age.

Selurehl - the name of the second god to emerge after Tarvanehl, usually known as Void.

Selumari - commonly called coral elves. They have blue skin in addition to their elf-like features.

Shara – what the eldarim people refer to themselves as when they communicate with each other. It means "little god-in-the-making."

Soll – the sun.

Tarvanehl - the creator god who came first, according to all mythology and story; he is often known as Father Time, or simply The Father.

Teldrim - a race of extinct horse lords that bore many similarities to the Amazons. A creation of Tarvanehl, these were remarkable because the race could intermix with any other. They were eradicated by Melkior shortly after their emergence.

Trog - a synonym for goblin. trogs much prefer to live in boggy areas and tend to pollute the land.

Vagha - commonly known as dwarves.

Void - sometimes used interchangeably with the Abyss or, the power or person of Selurehl who is frequently referred to as Void just as his son Malgrimm is more widely regarded as Death. Context determines the meaning.

Warchief - a title of rank among the vagha. Below the king is a Warchief who leads Warlords and Warcommanders under them. It might commonly be understood as a sort of general.

Timeline

Included is the general timeline of major world events in Esfah. Please note that, during the time before the Mother, Ghaeial, became a goddess and the First Age began, prehistory spanned a scope of time measuring eons, and in that time, verily, only *Time* existed. Despite the sage's attempts to capture much data and ancient knowledge, they did not begin tracking time and dates until the first passing of the Daybringer. The first three years of history might very well have been hundreds or even a thousand years as the gods (and the earliest race of eldarim) kept time differently.

Prehistory N.D.

Tarvanehl exists and creates within the realm of Void/Abyss and Esfah and Leguin are born; Ghaeial realizes she is a goddess and falls in love with Tarvanehl.

Turambar courts Leguin.

Selurehl, third of the brother gods grows angry.

Eldurim, the firstborn (earth) god-son of Ghaeial and Tarvanehl is born.

Ailuril, the second born (wind) god-daughter of Ghaeial and Tarvanehl is born.

Firiel, third born (fire) god-daughter of Ghaeial and Tarvanehl is born

Aguarehl, fourth born god-son (water) of Ghaeial and Tarvanehl is born

Malgrimm, the cursed bastard son (Death) is conceived and birthed after Selurehl's violence upon Ghaeial

Eldarim are birthed by Esfah and slowly emerge from the mire of her lands and water, evolving over long periods of time. They call themselves the Shara in their own tongue.

The First Age

03FA the Daybringer Comet passes Esfah for the First Time, the Sisters of Fate are birthed of Turambar and Leguin, Dragons and the Drakufreet are created during the schism of the god-children.

04FA Earliest creations of the gods: "monsters" are formed

15FA selumari are created

16FA vagha are created, trogs are created

17FA morehl are created

19FA The Dawn of War. morehl invaders overthrow the first selumari

22FA Humans arrive on Esfah via Tarvanehl's intervention

28FA Davian Whisperwynd leaves Maris-ta-Sehlim

32FA The proto-empyreans are birthed in the whirlwind

42FA Gundraokh Shatterfist finds the Bands of Turambar and renames the city of Orelod to Gundakhor

96FA Sshkkryyahr the Dread rises to power

103FA Malgrimm attempts to create a new powerful, destructive force within the Shadowlands, but the Areosan's magic resistance helps them maintain mild independence from the Death god and he abandons them to the frost plains.

143FA Undead created, Melkior is defeated upon the Raithlan Plains by the gods' chosen Champions

167FA Dilution of the eldarim race and the reduction of the Dragon population via the Dragoncrusades that eliminated nearly all the natural dragons of Esfah; the spells that compelled natural dragons that still remained in the realm became forgotten after this date in favor of those drawing eternal dragons through the interplanar rifts

341FA Existence of the empyreans is discovered when they aid the elder races in the first major Undead uprising.

447FA *Book of the Land, 1st Ed.* is published and immediately begins revisions

520FA morehl city of Karakto falls to the selumari

532FA morehl discover cursed bullets and retake Karakto

544FA Large load of Eldrymetallum discovered on the Karakto slopes

562FA Final version of *The Book of the Land* completed after 23 quintennial installments

836FA The Magestorm Wars erupt with the tectonic cataclysm that opens the Netherwold and nearly splits Dereh'Liandor in two; the Arcana Veil stiffens

842FA Disappearance of the gremmlobahnd and the genocide of the drakufreet

863FA Final battle of the Magestorm Wars ends the first age, the faeli are birthed in the Firequags and captured by the forces of Death and subjected to torments in the pits of the World Wound.

The Second Age

01SA Ghaeial walks the earth and surveys the damage of the elder races.

03SA Ghaeial creates the ghwereste

79SA The plagues of the World Wound at its evils continue and the first of the sarslayan emerge from the nearby Snekdenn Bayou

153SA The areosa race emerges from the Shadowlands. They are known mostly as rumors, but their existence is verified to the outside world.

209SA Whether the faeli escaped the torments of the World Wound or were released, none know, but they were so twisted by the centuries of abuse that they have become more children of Malgrimm than Ghaeial

233SA Under Ghaeial's wishes, the sylvan efflorah, existing as trees since even before the humans came to Esfah, picked up their roots and first emerged from forest and grove

829SA Zephras "Thunderfist" dies defending in Cyrea defending Balgavarr from a dragon

967SA Geril sa'Ghuren "Dragonsbane" born

1021SA Geril sa'Ghuren rules in Balgavarr

1082SA Coryn Sa'Geril is born

1119SA Daybringer Comet makes its pass by Esfah

1122SA Kholkoro Wicebrow writes her commentary
Kholkoro's commentary on Book of the Land

1127SA The famed "Adventurer King" Hy'Mandr sa'Meril is blinded

1139SA Melkior is revived

1142SA Daybringer Comet makes its circuit